The Looking Glass Wars®

ArchEnemy

Also by Frank Beddor

The Looking Glass Wars

Seeing Redd

Praise for Frank Beddor

'*The Looking Glass Wars*, the series of bestselling novels by *Frank Beddor* that takes the classic 19th century children's tale off into a truly unexpected literary territory – the battlefields of epic fantasy' *The LA Times*

'Fantastic battle scenes, plot twists, character interest and slow-burning love make this an ace read for both sexes' Guardian

To say Beddor's revolutionary novel is an adaptation of Lewis Carroll's original would do justice to neither author . . . The magic with which Beddor has imbued each character really and truly brings them to life' *Independent*

'This series is a rich and original re-imagining of Alice in Wonderland. It blurs genre lines and is unlike any other series out there. *ArchEnemy* was a perfect conclusion to one of my favorite series. If you enjoy fantasy novels or *Alice in Wonderland*, I highly recommend *The Looking Glass Wars* series' www.revish.com

'Backed by electric, heart-pounding action, interesting subplots . . . *ArchEnemy* closes out Frank Beddor's *The Looking Glass Wars* in an exciting fashion and cements the trilogy as one of the best new YA fantasy series currently published' *fantasybookcritic.blogspot.com*

'The climactic battle for Wonderland is outstanding and extra-ordinary reading for all generations!' *comicstory-arc.blogspot.com*

'Frank Beddor's intriguing revision of the Alice in Wonderland mythos reaches its thrilling conclusion in his final act of *The Looking Glass Wars*, *ArchEnemy*. Beddor takes pains to create a fully realized world populated by multi-dimensional characters that draw readers into the tale. theres also plenty of ancillary action with the supporting players that continues to flesh out the intricately designed and magical Wonderland' *www.blogcritics.org*

'A storming, imaginative tour-de-force . . . Inventive, dramatic and clever, with a colourful cast of characters to die for . . . Beddor has created something new and original, something fresh and exciting' *John McLay, children's literary scout*

'Great for teens and adults of all ages' *www.shakefire.com*

'One of the best books I've ever read – I would recommend it to anyone – fantasy lover or not' *www.livejournal.com*

The Looking Glass Wars®

ArchEnemy

Frank Beddor

EGMONT

For my little princess, Ava

EGMONT
We bring stories to life

First published 2010
by Egmont UK Limited
239 Kensington High Street
London W8 6SA

Text copyright © 2010 Frank Beddor
The Looking Glass Wars® is a trademark of Automatic Pictures, Inc.
All art copyright © 2009 Automatic Pictures, Inc. All rights reserved

The moral rights of the author and illustrator have been asserted

ISBN 978 1 4052 5193 8

1 3 5 7 9 10 8 6 4 2

www.egmont.co.uk
www.lookingglasswars.com

A CIP catalogue record for this title is available from the British Library

Typeset by Avon DataSet Ltd, Bidford on Avon, Warwickshire
Printed and bound in Great Britain by the CPI Group

A word of warning to my readers:

A number of years ago, while on a business trip to London, I went to the British Museum and came across an exhibition of ancient playing cards. At the very end of the exhibition was an incomplete deck of cards, illuminated by an unusual glow. The cards showed *Alice in Wonderland* as I had never seen it before.

On the way to the airport the next morning, I went to an antiques shop specialising in playing cards. When I told the dealer about the unusual exhibit, he revealed that he in fact owned the other cards missing from the deck. He then proceeded to tell me the story of *The Looking Glass Wars*®. That story is the one you now hold . . .

But one word of warning: the true story of Wonderland involves bloodshed, murder, revenge and war. I apologise in advance to those of you who might find some of the scenes in this book distressing, but I feel it's important that the facts are set down as they actually happened. Those of you of a more sensitive disposition might prefer reading Lewis Carroll's classic fairytale.

Frank Beddor

♥ ♠ PROLOGUE ♣ ♦

Oxford, England. 1875.

Alyss of Wonderland raced up the front walk, using her imagination to unlock the door and turn the latch. Inside the house, nothing had changed. The umbrella stand and hat rack, the family pictures hanging in the hall, even the gouge in the skirting board marking where she'd thrown her ice skates one winter afternoon: everything was exactly as it had been when she'd lived there ... so long ago, it seemed.

'Please, what do you want?' the dean's voice reached her from the back of the house.

She sighted them in her imagination's eye: the dean and Mrs Liddell, Edith and Lorina. Their clothes a good deal ripped, they huddled together on the drawing-room sofa in fearful silence while Ripkins – one of King Arch's bodyguards, and a deadly assassin – stood ominously before them. Ripkins: the only Boarderlander who could flex his fingertips – deadly sawteeth

1

pushing up out of the skin in the pattern of his fingerprints.

'Please,' the dean said again.

Fingerprint blades flexed, Ripkins moved his hands fast in front of him, shredding air. Mrs Liddell flinched. The assassin took a step towards the dean, the sisters each let out a sob and –

'Hello?' Alyss called, walking directly into the room. She had imagined herself into Alice Liddell's long skirt and blouse, her hair in a tight bun. 'Excuse me, I didn't know there was company.'

She tried to look startled – eyes wide, mouth half open, head tilted apologetically – as she thought her double would. Wanting to catch Ripkins off guard, she pretended to be meek, cowed, and let him grab her and push her towards the Liddells.

Where he'd touched her, there was blood.

Ripkins's hands became a blur in front of him, churning air and moving in towards the dean's chest. Alyss had no choice but to expose her imaginative powers in front of the Liddells. With the slightest of movements, she conjured a deck of razor-cards and sent them cutting through the air.

Fiss! Fiss, fiss, fiss!

In a single swift motion, Ripkins spun clear and unholstered a crystal shooter, firing a retaliatory cannonade.

Alyss gestured as if wiping condensation off a looking glass and the shrapnel-like bullets of wulfenite and barite crystal clattered to the floor.

The Liddells sat dumbfounded, their fear muted in the shock of seeing their adopted daughter engage in combat, producing otherworldly missiles out of the air – flat blade-edged rectangles resembling playing cards, bursts of gleaming bullets. She conjured them as fast as she defended herself against them, what with the intruder making expert use of the strange guns and knives strapped to his belt, thighs, biceps and forearms.

'Father!'

A fistful of mind-riders – ordinary-looking darts infused with poison that turned victims one upon the other in rage – rocketed towards the family.

Alyss threw out her hand and the weapons changed trajectory, shooting towards her. She annihilated them in midair with a pinch of her fingers, becoming like gravity itself, pulling whatever Ripkins hurled at the Liddells towards her until –

The wall pushed out a score of daggers. Ripkins, knocked backwards by a steel playing card as big as a man, slammed against them and slumped to the floor.

Silence, except for the ticking of a grandfather clock.

'Oh!'

In the doorway stood Alyss's double, the woman she had, with utmost effort, imagined into being to take her place in this world: Alice Liddell who, with her gentleman friend, Reginald Hargreaves, stared at the dead assassin and Wonderland's Queen. The dean, his wife and his daughters looked from Alyss Heart to Alice Liddell and back again.

'I –?' the dean started.

But that was all he managed before Alyss bolted from the room and out of the house, sprinting until she was well along St Aldate's Street. Certain the Liddells weren't following her, she walked briskly in the direction of Carfax Tower, towards the portal that would return her to Wonderland: a puddle where no puddle should be, in the middle of a sun-drenched pavement behind the tower. But even from this distance she could see that something wasn't right. The portal was shrinking, its edges drying up fast. She started to run, her imagination's eye scanning the town.

'How can it be?' she breathed, because all of the portals were shrinking, the tower puddle already half its former size when she leapt for it, closing her eyes and sucking in her breath, anticipating the swift watery descent through portal waters, the reverse pull of The Pool of Tears, the –

Knees jarring, she landed on pavement. The portal had evaporated.

Alyss Heart, the rightful Queen of Wonderland, was stranded on Earth.

PART ONE

♦ CHAPTER 1 ♣

Bibwit Harte, most learned albino in the land, tutor and advisor to four generations of Heart Queens, bustled along a path in the grounds of Heart Palace. The flowers and shrubs he passed riffled their blooms and called out in respectful greeting.

'Good evening, Mr Harte!' said a purple sunflower.

'We trust you're well, Mr Harte!' cried the blossoms of a hollizalea shrub.

The tutor returned their well-wishes, though more than a few tulips found it strange he didn't say more; Mr Harte rarely missed an opportunity to chat. Stranger still, the royal tutor didn't even chat with himself as he approached a hedge indistinguishable from those around it. His bald head glistening like a second moon in the evening's light, his large ears – twice the size of an ordinary Wonderlander's – pivoting to catch any sound that might indicate the return of expected friends, he stepped into the hedge. Its roots shifted, unlocking a hatch, and he descended through the opening.

On a platform halfway to the floor of the subterranean chamber stood Queen Alyss, dressed in an ankle-length dress of shimmering, opalescent white. Her long, black hair elegantly dusting her shoulders, she held her bejewelled royal sceptre in one hand while her other was extended towards The Heart Crystal's unsteady pulse as if trying to physically draw inspiration from it.

A new moon had come and gone since a web of caterpillar thread spanning the sky over Wonderland – WILMA, King Arch's Weapon of Inconceivable Loss and Massive Annihilation – had reduced The Heart Crystal to what it was now: a sputtering, blinking, useless thing. The imaginative source for all creation, the means through which Wonderland's most ingenious inventions passed to Earth and other worlds, had become little more than a font of frustration.

'Shouldn't the effects be wearing off by now?' Alyss asked as Bibwit stepped down beside her. 'I can't conjure so much as a tiny opal.'

'You could enlist the help of an imagination enabler, Queen Alyss,' said General Doppelgänger, who sat monitoring the viewing screens at a control desk. 'Someone residing outside Wondertropolis and not so affected by King Arch's Weapon.'

Bibwit's ears quivered, his scholar's robe swished at his bare feet. 'It is indeed horrible for all imaginationists within Wondertropolis to have lost their imaginations on account of King Arch. And although we may find some relief in the fact that those in rural quadrants, while weaker in imagination than before, have not been left completely bereft – a circumstance I ascribe to the web of caterpillar thread having been more tightly knit over our capital city; what I mean to say, in short –'

Alyss laughed. When had Bibwit ever given a short speech instead of a long one?

'– in *sum*,' the tutor continued, 'while it is possible for us to send for an imagination enabler, I don't think we should let more Wonderlanders know of the Queen's loss than is absolutely necessary. An imagination enabler cannot help matters. The Queen's powers *will* return.'

'I'm glad *someone* is sure of it,' Alyss said.

'My dear Alyss,' Bibwit bowed, 'in this world I can be sure of nothing so much as my own wisdom.'

It was strange, Alyss thought, that she should seem more

concerned about her loss than Bibwit and the general. True, it was *her* imagination, but hadn't they always urged her to exploit it for the Queendom's benefit and for the glory of White Imagination? She had felt such freedom upon first discovering the absence of her gift and already, here she was, worrying enough for the three of them.

Because my responsibilities as Queen haven't disappeared along with my imagination.

Whatever freedom she'd felt had been illusory. It wasn't just *her* imagination, after all. Being sovereign of the people, she was not at leisure to be sovereign of her own actions, doing what she liked whenever she pleased, no matter how much she might wish for it. Love, justice, duty to the populace – the guiding principles of the Heart dynasty and of White Imagination were a part of her. She would defend what she thought best for the Queendom as long as she occupied the throne.

'Club soldiers are amassing in Rocking Horse Lane,' General Doppelgänger reported into his desk's talkback module. 'Repeat: Club soldiers in Rocking Horse Lane. Decks one and three converge.'

Lack of imagination throughout the realm had given rise to new problems. These in turn had brought her here, to The

Heart Chamber, to try and coax a hint of her former power from the Crystal.

'We'd do well to remember, Alyss,' Bibwit said, 'that when The Crystal Continuum was contaminated by – what shall I call it? – by Homburg Molly's mishap, yes, any imaginationist travelling inside of it at the time found herself without her abilities. Much as imaginationists now suffer as a result of King Arch's attack on Wondertropolis and The Heart Crystal. In the case of Molly's mishap, the effects wore off, and the continuum is now perfectly functioning. I therefore assume the effects of WILMA will similarly wear off.'

'Unless, of course, they don't,' Alyss said. 'I'm no stronger now than when the weapon first detonated.'

Bibwit shared a quick glance with General Doppelgänger. 'We obviously have longer to wait than we did with the continuum incident, the power of WILMA being much greater.'

Alyss again turned her energies towards The Heart Crystal, envisioning a smooth polished rock of clear agate at her feet. The Crystal fizzed and crackled, but no agate materialised.

'It's not as if Arch's caterpillar thread is still radiating its power!' she cried. 'It disintegrated!'

Nor had it ever unleashed the full extent of its paralysing energy. She and Hatter Madigan had seen to that.

'By now,' General Doppelgänger said, his eyes on the control desk, monitoring the movement of his card soldiers, 'Redd might know that Queen Alyss is without imagination.'

'And the only reason she continues to retreat is because she's lost *hers*,' Bibwit agreed. 'A confrontation at this juncture would be nothing more than brute force against brute force. Redd cannot be so sure of victory without her imagination. We should start incorporating into our military the new weapons made before WILMA's detonation, in case we find ourselves having to cope with both Redd's army and the Clubs.'

Alyss lowered her sceptre and turned from The Heart Crystal. 'During her attack, Redd couldn't have known about WILMA or its effect on imagination. If she had, she never would have entered Wondertropolis and made herself vulnerable to it.'

Bibwit nodded. The veins visible beneath his head's translucent skin pulsed, keeping time to his thoughts. 'There's a question I've much been puzzling over,' he admitted at last. 'Where did Arch get so much caterpillar thread and the knowledge of how to use it to create WILMA? As aged as I am, Alyss, I have never before seen the thread of all six caterpillar-oracles together in one place.' Then, with a flourish of his robe, as if this could wipe away all stress and uncertainty from the land, he added, 'But enough of unsettling topics. I originally came here to tell you, my dear, that I've received word we should expect Hatter and Molly before the next eclipse.'

'That *is* good news!'

'Yes,' General Doppelgänger brooded, 'because we'll need all the bodies we can get. The Clubs are growing –'

The General's desk rattled with the sound of a distant explosion, he split into the twin figures of Doppel and Gänger, and both of them shouted to the card soldiers converging on Rocking Horse Lane, to the chessmen patrolling the outskirts of Wondertropolis, to anyone anywhere who could help:

'Attack!'

♦ CHAPTER 2 ♣

For as long as anyone could remember, imaginationists had mingled with ordinary Wonderlanders throughout the Queendom, living in the same residential complexes, working at the same firms, shopping at the same stores and educating their children at the same schools. If, in the rugged resort towns of Outerwilderbeastia or the scrubland communities between The Everlasting Forest and The Chessboard Desert, there was a higher concentration of ordinary Wonderlanders, it was owing to nothing more sinister than a group of them having settled there long before; over the years, their families had prospered. Just as there was nothing ominous about the Croquet Court Lofts in Rocking Horse Lane being home to a high concentration of imaginationists. Writers, architects, scientists, painters, sculptors, inventors, White Imagination enthusiasts – these and more had taken up residence at the Lofts, bound together by the alternating elation and melancholy, the moments of inspiration offset by self-doubt and dissatisfaction, that came with all imaginative endeavours. Lately, however, the dissatisfactions had been more poignant than usual, the bouts of inspiration less frequent, and Croquet Court's imaginationists gathered to complain in the building's lobby at the close of each day, much as they used to gather to brag of what they'd accomplished when their imaginations had been ripe with ideas.

'I think I almost had a thought today,' a writer said.

'That's more than I had,' grumbled a sculptor.

'There!' a stymied inventor blurted to an architect, pulling a clump of hair from his head and holding it in his palm. 'I've just now invented this ball of hair!'

In a corner of the room, not wanting to admit she'd suffered another clutch of unproductive hours, a painter stood before a canvas decorated with three hesitant lines, one for each of the days she'd spent with her brush poised to capture the likeness of . . . anything.

'Can I go play yet?' the painter's daughter asked, posed before her as if in punishment.

'Just a little while longer.'

But then – *chhrrrkkkkkshhhhh!* – the lobby door blasted off its hinges, the room filled with dust, and several hands of card soldiers stormed in with weapons drawn. Not the oft-seen soldiers of Alyss Heart's army: with their angular helmets, their shields shaped like the suit symbols laser-etched into their breastplates, shoulderplates and kneeplates, these were soldiers from the Club decks.

'You have till my shield stops spinning to gather your families and your belongings and board the transports outside!' a Four of Clubs commanded, stabbing the bottom point of his shield into the floor and, with a heavy push of his arm, setting it in motion.

The imaginationists were too shocked to move.

'Why should we go anywhere?' a playwright finally managed. 'You have no authority over us.'

'Oh, no?'

The Four of Clubs aimed a fist at the fellow and – *shink shink shink!* – skin-splitting club emblems shot out from a slot in the armour of his forearm and lodged in the playwright's vitals. The Four of Clubs looked at his spinning shield. 'Until it stops!' he announced again. 'Not a moment more!'

Under guard, the imaginationists hurried to their lofts, gathering their clothes and valuables, trying to comfort the confused murmurings of wives and husbands, to hush the protests of children forced to leave prized possessions behind, until –

A muted thunder, as of an orb generator exploding underground. The floors trembled. Outside, a fountain of shattered glass rose five storeys into the air.

In the Croquet Courts lobby, the Four of Clubs muttered, 'Heart soldiers,' and grabbed his spinning shield. 'Time's up! Everybody out! Move! Move!'

Throughout the building, Club soldiers cocked their heads, receiving the order, and in the crush caused by their impatience to herd the imaginationists outside, children were separated from parents, husbands from wives. Had the prisoners eyes for anything but their own fear as they walked to the waiting smail-transports, they would have seen – at the nearest intersection, where Heart soldiers battled Clubs and Spades – a hand of Heart Cards emptying the ammo cartridges of their AD52s at the enemy and a fiery orb tearing through the sky towards them, bringing the bright light of midday and death.

♦ CHAPTER 3 ♦

Dodge Anders – head of the palace guard, son of the late Sir Justice – was half-dressed in his quarters, but to the walrus-butler standing uncertainly before him, he seemed, even without the trappings of his military uniform, a man as fierce in combat as any Milliner. The guardsman's undershirt was obscured by an ammunition belt that crossed in an X on his chest, AD52 projectile decks and shooter cartridges strapped along its surface save for areas taken up by a crystal communicator's microphonic patch, audio output and vid nozzle. And what with an AD52 holstered under each of Dodge's arms, a crystal shooter strapped to each thigh, and whipsnake grenades pinned and dangling about his person, the walrus-butler might have been forgiven for thinking that weapons *were* the guardsman's underthings.

'What do you think of this ratty old gown, Mr Anders?' the creature asked, holding up the garment in question.

'Too showy,' Dodge said.

The walrus's eyes widened at the gown's plain weave, its dim colour as of dried clay. The guardsman was proving impossible to satisfy, and the past lunar hours the butler had spent hurriedly waddling about the palace's environs on his behalf had made him more anxious than usual. Trying to deposit the gown on to a heap of discarded clothes, he somehow got himself tangled up in it.

'Oh!' he cried, flippers flailing. 'This is troublesome! Help!'

Dodge pulled the gown free, dropped it on the floor with the rest of the rejected items. 'Anything else?'

'Anything . . .? Oh, Mr Anders, I have raided the servants' closets. I have picked through the Bandersnatch Avenue Donation Bins, and I've begged among the shops on Heart Boulevard for whatever they might be willing to dispose of. I have, Mr Anders, exhausted what I believe are the best sources of supply, but if you wish, if you insist, I will seek further afield for more.'

Dodge eyed the scant items brought by the walrus that he'd not yet dismissed as unsuitable: a wig, a sack-like smock, a pair of soiled stockings and another of worn sandals. In one respect, he admired Alyss for refusing to hide safely behind the palace gates, not content to rule according to reports delivered to her from advisors. He respected her warrior Queen spirit, her determination to get into the muck of things, the better to decide what was best for the Queendom.

And yet . . .

He wished she *would* hide safely behind the palace gates, abandon her plan of venturing out into a city so recently under siege by a foreign army and now being nipped at here and there by the Clubs' rogue military. Why couldn't Alyss rely on relayed intel like a normal Queen? Why couldn't she have conceded to him when – early in the afternoon, over tea and wondercrumpets – he'd asked her not to expose herself to undue risk? Especially because he'd appealed to her not as a guardsman concerned for his Queen, but as one who cared for her above all others.

Just a single lunar phase earlier – though he'd wished otherwise, wanting always to keep her safe – Alyss's need for his protection had been largely unnecessary due to her tremendous imaginative gift. But now that she was without imagination . . .

'You understand the importance of what we're about here, walrus?' he asked. 'To protect Queen Alyss, I need to dress her in clothes not *in the least* fit for a Queen.'

The walrus-butler glanced at the mound of discarded garments, none of which he suspected any Queen in any land would deign to wear. 'I will go in search of more, Mr Anders.'

The creature turned to leave, but Dodge stopped him with a sigh.

'No. It's getting late.' He extended a hand towards the smock, wig, stockings and sandals. 'These will have to do.'

They had better. The life of the woman he loved depended on it.

♥ ♦CHAPTER 4♣ ♦

The smail-transport came to an abrupt stop and the imaginationists crammed inside were ordered to disembark. One by one they emerged into the night, glad to be free from the transport's stifling heat and humidity. Voices cluttered the air, crying out for mothers, fathers, brothers, sisters, husbands, wives – family members who had been loaded on to transports and randomly dumped in different limbo coops. But there were other voices too, unfamiliar to the Croquet Court Lofts, belonging to imaginationists residing throughout the Queendom, unwilling passengers of yet other transports, kidnapped from their everyday lives and calling in vain for their own missing relatives.

Sheer walls of dolomite seven metres thick rose to unseen heights around them. The road was unpaved, the structures on either side dilapidated, as if hurriedly thrown together out of garbage collected from construction sites.

'Welcome home!' a Six of Clubs mocked from his perch in a guard tower.

An imaginationist, desperate to escape, ran at the lone opening in the limbo coop's wall. Like the demarcation barrier between Boarderland and Queen Alyss's realm, it was secured by an impassable weave of lightning-like soundwaves, and the imaginationist could force only an arm and shoulder through it before his whole body spasmed and he was caught, his internal organs vibrating, generating ever increasing heat and burning him from the inside out.

'Congregating on the street is not allowed!' the Six of Clubs yelled, aiming a mauler rifle at the imaginationists, threatening an onslaught of quicksilver shards from its double barrel. 'Idling is not allowed!'Dragging their luggage, not knowing what to do or where to go, the crowd began to disperse, slowly at first, but more quickly when it became known that there weren't enough living quarters to accommodate everyone. In single-room flats throughout the limbo coop, a scene played out over and over again, of broken families seeking adequate space for themselves having to confront a new enemy – not Clubs but their fellow prisoners.

'We were here first,' a voice said when a musician and his son entered a flat on the main thoroughfare. 'Get out.'

'But *all* of the flats are occupied,' the musician answered.

From the dark where he'd been huddling with his family, an inventor emerged. At the Croquet Court Lofts, he and the musician were friends and had often enjoyed dinner together.

'Gebling?'

'There's no room for you here,' the inventor said.

'But –'

The inventor shoved the musician's son towards the door.

'Don't *ever* touch him!' the musician yelled, and threw a punch, and then both men were on the floor, at each other with fists and elbows, their children trembling in silence, the inventor's wife wailing for them to stop.

Thimp thimp thimp thimp!

Razor-cards splintered the floor. The fighting Wonderlanders paused, looked up and saw a pair of Club soldiers at the door. The Four of Clubs pushed in a large litter of a family.

'At least ten to a flat. No exceptions.'

The Three of Clubs, cradling his AD52, smirked at the musician and inventor. 'You're not allowed to kill each other. You leave the killing to us.'

Then the soldiers laughed, and were gone.

♥ CHAPTER 5 ♦

In the chamber beneath the palace grounds, Alyss, Bibwit and General Doppelgänger had gathered at the control desk to monitor the activity on Rocking Horse Lane, where surgeons were tending to wounded Heart soldiers.

'We're certain the Diamonds and Spades have nothing to do with this?' Alyss asked.

At a nod from Bibwit, General Doppelgänger punched a code into the control desk's interface panel. One of the viewing screens displayed the inside of a long, rectangular dormitory at The Crystal Mines – that system of tunnels in which Wonderlanders who violated the laws of society laboured to excavate crystal from a mountain's stubborn bedrock; where the wardens were strict but officious in their duty to rehabilitate prisoners and there was always an opportunity to regain one's freedom. Unlike during Redd's reign, when wardens had been commanded to turn every prisoner's stay at the work camp into a death sentence.

'Is that . . .?' Alyss said, watching the transmission from The Crystal Mines dormitory. *Hard to recognise her without all the finery, her haughty bearing, but could that be ...?*

'The Lady of Diamonds, yes,' said Bibwit.

The lady was sitting up in bed, her eyes squeezed shut and her hands pressed to her ears to keep out her dorm mates' pestering.

'I can't hear you!' she whined.

'Didn't have the luxury of swinging a pickaxe at that mansion of yours, eh?' a dorm mate teased.

'Tell us a story of wealth and power,' laughed another.

'I can't hear you!' the Lady of Diamonds insisted. 'I'm not in these dirty mines! I'm at home! I'm imagining that I'm home and –'

Splat! A sopping rag hit her in the face. The dorm filled with laughter and General Doppelgänger directed the viewing screen back to Rocking Horse Lane.

'Lord Diamond is having a similarly difficult time adjusting to his new life,' Bibwit explained, 'and so far we've found nothing to link the Diamonds to anti-imagination activities. As for the Spades . . .' he again nodded to the general, who brought up a visual of the Spades' estate, on

whose grounds Ten Cards from the Heart decks were training
Spade soldiers, 'they've offered you their full support and I'm
sure they have nothing to do with fomenting strife within
the Queendom. It's against those who have claimed their
innocence throughout WILMA's aftermath that we must
direct our efforts.'

'The Clubs,' said General Doppelgänger. 'The recent
maraudings of their soldiery have turned rumour into
confirmed fact: the lord and lady are in open rebellion.'

'You have proof that the Lord and Lady of Clubs are
to blame and not a renegade general of their military?'
Alyss asked.

'I have reports from my Ten Cards.'

'Which to my mind, General, rely too much upon
assumptions.'

It had been a shock to learn: her mother's noble
intentions, the principles of White Imagination inspirational
to so many Heart Queens in the exercise of their power,
meant nothing to citizens who had always resented the ruling
family. Not Black Imaginationists, but a more subtle and thus
perhaps more subversive group – ordinary Wonderlanders
jealous of anyone possessing imagination, regardless of how
weak. Alyss wanted, needed, to see these unhappy citizens

for herself, to find some clue that would help her understand their resentment. Which was why she'd made certain plans for tonight.

'Chessmen have been despatched to question the lord and lady?' she asked.

Bibwit's ears swivelled. 'Yes, my dear, but now that their machinations are out in the open, they themselves seem to have gone underground.'

'Surely, their absence confirms their guilt,' pressed the General.

Tzzzz.

Up above, the chamber hatch opened. Footsteps descended towards Alyss and her two advisors, the tread familiar yet somehow strange, as if whoever it was had sustained an injury that altered his usual gait or –

'Let's do this.'

A stiff, unsmiling spirit-dane wrangler stood before them, the dirt of the stables staining his beard and the hair that poked out from beneath his helmet. Reins and spurs hung from the belt of his faded jumpsuit. He wore thick-heeled boots that reached nearly to his knees and carried under his arm what looked like a bundle of saddle blankets.

General Doppelgänger's hand went instinctively to

his holstered crystal shooter. Bibwit's ears folded back and his mouth opened in disbelief. How could a stranger have managed to locate, let alone enter, the Queen's secret Heart Chamber?

'Dodge,' Alyss said.

The General released his weapon and Bibwit pretended to yawn.

'Had you and the General fooled for a gwormmy-blink, Bibwit?' Dodge asked.

'I am *not* pleased to admit it.'

'But I'm glad to hear it, because if we can fool you . . .' Dodge handed his bundle to Alyss. 'I brought this so you could change here. We need to leave. Now.'

Alyss hesitated, picked at the bundle's fabric. 'It was so much easier to disguise myself when I had imagination. I simply envisioned myself in an unfamiliar costume and there I'd be, wearing it.'

Dodge stroked her hair – hair that was his responsibility to save from harm, that he wished to see turn grey with age in future years. 'By the time your imagination returns,' he said, 'there won't be a need for disguises. I promise.'

Alyss smiled, not without sadness, and retired to the floor of the chamber to change clothes.

Bibwit cleared his throat. 'Having spent several lifetimes in study,' he said to Dodge, 'I should point out that disguises are a necessary part of our daily lives. For instance, a Wonderlander might disguise herself as duly impressed with a friend's quartz mosaic, all the while thinking the piece poorly executed. Half a lunar cycle later, this same Wonderlander might give a colleague a poem she'd written, and this colleague, instead of saying what he thinks, which is that it's the worst poem ever conceived, pretends to enjoy it.' (Here, Dodge stopped listening, though he appeared attentive enough.) 'It would be a rude world indeed,' the tutor continued, 'if Wonderlanders didn't disguise themselves thus, with everyone constantly scoffing at everyone else. Can you imagine? No, excuse me, bad choice of words in our current predicament. But try to picture a Wonderland in which every citizen fails to disguise their true feelings, unable or unwilling to mask hurt, anger, dislike and dissatisfaction, however momentary.' (Here, General Doppelgänger fell to polishing the buttons of his uniform with his coat sleeve.) 'I realise I'm just a scholar with infinite wisdom, but I submit to you that disguises are as much a part of ourselves as our arms or legs, our –'

'Here she is!' Dodge cried, relieved, as Alyss returned from the chamber floor.

'My Queen,' General Doppelgänger observed, 'you look just like a farmer's maid.'

'That *is* the idea,' said Dodge.

Alyss had tucked her shoulder-length black hair beneath a wig of blonde curls. By means of a dye-pen, she had given herself freckled cheeks, and her smock – a dull, rough-fibred affair – must have been padded on the inside because her slim figure was gone and she appeared thick-waisted, her body shapeless.

Bibwit's brow took on the look of lined papyrus. 'Being an ancient specimen lacking in melanin, forgive the question, but why are Wonderland's Queen and the leader of her palace guard dressed in this manner?'

'Because we have a meeting to attend, Mr Harte,' Alyss said.

'A meeting? But I wasn't notified. Why wasn't I notified? Were *you* notified?' Bibwit asked General Doppelgänger, who shook his head. 'Why weren't the General and I informed of this so-called meeting? Why were we not at the top of the list of attendees, or at least –'

Dodge pulled a dull grey rock from his pocket and handed it to the tutor.

'A lump of dolomite is to explain our lack of an invitation?'

31

'Rub the smooth side of it.'

Bibwit, so accustomed to being the instructor, did as he was instructed. *Brumalia salvage lot, Plattnerite Quadrant, Wondertropolis* glowed briefly on the rock's flat surface, along with the date and the symbol of the upcoming hour. He understood at once: Alyss and Dodge were going to a Clubs' anti-imagination rally.

'You must not attend, Alyss. There's too great a chance you'll be recognised.'

'I've already tried to convince her,' Dodge mumbled.

'You're at your most vulnerable, my Queen,' said General Doppelgänger. 'I will unshuffle a deck of soldiers to prevent the meeting.'

'No!' Alyss's vehemence took everyone aback – herself not least of all. 'One founding family has already fallen into disgrace,' she said, 'and at this precarious time in Wonderland's history, we do *not* need to lose another if we can avoid it. You all know that I don't care for them personally, but the Lord and Lady of Clubs have too much influence politically and economically to be arrested without absolute proof.'

'Let me go alone,' Dodge said. '*I* will bring you proof.'

Alyss turned an exasperated eye on The Heart Crystal and its blinkered, apprehensive glow. 'The reason I'm Queen has been taken from me. The three of you should consider the likelihood that without my powers, I'm not so important to Wonderland, or to White Imagination. As for attending this meeting,' she turned to Bibwit and the General, hooked an arm under Dodge's, 'I have this brave guardsman to protect me. As for the meeting itself . . . we cannot prevent Wonderlanders from gathering, simply because we don't like what they've gathered to hear; they must first break laws. Nor are the innocent to suffer with the guilty. General, you're to deal the decks, if and only if you receive communication from Dodge.' She handed her royal sceptre to Bibwit. 'Please hold on to this while I'm gone.'

The Queen and her guardsman were at the top of the stairs to the outside world and no longer in sight when the tutor blinked at the sceptre, surprised to find it in his hand.

'This is not a good idea!' he called.

Alyss, knowing she didn't have to raise her voice for him to hear, watched the chamber hatch slide open to reveal a blood-dark sky speckled with stars, and murmured, 'The best ideas rarely are, Bibwit.'

♦ CHAPTER 6 ♣

Alyss and Dodge were required to surrender the dolomite, the Two of Clubs at the salvage lot entrance reaching for it and scraping the guardsman's palm with the sharp-angled steel of his gauntlet. Citizens from all strata of Wonderland society had shown up for the rally: kitchen workers in their splatterproof wear, on breaks from nearby restaurants; upright gentlemen sporting the collar-pins that signified them as law court arbiters; travelling merchants with their cases of goods; shop owners handing out advertisement crystals for their establishments; entire families come as if for a night's picnic. There was even, as Dodge indicated to Alyss with a jut of his chin, a trio of off-duty palace guardsmen.

Alyss held Dodge's hand as the crowd carried them to a space cleared amid the old transports in various stages of disrepair, the heaps of bent and broken hovercycles.

'This is my fourth time at one of these,' a Wonderlander

next to Alyss confessed. 'I don't agree with *everything* they say, but they *do* make sense on a number of points. And sometimes they serve mostly toasted oaties afterwards.'

Alyss smiled politely, not daring to speak in case her voice gave her away.

'So many people,' another said. 'A half-moon ago, the audience wouldn't have filled a space half so big.'

The rally couldn't have been more than a few hundred Wonderlanders strong: not the largest Alyss or Dodge had ever been to, but not the smallest either.

And if their numbers are growing …

'I know what it's like to deceive myself!'

The amplified voice seemed to come from all sides simultaneously, echoing off the hard surfaces of ruined vehicles and causing the fire crystals along the perimeter to gutter as if from the force of jabberwocky breath.

'I know what it's like to lie to myself!' the voice boomed.

'Over there!'

A matronly woman pointed to the Lady of Clubs standing atop a stack of flattened hovercycles with her husband and several Wonderlanders Alyss didn't recognise. Club soldiers – Twos and Threes and a pair of Fives – took up position around the makeshift stage, facing the crowd.

'I know what it's like to hate myself!' the Lady of Clubs announced.

Dodge squeezed Alyss's hand and gave her a questioning look.

Why couldn't it have been a renegade general instead of the Clubs themselves? For Wonderland's sake? wondered Alyss. *It would be best to take the lord and lady into custody when no audience was present. Don't want to turn them into martyrs. Arresting them now might provoke their followers.*

Alyss shook her head. Dodge should not yet signal for troops.

'I used to pretend I had a powerful imagination,' the Lady of Clubs was preaching, 'that I could rival Alyss Heart in any show of imaginative strength! I did this because I couldn't bear to admit I possessed none of what Wonderland has, for too long, valued above all else! But I no longer have to lie to myself!' The Lady spread out her arms and turned her face to the heavens. 'I HAVE NEVER BEEN GIFTED WITH IMAGINATION!'

The murmuring crowd went silent. Elsewhere, in limbo coops that were broadcasting the Lady's speech, imaginationists had stopped complaining of their sudden imprisonment to listen.

The Lady of Clubs let her pronouncement hang in the air, went on in a calmer voice. 'A Wonderland devoid of imagination is cause for celebration. No longer need we feel like lesser citizens because we cannot invent anything worthy of passing into The Heart Crystal. No longer must shame be our constant companion because we cannot conjure silly objects. The time of our suffering is at an end. I belong to one of Wonderland's founding families and yet I stand here,' with a turn of her hand, she indicated the Wonderlanders next to her husband, 'sharing the stage with a family of salvagers. Because where imagination is concerned, no one is superior to anybody else – not founding families and not Queen Alyss.'

Some in the crowd were nodding, muttering agreement.

'We have an opportunity, the first of its kind in Wonderland's history, to rise up against those who've made us feel bad about ourselves for so long. My fellow unimaginative citizens, let us not squander this momentous occasion! Let us unite to topple "our" Queen, whose family has flaunted their imagination over us with . . . yes?'

In the crowd, a squat little fellow with mutton-chop sideburns had raised his hand. 'But doesn't it take imagination to have thought of what you're proposing? And isn't imagination required for us to organise and, to use your words, "rise up" against Queen Alyss's administration?'

'Interesting,' the Lady of Clubs said, flashing a look at her Five Cards. 'I'd like to hear more of your thoughts on this matter in private. Kindly accompany my representatives to the smail waiting outside.'

Club soldiers roughly escorted the man from the premises.

'I trust no one else believes that I or my husband have any imagination whatsoever?' the Lady of Clubs asked the silent crowd. 'Good. What you choose to do tonight can reverberate throughout history. For your future welfare, for the welfare of your children and grandchildren, every one of you must etch your names into what will be the foundation of a new government in Wonderland: the Pledge of the Unimaginative!'

The Clubs stepped from the stage and the audience heaved, sympathetic Wonderlanders clamouring for a word from the wealthy couple or pushing to be among the first to add their names to the Pledge: an edifice of marbled dolomite sculpted to resemble an oversized *In Queendom Speramus* – the tome that for generations had provided the foundation of a Queen's education. In the commotion, Alyss's hand was yanked from Dodge's. *No!* Her freckles smearing, she struggled to reach him again, to be free of the pressing bodies, while he bumped people out of his way, clearing a path towards her as –

A news tweaker noticed the struggling Wonderlander with the stained cheeks. Something about her struck him as familiar. Then a stray arm knocked her wig askew. 'Queen Alyss?' he breathed. He tugged at those around him, pointing. 'The Queen! Queen Alyss is here!'

His cries attracted the Clubs' attention. Soldiers forced their way through the crowd, closing in fast on Wonderland's sovereign and finding –

A dirty wig on the pavement.

'Block the exits!' a Five Card ordered.

Access to and from the lot was immediately cut off, blockaded by Club soldiers, and somewhere within the gathering of suddenly nervous anti-imaginationists, amid all that scrap Wonderland steel: Alyss Heart and Dodge Anders trapped.

♣ CHAPTER 7 ♦

They could not remain at Talon's Point, the highest peak in the Snark Mountains, as oblivious to the world below as the Wonderlander they mourned. Hatter Madigan had said this more times than he remembered, trying to convince himself as much as his daughter. Yet they were still here.

'We can't stay,' he said again.

Homburg Molly merely stared at the faded glow of fire crystals in the pit. Since the last new moon, they had ventured from the cave only to forage for winglefruit lower on the mountain. They spent nights sitting in meditative quiet beside Weaver's grave, Molly fingering her mother's crushed Millinery ID chip, which hung from a strip of flugelberry vine she wore around her neck, while Hatter ran his fingertips over the formulas in Weaver's alchemy notebooks. The formulas themselves were meaningless to him. But Weaver had entered them into the books. Weaver, with her precise, delicate hands. He would have to learn to live with her absence. Molly, too. Leaving Talon's Point would not make it easier.

'She should have a Hereafter Plant,' Molly said, getting to her feet.

Hatter wasn't at all sure the plant would grow in the shadowy atmosphere of the cave. 'We'll bring a seed on our next visit.'

In a moody silence, Molly packed blankets, along with her mother's notebooks and diary, into the satchel left in the cave years earlier. She had allowed herself to watch the diary, once and only once . . .

Hatter pressed the covers of what resembled a pocket-sized hardback from Earth in every particular except that, splayed open, it projected on to the air an animated holograph of Weaver. Molly flinched when she saw her: Weaver concerned over what had become of the Queendom under Redd, for the toddler daughter she'd left at the Alyssian camp in The Everlasting Forest. Everyone else supposed Hatter dead or lost to Earth forever, but not Weaver. She'd wanted to leave him word – at Talon's Point, where the two of them had, in better times, made a refuge for themselves – of the daughter he didn't know existed. Hatter said he hoped the diary would help explain things, but afterwards, Molly was quiet and she never asked to view it again.

She stood at her mother's grave with her head lowered while Hatter stepped to the hollow in which he'd stowed his Millinery gear: his top hat and wrist-blades; his belt that could flick out sabres with a punch of its buckle; his backpack with its seemingly endless supply of body-puncturing weaponry. Not long ago, Molly wouldn't have been able to leave the gear alone, wanting to prove her combat skills. But since her mother's death, she pretended not to see it.

Hatter brushed his top hat clean of dust, held it by the brim and with a quick sideways jerk of his wrist flattened it into a coptering fan of S-shaped blades connected by a common axis-bolt. He sent the weapon slicing through the air towards the mouth of the cave. It boomeranged back to him and he caught it effortlessly, returned it to its conventional hat shape and flipped it on to his head. Molly was watching him.

'Seems to be working all right,' he said. 'When we get back to Wondertropolis, we'll have a new homburg made for you.'

'Whatever.'

Her lack of concern for her lost homburg, her disinterest

in all things Millinery, were more troubling than her insolence had been back when Hatter naively thought her untrustworthy because she was a halfer. Locking his Milliner bracelets into place, he squeezed his hands into fists to activate first one set of blades, then the other: deadly steel spun at the outside of his wrists. Relaxing his hands and forearms, the blades retracted and the bracelets clicked shut.

'I'd better contact Bibwit to tell him we're on our way,' he said. 'The communicator doesn't get reception in here, so . . .' he gestured at the open mouth of the cave. 'Would you make sure my backpack works? All this dust, its inner mechanics might be gunked up.'

By the time he was on the ridge outside, slyly peering into the cave, Molly had set down her mother's satchel and strapped the backpack over her shoulders. She shrugged, unenthused, and a host of daggers snapped to the ready. With a second shoulder twitch, the weapons sank into the backpack. Another annoyed little shrug and knives and spearpoints again pushed out of the backpack, but Molly made no move to reach for one, to pretend she was mid battle, as she used to do. She shrugged; the weapons folded away.

'It works!' she said loudly. So she knew he'd been spying.

He stepped into the cave and, taking the backpack from her, cupped her chin in his hand and lifted her face to his. He wanted to tell her what he'd told her countless times already – that Weaver had left her at the Alyssian camp out of love, not the opposite; that Weaver had intended to return to the camp until she became afraid of Queen Redd discovering that Hatter Madigan had a daughter – Queen Redd, who was intent on wiping out the Milliner breed. He wanted to tell her what he'd told her two nights earlier, as they stood at the cave entrance watching the setting suns – that, yes, King Arch had used her to satisfy his own ambitions. But if it hadn't been Molly, he would have found another way. Lives would have been lost no matter what. The responsibility lay with Arch, not with her.

'It wasn't your fault,' he said, meaning Weaver, everything.

'I know.'

Molly didn't look as if she believed it. He kissed her forehead, reminding himself not for the first time that he probably couldn't underestimate the effect her years as an orphan had had on her.

They shared a solemn moment together at Weaver's grave, then started down, hiking the passage Hatter had tunnelled through the mountain with his wrist-blades a lifetime ago. At day's end they emerged from the passage on to the lower slope, the velvet-petalled daphnedews shivering in the coolness of oncoming night. Molly tramped on, a good ten paces in front of Hatter, and she almost didn't realise it when he stopped, tense and staring at a bushel of shady greens. A sort of spicy liquorice smell laced the air, her nostrils tingled, and out from behind the bushel's thick, broad fronds a blue caterpillar four times her size floated on a cloud of hookah smoke, his lipless mouth puffing at his waterpipe as if this were propelling him forwards. Molly had read about caterpillar-oracles in her classes at the Millinery. But here was the first she'd ever seen, sailing straight for her, and it was all she could do to remain motionless as he drifted to within arm's length of her, exhaling three blasts of hookah smoke that spelled out, in letters shivery with foreboding, Y-O-U.

♦ CHAPTER 8 ♣

Boarderland: Wonderland's largest, most powerful neighbour, consisting wholly of nomadic towns and cities, any one of which might be situated amid the sandy dunes of Duneraria one week but spread out alongside Bookie River the next; an uncultivated, expansive place where itinerant settlements had always been separated by large tracts of unpopulated, rugged terrain; a land where, except for clashes, tribes used to keep to themselves, allowed to observe their own customs and rituals so long as they submitted to Arch as King of *all* Boarderland.

But that was before Arch had been reunited with an old friend and his practice of perpetuating hostilities among the tribes revealed for what it was: the method by which he maintained his authority, stoking animosities so that the Astacans and Maldoids and others wouldn't unite to form an army his own could not hope to rival.

That was before Redd Heart.

'WILMA was *not* activated as she should've been, but I recognise her effects,' the former King whispered to one of his intel ministers, who was crouched behind an orb cannon to avoid notice. 'I'm willing to bet Redd is without her powers. We wouldn't be returning to Boarderland if she had them.'

'You don't know for sure she's without imagination, My Liege.'

'Not yet. But I will.'

The military caravan had halted in Outerwilderbeastia before the final push back into Boarderland. With the prospect of it before him, the country Arch had so recently ruled suddenly seemed inhospitable and miserly, a dusty landscape of wind-battered tenements and few natural resources. It had never been enough. He didn't want to be King again, not if it meant being King of Boarderland alone.

'Nor can you know if such a loss of imagination is permanent,' the intel minister said.

Arch looked off to where Redd lounged beneath a canopy at the edge of the sparring arena, an open space surrounded by tribal warriors and Earth mercenaries. Sitting with Mistress Heart in the shade along with the rest of her top military rank was The Cat – half feline, half Wonderlander, total assassin; and Vollrath, that member of the tutor species devoted to Black Imagination. All unengaged troops had been ordered to gather for a series of brawls. It was supposed to be entertainment.

'You see how Redd pretends to give no thought to the fact that even now,' Arch said to his minister, 'both in front of us and behind, her recruits are fighting Alyss's forces? She's overacting. With this leisurely retreat of ours, she's trying to prove that clashes with her niece's armies are nothing and she can go where she likes, Wonderland is as good as hers. I don't believe it.'

Arch knew Redd's impatience too well: in taking back the crown, in putting an end to Alyss Heart, Redd would never have been leisurely if she could help it.

'Had WILMA wreaked what she was supposed to,' the minister said, 'Boarderland and Wonderland would already be yours, My Liege.'

Arch nodded. 'If Redd's without her imagination, so is Queen Alyss. I have to take a chance and make my move while they're without their powers.'

Shouts rose from the troops around the sparring arena. Hoofs and fists pumped the air. The first brawl had begun.

'Arch!' Redd's voice cut through the cheers and

catcalls, her eyes on the former King.

Arch dipped his head, the closest he would ever come to a bow. 'Coming, Your Imperial Viciousness!' Turning away to take his position at Redd's side, keeping his lips as still as possible, he told his minister, 'You're going to pay a visit to the Glass Eyes' tent and you're going to do and say exactly as I instruct . . .'

It could not have been going worse for her niece, chessmen succumbing to slashing blades, card soldiers falling a pack at a time under a barrage of orb generators and cannonball spiders. How invigorated Her Imperial Viciousness had felt, watching Alyss's pathetic defensive manoeuvres as Boarderland's twenty-one tribes, under *her* command, stormed into Outerwilderbeastia, each tribe wielding the weapons they most favoured: gossamer shots (Awr), mind riders (Maldoids), kill-quills (Scabbler), death-balls (Gnobi), knobkerries (Astacans), and the crude tools of less developed tribes hardly worth her notice. No, her attack on Wonderland couldn't have been going better. Her Boarderlanders and Earth recruits had laid flat shuffle after shuffle of Heart soldiers, rampaging through Outerwilderbeastia into The Everlasting Forest and The Chessboard Desert, converging on Wondertropolis. How she had frowned with appreciation as The Cat swiped claws across the chests of Six Cards and swatted down pawns! How she had grimaced with pride as her foremost military rank, the most gifted of her Earth recruits, proved their worth: Sacrenoir, who raised the bones of the dead into skeleton-zombies desperate to satisfy their insatiable hunger for live flesh; Siren Hecht, unhinging her jaw to release high-pitched screams that sent platoons squirming to the ground in pain; Alistaire Poole, the surgeon/ undertaker who conducted autopsies on living card soldiers; and Mr Van de Skulle, dexterously lashing chessmen with his spike-tipped whip.

And at last she'd been making her way down Heart Boulevard, towards Heart Palace and a final victory over her presumptuous upstart of a niece! But that's when things had gone instantly, horribly –

Odd.

She awoke, lying in the middle of the boulevard, her head hazy, her soldiers splayed about in various stages of unconsciousness. She had tried to view Alyss with her imagination's eye but saw only blackness. Whether or not her niece had harnessed some sort of reserve power from The Heart Crystal, as Arch had suggested, Redd didn't know.

The infusion of strength she'd experienced when nearing The Heart Crystal had gone in a moment. She'd been barren of imagination ever since.

'Not bad,' she said, applauding listlessly as Ripkins dragged a defeated Glass Eye from the sparring arena.

She had called for the fights in order to boost morale. The tribes were fitful, having never remained in such proximity to one another for any length of time and not understanding why they hadn't stormed Heart Palace when they had been so close. But she couldn't have risked entering the palace when Alyss might have had her powers while she . . . no, she hated to admit it even to herself. Besides giving her an opportunity to observe what Arch's bodyguards were capable of, the sparring matches would distract the troops from their unease.

Redd nodded in Blister's direction. 'Your turn.'

The bodyguard stepped into the sparring arena, pulled off his elbow-length gloves and placed them neatly in his pocket. Her Imperial Viciousness glared out at the troops.

'Anyone wishing to earn my special regard, which should be every one of you, will step forwards and earn it!'

Blister waited for an adversary, but none came forwards.

'Are this Doomsine's talents so great that you'd all risk *my* wrath as cowards?'

51

'Let me fight him.'

The Cat's words had come out as a growl. He was standing between Redd and Arch in humanoid form, erect on two heavily muscled legs, his strong arms reaching down past his waist, his paws unsheathing claws sharp and long enough to run through an average-sized Wonderlander. His fangs showed beneath his flat pink nose, his twitching whiskers.

'You've only one life left,' Redd reminded him.

'And it's worthless if I don't risk it doing what I do best.'

'I like your rashness, feline. Take your position.'

The Cat leapt into the sparring arena. He and Blister eyed each other, unmoving.

'Is this supposed to be impressive?' Redd snorted.

Like one warming up for more strenuous exercise, Blister tossed a whipsnake grenade, but The Cat easily sidestepped its slithering, snapping electric coils. Blister would try to work his way in close, The Cat knew. Every swipe of a paw could prove as deadly to himself as to Blister. He should be careful. But he wasn't here to be careful, so he ran straight at his adversary, his powerful legs carrying him forwards with such thrust and purpose that anyone else would have tried to flee, but Blister merely remained where he was.

The Cat pounced – a low, perfectly horizontal leap forwards. He morphed into a kitten in midair, ducking Blister's outstretched hands, and transformed back into a humanoid as he passed, raking his claws across Blister's shin. He came to a stop three spirit-dane-lengths away, a full-formed assassin again.

Blister showed no sign of feeling the bloody gash in his leg. He produced an AD52 from somewhere beneath his coat and held down its trigger, shooting a full deck of razor-cards at The Cat and stalking after it. The Cat avoided what projectiles he could and batted down others, smacking the tops of them without touching their sharp edges, but Blister was able to get within arm's reach and –

The Cat hissed, leapt back. Blister had grazed his shoulder with a finger. The fur immediately swelled; the skin underneath it bubbled. The Cat popped the swelling with a claw and spat.

Beneath Redd's canopy, Arch leaned towards his mistress, smiling and flirtatious.

'You're looking particularly grim, Your Imperial Viciousness.'

'Flatterer.'

'I *was* going to woo you with lies, Redd, but I have to say, the blurriness that's been part of you and The Cat since your return to our world –'

'What of it?'

'I know you said something about its being the result of your unprecedented journey through The Heart Crystal, but . . . well, it's pretty much gone.'

Redd crinkled her nose in what was supposed to be a teasing manner. 'Again I ask: what of it, Archy? Does it surprise you that I used my powerful imagination to rid myself of a loathsome blurriness? It's just taken longer than I'd liked. What The Heart Crystal gives isn't so easily done away with . . . even for me.'

'Hm,' Arch said.

Blister and The Cat stood breathing heavily in the middle of the sparring arena, each waiting for the other to make the next move. Blister's clothes were shredded, thin lines of blood showing where The Cat's claws had dragged across his chest, back, leg and arms. The Cat's shoulder and forearms were leaking – wherever Blister had even lightly touched him, yellow pus dribbled from popped bubbles of skin.

'Caterpillar,' Vollrath noted, his ashen finger pointing at a series of green smoke rings drifting out from behind a fried dormouse hawker's stall.

In the sparring arena, Blister threw a dagger at The Cat. The feline dropped into a crouch, about to spring forwards.

'Enough!' Redd shouted. 'As much as we're all dying to see the outcome of this little dalliance, I may still have use for *both* of you.'

Though she'd always deemed caterpillar-oracles to be ugly, annoying creatures, Her Imperial Viciousness stomped towards the dormouse hawker's stall, leaving Blister and The Cat to believe they had lost their sole chance to prove which of them was the greater fighter. They couldn't know there would soon be another.

♦ CHAPTER 9 ♣

Alyss didn't think they would survive. Too many anti-imaginationists in the salvage lot had seen Dodge hurry her into this rotting smail-transport to avoid the Club soldiers . . .

We've a few steps headstart at most.

. . . and now he was leading her up a buckled aisle to the pilot's station, pushing a hand under the sleeve of his jumpsuit to touch the keypad strapped to his forearm.

'Deal the decks!'

He's wearing his ammunition belt.

'Alyss has been recognised! Lord and Lady of Clubs on premises! Deal the decks!'

The General's voice sounded from somewhere beneath Dodge's jumpsuit. 'Decks dealt! Decks will –'

Pffffffffffffaaa!

The transport shook. Outside, Alyss could hear the

metallic wheeze of unfolding cannonball spiders, the scuffle of running feet, panicked voices.

'This transport's positioned against the lot's outer fence,' Dodge said, pulling an AD52 from under his jumpsuit, 'so if we can just . . .'

He aimed his weapon at the side of the pilot's station and hit the trigger. *Fith fith fith fith fith!*

Razor-cards embedded in the wall, forming a rough circle.

Everything's moving so quickly and yet so slowly . . . Dodge kicking at the wall panel outlined by his razor-cards, and there, a Three of Clubs entering where we did just a gwormmy-blink ago. Has it only been a gwormmy-blink or – ?

'Dodge?'

Before the Three of Clubs had even planted a second foot in the transport, Dodge somehow armed himself with a crystal shooter and sent out a swarm of luminous bullets. The soldier fell, but more were coming, shoving aside the lifeless Club and scrabbling into the ruined vehicle, their mauler rifles spitting shards of quicksilver.

Dodge pulled a slender rod from the top of his boot, and –

Fwathump!

The rod opened like an umbrella from Earth, its webbing shielding him and Alyss from incoming shards.

'Get that off,' Dodge said, nodding at the would-be escape hatch and handing Alyss his AD52.

He sent a steady spray of crystal shot around the shield, aiming at anything and everything. Only enemies were on the other side of the shield.

Alyss kicked at the pilot station's wall. *Focus, concentrate.* But it was hard, trying to conjure, as she'd been forced to do in past battles with Redd's card soldiers and Glass Eyes, swaddling herself and her forces in a cocoon of deflective NRG. She had to sharpen her attention to a pinpoint while still kicking at the –

Eeeeeeeeeeeeeeeesh!

A mauler shard whistled by her head.

'I can't hold them off much longer!' Dodge said.

Alyss stepped back and held down the AD52's trigger until the ammo cartridge clicked, empty. At least three decks of razor-cards outlined a circle on the pilot station's wall. She aimed her foot at the circle's centre, kicked as hard as she could.

The wall panel came loose, clattered to the floor.

The outer fence.

She could reach out and touch it, but pressed up against its other side, blocking any chance of escape: the solid windowless side of another transport.

'What's wrong?' Dodge shouted. 'Go! Go!'

He backed towards her, shield still held to their advantage and crystal shooter spewing its life-ending spatter. Club soldiers continued to advance, sheltering behind rusty benches, progressing cautiously up the aisle to the pilot's station.

Then Dodge saw it: the second transport.

But in the quarter-instant he and Alyss stood staring at its impenetrable side wall, with mauler silver ricocheting dangerously around them, swatches of it began to vanish, swiped into nonexistence by an unseen hand, like figures being erased from a blackboard.

A man's face appeared in the opening – the man with mutton-chop sideburns who'd been roughly escorted from the salvage lot.

'I thought I heard something,' he said.

He was holding what looked like a kaleidoscope, no longer than his forearm, the larger end of which he now dragged back and forth against the fence that separated the two transports. Wherever the instrument touched, the fence faded to nothing.

'You're both welcome onboard,' he said. 'Although I

doubt you'll like where we're going, it *should* be safer than staying here.'

The man's transport jerked into motion. Alyss and Dodge had no time. Mauler shards were pinging and bouncing off the pilot station's controls. Dodge's jumpsuit had already been sliced through in several places. Another few paces and the Club soldiers would be upon them.

They jumped out of one transport into the other, landing awkwardly in the aisle, and Alyss immediately found herself attacked by scarves, blouses, a hooded cloak: imaginationist-prisoners offering what they could for further disguise.

'They'll be looking for you dressed as a farmer's helper,' the sideburned man explained, inclining his head and adding an almost inaudible 'Your Highness' to indicate that he knew who Alyss was. He moved his kaleidoscope-like instrument back and forth over the hole in the side of the transport. Wherever the instrument passed, the wall re-formed until the transport was entire again. Up and down the aisle, prisoners had gathered in twos and threes to prevent the Club soldiers in the heavily partitioned pilot's station from noticing the disturbance, but they now settled quietly into the shadows. Alyss and Dodge sat among them as if they had been there all along.

'Where are they taking us?' Alyss asked the whiskered Wonderlander.

'I couldn't tell you the exact location, but my guess – and my hope – is that we're going to one of the limbo coops.'

The limbo coops.

Dodge – surreptitiously tapping at the keypad on his forearm, transmitting tracking codes to General Doppelgänger – looked at her. They had heard unsubstantiated rumours of limbo coops, in which imaginationists were being imprisoned. But they had known for sure only that Wonderlanders were being routed from their homes and deposited *somewhere* . . . if not suffering worse.

The noise of the salvage lot was growing faint and, as the smail hummed through darkened neighbourhoods towards the Clubs' extensive land holdings, Alyss studied the diminutive hairy-cheeked man. He had a single eyebrow nearly as coarse and bristly as his sideburns. Squiggles of hair pushed out from his shirt cuffs, and tufts of the stuff grew thick on the first digit of each of his fingers. The only place he didn't have hair, it seemed, was on top of his head, which resembled the rounded point of a gwynook's egg. And unlike Dodge who, finished with his keypad, sat as tense as wire, and unlike the others in the transport, the man's status as a prisoner apparently did not weigh heavily upon him; he wore an expression of pleasant anticipation.

'Who are you?' she asked.

Again, he inclined his head ever so subtly. 'Just an average tinker who makes his living by travelling the Queendom, offering for sale the modest gadgets I design and manufacture myself, and which I trust either amuse and educate my customers or make their daily chores a touch easier.'

'But you have a name, I take it?'

'My name is Mutty P. Dumphy. But as I said, I'm a simple tinker who lives by what modest wit and imagination I possess, as all of my kind must.'

'You live by your inventiveness, but you subscribe to the Clubs' anti-imagination propaganda?' Dodge asked.

'I don't subscribe to it at all, sir.'

'Then why were you at the salvage lot to hear them speak?' asked Alyss.

'I see no harm in my tinkering with ideas as I do objects, if only to better understand why I don't believe what I don't believe. But mostly I was there in hopes of getting myself reunited with any number of friends who've been taken to the limbo coops. I can't be sure to which coop I'll be taken, of course. I don't even know how many there are. But I can't help being optimistic. I trust I will meet at least one of my friends, yet if not, others might benefit from seeing me, as I have encouraging –'

The smail-transport came to a sudden stop and Mr Dumphy, who'd been standing in the aisle, went tumbling into the pilot's partition. Ordered to disembark, the prisoners filed out on to an unpaved street, both sides of which were crowded with ramshackle structures that appeared on the verge of collapse – multi-level, if none-too-well constructed lean-tos complete with slanting floors and out-of-plumb corners. Around all, sheer walls of dolomite rose to unseen heights.

'Welcome home!' a Six of Clubs mocked from a guard tower, his mauler rifle aimed at the imaginationists. 'Congregating on the street is not allowed! Idling is not allowed!'

Limbo coop residents had shuffled from buildings to prevent the newcomers from settling into already overcrowded rooms. Slowly, not knowing what to do or where to go, Alyss, Dodge and the tinker walked the gauntlet of broken, defeated Wonderlanders. Dodge was half a step in front of Alyss and using his body as a shield. Alert for threats, he returned the goggle-eyed stares of families – dirty, hungry and growing more haggard by the hour; he scanned the cramped street, the condemnable buildings and the imposing dolomite walls rising into the night sky . . .

'Why would anyone *want* to come to a place like this?' Alyss murmured.

The tinker glanced about to make sure no one was near enough to hear but still spoke as softly as he could: 'Your Highness, I was trying to tell you I have encouraging news, and it is this: I've reason to believe imagination is returning to Wonderland.'

♦ CHAPTER 10 ♣

It should have been an uneventful journey from Talon's Point to Hatter and Molly's new flat in Wondertropolis's Gimble Lane. The skirmishes that intermittently flared up between Wonderland card soldiers and Redd's retreating forces were nowhere near the Snark Mountains. It should have been nothing more than a plodding trek from the lower slope of Talon's Point to one of the public hikers' cabins in the foothills, where Hatter and Molly could enter The Crystal Continuum and travel quickly to the capital city. Instead, they didn't even make it to the base of Talon's Point before –

'What was *that* about?' Molly asked, waking with her father next to a bushel of shady greens, the faint stink of caterpillar in the air. They had not been unconscious long. 'I knew oracles were big, but . . . do they always act so weird?'

'Not always,' Hatter said.

He'd been as still as a fossil – he, who knew precisely what to do when facing an enemy of terrible violence and power, had made no move and uttered no sound as Blue confronted his daughter, issuing his one-word prophecy. Never before had a caterpillar revealed itself to a Milliner not in company of the Queen, let alone a halfer whose confidence in her abilities had been shattered by a conniving king. Whether Molly didn't remember being singled out by Blue or didn't care, Hatter couldn't determine. Without a word, she got to her feet and started down the mountain again, sullen, uncommunicative, her eyes on the uneven ground. As if nothing had happened. As if she didn't care whether he followed her or not.

The hiker's cabin was equipped with two looking glasses. The first, unfocused, provided access to the elaborate crosshatch of sparkling passages that made up The Crystal Continuum; entering it, father and daughter would be able to go anywhere within the Queendom so long as their destination was equipped with an exit glass out of which they could be reflected. The second mirror was focused, bypassing the continuum's major arteries and communicating directly with a few locations in the capital city, including Genevieve Square.

'Not Gimble Lane, but it'll get us close enough,' Hatter said, referring to the focused glass.

'You shouldn't have left us,' Molly pouted suddenly.

She was staring at her reflections in the mirrors – *hers*, not his. Hatter was taken aback. He thought Molly knew better. He hadn't left them so much as he'd fought to prevent Redd from murdering Princess Alyss. At the time, there had hardly been a 'them' to leave.

'I had my duty to Queen Genevieve,' he said, 'to the Queendom and to the Millinery. Your mother understood –'

'You should have come back for us. You should have stayed.'

That stopped him. She *did* know better, but knowing it didn't help. He could not, he realised, reason Molly out of her feelings. And maybe she was right. He shouldn't have jumped into The Pool of Tears and spent thirteen years on Earth, searching for Princess Alyss. Impossible for him not to have done it, yet he shouldn't have done it, shouldn't have left Weaver. He couldn't have known about Molly, yet he should have known. He should have known and returned to his family.

'Do you have a lot of experience in looking glass transport?' he asked, which only seemed to give support to

67

Molly's complaints; he knew too little about her, not even if she was familiar with Wonderland's most efficient means of public transportation.

'I have enough,' she said, and bent into the focused glass.

He stepped into the continuum after her and, rushing headlong through the vein of ethereal glitter and shine, couldn't help being impressed. Molly travelled well, without any show of concentration on her destination, without any of the stuttering forwards motions typical of less experienced travellers who visibly struggled against the pull of entrance portals, near which the body fought hardest to be reflected back out into the world.

Midway to Genevieve Square, Hatter and Molly relaxed, as if floating in water, and let the gravity of its exit glass pull them onward.

Every hour of every day in Genevieve Square, businessfolk, shoppers, tourists, entertainment seekers and countless more stepped from the Crystal Continuum on to the pavement without attracting a second glance from passers-by. But Hatter Madigan emerging from a looking glass portal was no common occurrence. Hardly had he and Molly stepped to the pavement before Wonderlanders were pointing and calling out to the Millinery's most famous graduate. Hatter didn't appreciate being the centre of public attention. Aware that Molly was watching him, he tipped his top hat to fans and well-wishers, thinking he could not arrive at Gimble Lane fast enough, not near fast enough. But finally –

'I guess this is it,' he said, squinting up at the beryl slab of a building in Gimble Lane. 'We're on the top floor.'

One of the Millinery's attendants had arranged for the rental of the flat, outfitted it with necessary furnishings and bedding, and transferred Hatter's few belongings to its sleek, spacious rooms. No doubt a large number of Wonderlanders would have been happy to live there, with its expansive view of the city, its automatic bedmakers and self-cleaning kitchen and bathrooms. But that was part of the problem. Entering the flat, glancing round at the gleaming sterility of floors and countertops and crystal hearth, at the pristine furniture the Millinery attendant had chosen and the walls barren of decoration, it didn't strike Hatter as a home for a father and daughter. Where a conventional family might have had an entertainment matrix containing thousands of programs and games: a collection of training manuals, delineating decades' worth of the Millinery's pedagogical techniques. On a shelf where holo-crystals etched during family outings might have been arrayed: the bottled cleaning solutions Hatter used on his top hat, wrist-blades and belt sabre. Aside from a scarf and the other little presents Weaver had given him, everything Hatter owned had come from the Millinery.

'You like that?' he asked, because Molly had run excitedly up to a purple dog flower, which was wagging its petals and barking happily under her touch.

The girl tensed, as if ashamed by her sudden eagerness. 'It's OK,' she shrugged and, without another word, loped off to explore the bedrooms.

A note crystal was leaning against the flowerpot. Hatter cracked it open. The dog flower was a housewarming present from the Millinery attendant. Moving from entry hall to kitchen, Hatter passed a square of translucent rock embedded in the wall, activating the flat's message retrieval system. A recorded hologram of Bibwit projected on to the air:

'Hatter, Molly, I apologise for intruding upon you so soon after your return. You have my sympathy as you cope with your recent loss, but unfortunate developments require your immediate presence at the palace. National security prevents me from disclosing more in this message. Please hurry.'

Hatter found Molly sitting on the edge of the sleep-pod in her room.

'What are you doing?'

'Nothing.'

Here was an enemy against which his blades were useless: his daughter's pain and resentment, her confusion. 'I'm sorry, Molly.'

'For what,' she snorted, 'doing your Millinery duty?'

He felt a spike of temper. 'You're not the only one . . . with feelings. Bibwit has requested us at the palace.'

'I don't feel like going.'

Should he *make* her go, as a father demanding obedience? She would have to see Alyss sometime, but maybe it was best that she stayed in the flat. For now. Because whatever Blue's historic visitation meant, the Queen had to be informed. Bibwit Harte and General Doppelgänger had to be informed. And Hatter was pretty sure he preferred Molly not being there to hear it. She'd seen more violence and suffered more heartache than any Wonderlander ever should, but – as he guessed from Blue's prophecy – she was due to see and suffer yet more.

Because he hadn't lied. He just hadn't admitted the entire truth: caterpillars *didn't* always act so weird; but when they did, it was never good.

♦ CHAPTER 11 ♣

Redd stomped towards the green smoke rings that funnelled out from behind the dormouse hawker's stall, The Cat and others following at a short distance while Arch and Vollrath hurried to keep pace with her.

Arch, and all his coy talk about her blurriness.

He never flirted without an ulterior motive, Redd knew. He'd been trying to lull her into complacency, to disarm with soothing words in order to extract information he might find useful. She usually admired his deviousness, even when practised upon her, but something in his tone . . . he'd been goading her. As if he knew something. As if . . .

Could he have guessed she was without imagination?

Every other stride, she jabbed her rusty sceptre topped with shrivelled grey heart into the ground. Doubly irksome was the subject of Arch's flirtatious babbles. She had noticed it too – the edges of her body and The Cat's gradually becoming more distinct. She and her assassin now looked as they used to, before they had passed through The Heart Crystal and an amateur painter birthed them on Earth with his soft, smeary palette. Maybe the longer she and The Cat lived in actual flesh and blood, the less dependent they were on the imagination from which they had sprung? What did she care, so long as she'd got her old hard-edged self back?

She stepped behind the hawker's stall. The green caterpillar was alternating nibbles of double-fried dormouse snout with tokes from his hookah.

'Not a tarty tart,' he said, his mouth full of crunchy bits, 'but it'll have to do.'

Arch showed neither surprise nor awe at being so close to an enormous larva. Vollrath, however, bowed.

'You honour us with your appearance, all-seeing oracle.'

The tutor sneaked a glance at his mistress, knowing how much she disliked the creatures, but she seemed hardly aware of him, her jaw squared, her eyelids half-closed in suspicion and ill-concealed disgust.

The caterpillar motioned towards Redd's sceptre with a front leg and the legs immediately behind it mirrored the gesture. 'I see you navigated your Looking Glass Maze and retrieved your sceptre.'

'A great, wise oracle has come to point out the obvious, has he?'

The Cat, Sacrenoir and the rest of Redd's most senior military rank were gathering round. Boarderland's tribal leaders moved closer to listen while the common troops lingered at the sparring arena, curious to witness this meeting between Her Imperial Viciousness and an oracle.

'You must be feeling particularly *imaginative*,' the caterpillar said, sucking deep at his hookah and letting the sentence hang in the air.

Redd would have lashed out at this smoking-obsessed mushroom-hugger if she hadn't remembered what Vollrath once told her: that caterpillars could see all things past, present and future; there were no secrets from caterpillars. Which meant that this slinking annoyance before her knew she was without imagination.

What if, in his wormy wisdom, he revealed her lack to Arch or the tribal leaders? To Vollrath and her Earth mercenaries? She couldn't allow it. And if he knew what she was thinking right now? Let him know. Let him understand: oracle or not, if he dared speak a single word of her loss . . .

He was circling her, making a show of looking her up,

down, all around. 'I notice you're without Wonderland's crown.'

'You're nothing but a glorified worm,' she spat, each word like a burst of crystal shard from a muzzle.

'More "glorified" than "worm", I should think,' said the caterpillar, tossing the last of the dormouse into his mouth. 'You might want to think so too, since I'm willing to help you reclaim Wonderland's diadem.'

Redd's eyelid twitched. She breathed slowly, evenly, trying to control her temper. 'Why aren't you speaking in riddles, worm? Why no indecipherable symbols in a fog of sickening hookah smoke?'

The caterpillar shrugged, which surprised everybody since he didn't have shoulders.

'Oh wise and slithering one,' Vollrath said, his ears genuflecting, 'while I would never speak for Her Imperial Viciousness, who doesn't require help from anyone on account of her formidable imagination, I'm nonetheless sure she recognises the privilege you do her by offering aid. But . . .' the caterpillar, with a bored look on his face, mouthed the tutor's words as he said them, '. . . doesn't *In Queendom Speramus* state that caterpillars don't interfere in the workings of government, nor involve themselves in rivalries – whether

75

blood or strictly political – unless it's to ensure The Heart Crystal's safety? And even then, but rarely?'

The caterpillar grumbled and said, 'Have you considered, tutor, that by helping your mistress to reclaim the throne, I *will be* ensuring the safety of the Crystal?'

Vollrath had not considered it; his ears did a little embarrassed dance atop his head.

'I do as I have always done – what Everqueen requires if she is to reign,' the caterpillar said.

'Everqueen?'

Vollrath had never heard the term and silently turned it over in his mind. Her Imperial Viciousness, meanwhile, brooded . . .

The Heart Crystal safer with her on the throne instead of Alyss? Of course it was safer! A nation suffused with White Imagination was weak, exposed. For long-term strength and security, the Queendom's future had to be Black. And of course *she* was the Everqueen! *She'd* been born into the line of succession, not her niece. No edict from a mere monarch – not even if it had been her mother, Theodora – could change that. Alyss Heart: Neverqueen, the never-should-have-been Queen.

'What's that interesting thing over yonder?' the

caterpillar asked, gazing at something behind them.

Redd, Arch, Vollrath, The Cat and the other militants turned to look, but there was only the sky over Outerwilderbeastia. When they turned back, the caterpillar had gone.

All were silent, contemplative.

A ripple of movement passed through the troops nearest the Glass Eyes' tent, where what was left of that assassin force – cloned by Arch from Redd's originals – were being readied for combat. One of them had bolted out of the tent, startling the troops, and was speeding towards Mr Van de Skulle. The Dutchman firmed himself for attack, his spiked whip gripped in his fist. But the Glass Eye raced past. Daggers appeared in its hands and it launched itself at Redd, who did not seem in the least put out as –

Fwummp!

Her sceptre protruded from the Glass Eye's chest. The assassin staggered, sparks sprayed from its wound. Mr Van de Skulle stepped forwards and put an end to it with a well-placed lash of his whip. Pulling the sceptre out of the Glass Eye, he wiped it clean and presented it to Redd, and she held its spear-like butt-end to Arch's throat.

'Tell me, Archy. Why would I be ambushed by a Glass

Eye programmed to recognise *you* as its master?'

With an amused expression, Arch pushed the sceptre from his jugular. 'I gave orders for it to be done, Redd.'

'You – ?'

'Call it a test. To confirm what I suspected. You're without imagination.'

'And you'll be without a head!'

She swung her sceptre at him, but Arch ducked.

The Cat, Sacrenoir, Ripkins, Blister – everyone was stilled by uncertainty.

'My thinking,' Arch said, thrusting his knobkerrie vertically in front of him as – *klungk!* – Redd's sceptre clashed against it, 'was that if you had imagination, you would have conjured something to do away with that Glass Eye. But instead, you defended yourself as any one of us would have done. And –'

'Shut up!'

'– now you're swinging your ugly stick at me like an uncontrollable shrew instead of imagining me –'

'Shut up!'

She ran at him, her sceptre a deadly javelin. Arch held his knobkerrie at both ends to deflect the attack, leaving himself vulnerable, and Redd kicked him in the chest, slamming him backwards. Before he recovered his balance, she charged him again, but this time he managed to swing first. Knobkerrie smashed against sceptre. Redd lost a handle on her weapon, retreated a short distance to readjust.

'You've relied too much on your imaginative powers,' Arch smirked. 'Your everyday combat skills have suffered, Rose, if you'll allow me to say so.'

He snatched a second knobkerrie from the sash of an Astacan warrior and, one in each hand, twirled them baton-like as he advanced, driving Redd back on her heels and raising his voice to address the surrounding army.

'I have asked myself why Boarderland's tribal leaders would unite against me when, as king, I only ever strived for lasting peace among them!'

Redd tripped over a tree root and fell, hard. The Cat made a move to jump at Arch, but a stand of Doomsines – the King's own tribe – stepped forwards to defend him. Mr Van de Skulle took hold of his whip, Alistaire Poole his scalpel. Ripkins flexed his fingerprints. Siren Hecht loosened her jaw, threatening a scream, and Blister tucked his long gloves in a pocket, leaving his hands bare.

'I've since learned the reason for the mutiny!' Arch said to the tribes, foisting his knobkerries down at Redd who, flat on her back, spun her sceptre parallel to her body and knocked them away, somersaulted backwards and regained her feet. 'The late Jack of Diamonds claimed I kept you at odds to maintain control over you! But Jack was in Redd Heart's service! He would have said anything to get you to join together under Redd's command!'

'But he knew things that convinced us,' Myrval, leader of the Gnobi tribe, said. 'Things he could only have known if –'

Arch felt how unused to physical exertion Redd was; her sceptre was colliding against his knobkerrie with less and less force, her sallies slackening in pace. 'Redd used her imagination to discover whatever she needed to convince you!' he said. 'But where is that imagination now? Why is Redd Heart brawling with me like a common do-badder? And why are we *retreating*?'

'No one's retreating!' Redd shouted, and went at him with renewed vigour.

Fwack! Fwack fwack! Fwack!

'I'll tell you why!' Arch said, countering Her Imperial Viciousness's lunges with several of his own. 'Because Redd Heart has lost her imagination and is afraid of Queen Alyss!'

'Lie!'

Fwack! Fwack fwack!

'My tribal brothers,' Arch urged, parrying easily with Redd's increasingly manic attacks, 'why conquer Wonderland only to surrender it to a selfish, malicious Heart? Why not do what's best for our country and keep Wonderland's mineral-rich lands for ourselves, to benefit all of us! We don't need Redd Heart! United, I can lead you to success where she has failed! As one, to Heart Palace! As one, to –'

With the suddenness of a cannonball spider crashing to ground, Arch hit the dirt. The Cat stood over him, hissing, about to rip claws through giving flesh when –

Four Doomsine warriors jumped him. The Cat scratched and gouged, and even before his attackers fell to the ground, he was surrounded by more.

Every tribal warrior went at every Earth mercenary: Ripkins's hands cycloned in front of him, sawteeth fingerprints shredding the skin of thugs Redd had recruited from England, hangmen she'd culled from Brazil; Sacrenoir led his skeleton-zombies against a swarm of Awr and Scabbler; Mr Van de Skulle and Siren Hecht did their part against Maldoids and Fel Creel.

The Cat was clawing yet another Doomsine warrior when he sighted Blister in a scrum of mercenaries.

They would finish what they had begun in the sparring arena. He started fighting his way towards the bodyguard, then –

A whistle. Redd's whistle.

The Cat focused narrowed pupils on his mistress. With Vollrath, Redd was making her way to a narrow trail that led deep into the manic vines and gnarled, snarling tree trunks of Antic Arbour, Outerwilderbeastia's most dense region. The Cat converged on the trail head with Sacrenoir, Siren, Alistaire and Mr Van de Skulle, and engaged with them against Myrval and his Gnobi warriors as –

Boarderlanders took up surrounding positions, aimed orb cannons to annihilate them. But Arch was removing a knobkerrie from an unlucky mercenary when he saw it: Redd and her top assassins fighting through the Gnobi into Antic Arbour.

Unable to escape, outnumbered by the twenty-one tribes, the remaining grunts of Redd's mercenary force gave up their weapons and dropped to their knees.

'You let Redd get away!' Arch said, turning on Myrval.

'I didn't . . . *let* her,' the Gnobi leader protested. 'She fought a –'

'Perhaps I failed to convince you? Perhaps you still believe the lies told you by the Jack of Diamonds?'

'We will convince you of our belief.' Myrval signalled to his warriors, who started down the trail into Antic Arbour, where trees were manic and dirt sentient.

'Stay where you are!' Arch ordered.

The Gnobi halted and the King stared out at the ranks of Boarderland warriors paused in various attitudes of attack, adrenaline making uneasy pacifists of them. He could not let Redd survive. She would plague him as long as she drew breath. But how much easier it would be to do away with her once he'd secured ultimate power.

'You *will* hunt down Redd and kill her,' he told Myrval. 'Afterwards.'

'Afterwards?'

Arch held his knobkerrie aloft in a gesture of triumph. 'After Wonderland submits to its first king!'

CHAPTER 12

The walrus-butler guided the tea tray into Heart Palace's ancestral chamber, expecting to find, as he usually did at this hour, Queen Alyss silently communing with her foremothers and fathers, images of whom hung in marbled frames around the room.

The monarch, he was sure, would take much pleasure in the night's tea selection. Indeed, so lost was the walrus in reveries of Alyss's anticipated enjoyment that he tottered halfway into the chamber before realising she was not there.

'She must be in the memorial wing. Come along,' he said, steering the tea tray to the rooms that were recreations of Queen Genevieve's private quarters in the former palace. Although the tea tray was inanimate, made mobile by its adverse reaction to body heat, the walrus-butler habitually treated it as a pet. 'That's very likely the frog messenger,' he observed to it when, at the foot of a tumbled stone staircase, a blur shot past him. 'But to whom could he be delivering a message at this late hour, do you suppose? Well . . . no point in speculating, no point at all.'

After thoroughly canvassing the memorial wing without finding her, the walrus's eagerness to witness Alyss's satisfaction as she sipped her tea was still greater than any concern for her whereabouts. 'It's unlike the Queen to retire without having at least one cup,' he mused. 'Let's try the sovereign suite.'

The sovereign suite, however, was empty of the Queen.

With increasing alarm, the walrus checked libraries, salons, state rooms, even the briefing room. Failing to locate Alyss in any of these, he abandoned himself to anxiety.

'I don't understand why things aren't as they ought to be! With Queen Alyss – with the Queen *especially* – things should *always* be as they ought!'

With no eye for the palace's artworks or pearl-inlaid floors, the walrus-butler turned hurried flippers towards the war room.

'Please don't be there,' he mumbled, the tea tray bobbing before him, tea slopping from the kettle's spout and the kettle itself dangerously close to falling off the tray. 'Please, please,

please. For nothing favourable ever comes from Queen Alyss having recourse to the war room.'

Arriving at the place in question, the walrus discovered Bibwit Harte pacing to and fro, his ears as scrunched as his vexed brow. Four General Doppels and an equal number of Gängers were ranged about the conference table, along with Hatter Madigan, the white knight and white rook. But Queen Alyss was not present. Everyone in the room was watching a holographic screen, on which, before a backdrop of some dusky attic, a Wonderlander with an oblong head and the bushiest sideburns the walrus had ever seen was holding forth.

'I by no means thought my imagination worthy of note,' the man onscreen was saying, 'but when my friends, many of whom possessed more talent than I, were being rounded up by Club soldiers, I thought it prudent to go into hiding.'

'Prudent, Mr Dumphy, but an unjust necessity,' interjected the four General Doppels, to which the General Gängers grumbled their agreement.

'I'm a man of modest ability,' Mr Dumphy continued. 'But this has never been a source of resentment for me, as it often is for others who, minorly gifted, regret they're not geniuses. Until recently, I've had talent enough to make a living.

My wants are as modest as my abilities and I've had all that I've asked for and been comfortable. But when even my lowly imagination deserted me . . . I admit, it's been frustrating.'

'Your frustration is ours as well,' said the four General Gängers, to which the General Doppels vigorously nodded.

'Since before Queen Alyss's inauguration, I've been working on this little device.' The Wonderlander held up a tubular contraption for everyone in the war room to see – the kaleidoscope-shaped tool that had helped Dodge and Alyss escape the salvage lot. 'I've never let a day pass without devoting some attention to its completion,' he said. 'While in hiding, this mostly involved staring idly at its internal parts, but this morning I experienced a surge of inspiration and in a moment realised what had to be done to bring the invention to completion. As I believe the Queen can attest, the Rearranger, as I call it, now works perfectly, and since this morning I've felt my imagination growing stronger.'

'We're hearing similar reports from others,' the white knight acknowledged.

'Not as many as we would've hoped for by now,' said Bibwit.

'Some are probably afraid to come forwards because of the Clubs,' the rook noted.

Bibwit stopped pacing and his ears bent forwards once, as if to allow for the likelihood of this. 'What about *your* imagination, Alyss? Do you feel . . . anything?'

The Queen's face replaced Mr Dumphy's on the holo-screen, and the walrus-butler, who had been standing unnoticed by everyone except Hatter and Bibwit, blurted, 'Queen Alyss, I brought your tea!'

The generals and chessmen turned to him, surprised.

'Thank you, walrus,' Alyss smiled.

'Yes, I'll just . . . I'll place it here,' the creature said, setting the tea tray on the table and sweeping a fretful glance at the number of bodies in the room. 'And I'd better get more cups.'

'Alyss?' Bibwit asked again, once the walrus had gone.

'I feel nothing,' said the Queen. 'I've conjured nothing, and I can't even remote view into the next room.'

'We should not suppose WILMA's effects will be the same for everyone,' Bibwit said, more thoughtful than disappointed, 'since imaginations differ as much as Wonderlanders them-selves. I suspect Mr Dumphy's imagination isn't as modest as he claims, yet it makes sense to me that weaker imaginationists will be the first to recover. The less one had to lose, the less one has to regain; thus, the time needed to regain it should be shorter than it will be for, say, Queen Alyss or Redd.'

'In that case,' said the rook, 'we'd better hope Redd gets hers back first, since it'd mean Alyss is the stronger of the two.'

'Mind you,' Bibwit added, 'I posit this just as a theory, but the evidence supports it, as we've only received reports of small imaginative doings and have yet to hear of any great feats. On top of which,' the tutor flattened his ears in contrition, 'when confronted with the unknowable, all we have are theories.'

'We should assume the Clubs are aware of imagination's return,' Alyss said.

Dodge pushed his face into frame on the holo-screen. 'And Redd.'

'And Arch,' added the rook.

'We've had to assume all of the above,' put in the General Doppels. 'Redd's forces are no longer retreating.'

'They've been fighting their way into positions around Wondertropolis,' the Gängers added. 'We've officially commissioned the Spade decks to help in our defence.'

'Then Redd either already has her imagination back or she's preparing her forces in anticipation of its return,' said the knight.

The rook stepped smartly over to the room's crystal control panel, which had started to blink and beep. 'We're receiving a communication addressed to Queen Alyss. It's from *Arch*.'

The chessmen looked at each other, then at the generals. The generals directed questioning eyes to Bibwit, who in turn consulted the faces of Hatter and Alyss.

'I'm unavailable,' the Queen said. 'But keep the audio line open. I want to hear what he says.'

The image of Alyss and Dodge faded from the holo-screen, replaced by a close up of Arch. Seeing only Alyss's advisors in the room, the King frowned, aiming a particularly hateful glare at Hatter.

'My transmission is intended for your Queen.'

'If it's not too unpleasant for you,' Bibwit said, 'she has requested you make do with us.'

'I can make *nothing* of you. But how typical that Alyss absents herself when her Queendom's in peril. I expected a little more, even from a woman who, like her Aunt Rose, is without imagination.' He paused to let the advisors fully comprehend: he *knew*. 'Together with a great mass of nasty specimens that Redd left me, the Boarderland tribes are back under my command. I'm sure you've noticed they're again closing in on Wondertropolis? I intended to give Alyss a chance to surrender Wonderland without violence, but as she's off perfuming herself somewhere, it seems a bit of violence will be in order. So be it. Let her feel how an army commanded by a man contends against one that answers to a woman. I look forwards to subduing you all.'

The holo-screen went white. The rook pressed a button on the room's control panel and the visual of Alyss and Dodge came back on line.

'Alyss,' said Bibwit, 'we need to get you out of that limbo coop. You should be with The Heart Crystal, in case –'

'– my imagination returns in time to be of help?' Alyss raised an eyebrow in doubt. 'That doesn't strike me as likely, Bibwit. Nor should energy be expended on my behalf when as much effort as possible should go to defending the Queendom from this foreign invasion. A clash of armies, without the support of imagination on either side, likely benefits Arch. Generals, chessmen, I must leave him to you for now. The Clubs' rebellion must also be dealt with, which is why I'll remain where I am. Dodge and I have a plan to bring down this insurgency. I will continue to test my imagination and contact you the moment I feel anything.'

'What about Redd?' the rook asked.

'If we're lucky,' Dodge said, 'Arch put an end to her.'

'My Queen.' Seeing that Alyss was about to sign off, Hatter had risen from his chair.

'Yes, Hatter?'

The Milliner bowed, then: 'Earlier, as Homburg Molly and I were returning to Wondertropolis, the blue caterpillar made himself known to us.'

Alyss and her advisors didn't need to be told that such a visit from an oracle was unprecedented.

'Did he speak?' Alyss asked.

'He spelled a word in smoke. As a prediction, a warning, perhaps both. And it was directed not to me, but to Molly. The word was "you" – y, o, u.'

Alyss sighed. 'I've been thinking it strange that Blue showed me a vision of how to sabotage WILMA but hasn't appeared to me since, when The Heart Crystal hardly seems less threatened. And now he presents himself to Molly?'

'The oracles, whatever their value, are nothing if not strange,' Dodge said, putting an arm around her.

Alyss nodded, but not in happy agreement. *Why, just once, couldn't the caterpillars be perfectly intelligible?*

'How *is* Molly?' she asked.

Hatter hesitated, unsure how to answer.

The Queen seemed to understand his silence. 'Please tell her, despite all that's happened, despite all that's currently happening, I look forwards to seeing her. I can think of no one I'd rather have as a bodyguard.'

'I will, My Queen.'

Hatter again bowed, knowing that momentous events, the stuff of a nation's history, were sometimes dependent on individuals commonly thought the least likely to set them in motion. He prayed his daughter would not be one of them.

CHAPTER 13

'Is it wise, My Liege, to scheme against a caterpillar-oracle?' a minister asked.

King Arch sat beneath the same canopy under which Redd had recently shaded herself during the sparring matches. The lights of Wondertropolis shone in the near distance. Shooting out of the surrounding dark country, where Doomsines were battling a deck of Heart soldiers, cries of enemy wounded vied with war whoops from tribesmen.

'Is it wise to scheme against a caterpillar?' Arch repeated to himself as –

Booooooooooaaaaashhhhhhhhhhhhhkk!

An orb generator exploded over a stand of gobbygrape trees, momentarily turning night into day, and revealing the King encamped in an untilled field, Ripkins and Blister standing behind his folding chair, one on each side, and his intel ministers gathered before him.

'It probably is *not* wise,' Arch admitted, 'but I'm not convinced I am scheming against a caterpillar. I'm inclined to think I'm scheming *with* one. And whoever among you wants to keep your position as "intel" minister during my new reign, now is the time to remind me of your intelligence. How is it I could believe I'm scheming with the green caterpillar?'

The ministers huddled together.

'Because the oracle, who must know Redd is without imagination, didn't tell her about WILMA,' said one.

'Nor did he tell her that the loss of her imagination was, in part, your doing,' said another.

'And he might have done this before you exposed her,' said yet another.

'Seeing all time as an oracle can,' said a fourth, 'the green caterpillar could have warned you that WILMA's ultimate strength would be compromised, but he didn't.'

'Excellent.' Arch smiled – he had chosen his ministers well. 'The caterpillar did not warn me of sabotage, or reveal the truth to Redd, because *he* is plotting something that apparently requires me and Redd still to be pitted against each other. The caterpillar knew if he gave me an opening, I'd take it. The question becomes: how long does he believe

I will continue to be a bit player in his subterfuge, whatever it is?'

'But, My Liege, what of this Everqueen he mentioned?' a minister asked.

'The caterpillar will say what he must to manipulate Redd.'

'Your Majesty,' another minister whispered, 'don't you think the oracle knows of this conversation?'

Arch waved off the question. He assumed the caterpillar was aware of everything he said. He was counting on it. 'The tribes have arrived at the various coordinates I assigned for the siege?' he asked.

'They have, Your Highness.'

'And Redd's old rabble?'

'They couldn't be more obedient if you'd recruited them yourself.'

Arch stood, thrust his head and arms into a coat of armour resembling reptilian skin, its scales medallion-sized plates impenetrable to blade and crystal shot, to whipsnake grenade and spikejack tumbler. He strapped on his leg armour and hefted his knobkerrie.

'Ripkins, Blister, stay close to me throughout, but if we should cross with Redd or Alyss in any of the fighting, you have my leave to stray. They're to be shown no mercy. The same goes for Hatter Madigan and that daughter of his – absolutely *no* mercy.'

'No mercy, no problem,' Ripkins said, flexing his fingerprint sawteeth.

'More like a pleasure,' Blister muttered, pulling off his gloves.

The bodyguards followed Arch into the Doomsine battle, and all along the perimeter of Wondertropolis, Boarderland's twenty other tribes – each with two platoons' worth of Redd's mercenaries mingled among them – marched out from their various locations to storm Wonderland's capital city.

♠ CHAPTER 14 ♣

Their numbers were greatly diminished. Thousands strong not half a lunar hour before, Redd's minions now amounted to no more than her top military rank. Vollrath, The Cat, Sacrenoir, Siren Hecht, Mr Van de Skulle, Alistaire Poole – with their mistress, they had paused deep in the Antic Arbour to catch their breath, none yet venturing a word aloud, as if waiting for Redd to deny she was without imagination. But each of them knew: if Mistress Heart had her powers, they would not now be in the arbour, nor so few.

Trees spat and snarled. A claw-like branch scraped across Alistaire Poole's shoulders. A vine slithered wet against Siren Hecht's arm, leaving a trail of sludge; another coiled briefly around Sacrenoir's foot before slinking into the underbrush.

'This place is gross,' Siren said.

The others grunted, nodded in agreement, but Redd was too preoccupied to care about her immediate surrroundings.

How had Arch known she was without imagination? Why would it ever have occurred to him to think of it? She'd not been dumb enough to betray the fact by her behaviour.

'How do you think he knew?' The green caterpillar glided out from the arbour's darkest depths, an impenetrable weave of vines untying itself to let him pass.

Redd's voice quavered with rage. '*You* told him.'

'Ah,' said the caterpillar, his face spreading with a grin, 'I might have supplied the King with a wealth of silk, which the other oracles and I produced. I might even have informed the King what effects certain combinations and patterns of this woven silk would have – if roughly positioned over The Heart Crystal – on imagination in general. But I cannot take credit for what he did not need me to tell him.'

'You mean *he* did this to me?'

'With my guidance.'

Redd lurched at the great worm, but he vanished before she could so much as aim the deadly end of her sceptre at his soft belly.

'Behind you!' Sacrenoir pointed.

At her back, the caterpillar was calmly smoking his hookah. Redd tried to catch him unaware and whipped her sceptre-wielding arm around without turning her head, but –

'Above you!' Alistaire pointed towards the arbour's uppermost branches, where the caterpillar hovered out of reach.

'Your Imperial Viciousness,' Vollrath interposed, 'might not the present state of our affairs – to say nothing of your alleged condition – suggest to you the justice of listening to this rather plain-speaking oracle?'

'You forget whom you address, tutor. I have an underdeveloped notion of justice.'

'Do you?' Vollrath's brow leapt up, then contracted. His ears fidgeted. 'But Your Imperial Viciousness, you've frequently complained of being unjustly removed from succession to Wonderland's throne, and you cannot be so embittered by what is *unjust* if you haven't a strong conception of what is *just*.'

Redd stepped close to the albino and, in a voice of quiet menace, asked, 'Are you trying to teach me something, tutor?'

'No, Your Imperial Viciousness. By no means.'

Vollrath bowed his way out of arm's reach, and Redd turned a challenging eye on what was left of her army, silently daring them to engage in *anything* they wouldn't have dared to do when she had imagination. The Cat, Sacrenoir, Mr Van de Skulle, Siren Hecht, Alistaire Poole – in the steady steam of Redd's fury, it didn't occur to her that the caterpillar's presence had assured these assassins' continued support and allegiance; because although not anywhere near as strong as she used to be, a caterpillar would not have been courting her if she was to remain forever weak, defeated.

'You are about to ask why I provided guidance to King Arch,' the slinking wise one said, alighting on the tiniest of branches above her head.

Redd nodded.

'I have already answered this. Everything I do is to ensure the safety of The Heart Crystal. For Everqueen.'

But how was that possible? Redd questioned. Hadn't the oracle previously told her the Crystal would be safe only after she had regained her throne?

'You showed Arch how to take away my imagination so as to help me reclaim Wonderland's crown?'

The caterpillar sucked on his hookah pipe, exhaled three puffs of smoke: y-e-s.

'And your coming to tell me this – that you instructed Arch in how to rid me of imagination – this too is to help me reclaim Wonderland's crown?'

The caterpillar again let three clouds of hookah smoke do the talking: y-e-s.

'Inscrutable, infuriating worm!' Redd shouted, not understanding.

'It is supposed that power corrupts,' the caterpillar said in a voice as untroubled as time itself. 'Yet the powerful are often corrupt *before* they are powerful. In fact, I find that they too often become powerful *by being* corrupt. Whether real or perceived, a lack of power can also corrupt.'

'What's that got to do with me?'

'Your imagination will return in all its strength, Redd Heart. What you do then will determine everything.'

'Since you know so much,' Her Imperial Viciousness scorned, 'why don't you tell me what I'm going to do?'

'Mistress,' said the caterpillar, exhaling a fog that left Redd and her assassins unconscious almost before he finished speaking, 'your understanding of the future is naïve.'

CHAPTER 15

It was her fault and nothing Hatter could say would convince her otherwise.

During the new palace's inaugural gala, Molly had attended a meeting between Queen Alyss and King Arch; the King had snickered upon hearing she was the Queen's bodyguard and she let pride and resentment get the better of her. Untamed emotion, lack of self-discipline – the internal enemies of every Milliner – had left her susceptible to cheap manipulation, the Lady of Diamonds gulling her with an exquisitely carved chest supposedly meant for the Queen. If she had had any control over herself, she never would have corrupted the Crystal Continuum with the chest's contents, she never would have become Arch's prisoner, and her mother would still be alive.

Or so Hatter's daughter believed as she wandered the flat in Gimble Lane, absently petting the furry leaves of the dog flower whose pot she cradled in the crook of an arm. Yes, *she* was to blame. The fault was *hers*. The desire to prove herself as capable and trustworthy as a full-blooded Milliner had proved, beyond any doubt, that she was *not* as capable and trustworthy as full-bloods.

'But who's to blame for me being a halfer, a worthless halfer unfit for honourable service in the Queendom?' she asked aloud.

Hatter and her mother, that's who. Hatter, especially. Because he was supposed to know better, to *be* better. A halfer might be expected to make the mistakes she'd made, bad as they were. But not him . . .

'Can't help thinking of him as Hatter,' she mulled, gazing out the living room's picture window at the city.

Almost from the time she could walk, she had known him as a public figure, an icon, the hero of innumerable programs for portable Interactive Crystal Entertainment Devices, which somehow, even in the absence of luxury that had defined life at the Alyssian HQ, one child or another always managed to have. Molly had been as enthralled by the ICED programs as anybody – more so, since she hadn't just watched them for amusement but studied them, the foundation of her self-training. The great Hatter Madigan hadn't belonged to her any more than he had to other Alyssians, and now she was supposed to put aside the experience of living through those years and call him 'father'?

The dog flower whined as she set it on the floor. She took her mother's notebooks out of the satchel she'd carried from Talon's Point, untied the flugelberry vine that bound them, and thumbed through the most care-worn, examining the formulae it contained as if they might reveal a secret about their author. Then she tied up the notebooks again and removed her mother's diary from the satchel. She pressed its sides; its covers popped open and a 3-D image of her mother took shape before her. She scrolled through the diary's final entry, past Weaver's description of Redd-controlled Wonderland and the genocidal treatment of Milliners.

'I understand that our relationship was difficult for you, Hatter,' Weaver's image said as Molly slowed the recording to normal speed. 'I know that despite how thoughtful and loving you always were to me, a part of you was angry with yourself for succumbing to your feelings for anyone, let alone a civilian. You thought your feelings a mark against you, an indication of weakness.'

Molly had expected fresh anger, renewed agitation. Instead, the tears dropped from her eyes as she'd not allowed them to do when she watched the diary with her father on Talon's Point.

'Hatter, I know how you feel about halfers,' Weaver's image said, 'and I was never sure how you'd react to hearing you had fathered one. Every time I thought to tell you of my joy – of *our* joy – I found an excuse not to. I did plan to tell you the next time we'd be on Talon's Point together. But as you know, there was no next time.'

The recorded Weaver then explained how, at the Alyssian HQ, she had given birth to a beautiful baby girl. Only once before had Molly heard her mother describe her as 'beautiful', but the sorrow that threatened to take her breath was little compared to what she felt when Weaver said Hatter should know his daughter's name and –

'Molly,' she whispered, as if afraid enemies might hear.

The flat echoed with silence. The diary lay open in Molly's lap, but she made no move to close it or to play the entry a second time. She had heard it was easy to blame others for one's own failures. But that wasn't exactly accurate. It was easy to blame herself for what had happened – hard to live with it. And if the others in question were Hatter and her mother . . . it was hard to blame them, harder still to live with the need to blame them.

Chk!

The flat's security system unlocked. Molly barely had time to slip her mother's notebooks and diary into a coat pocket before the front door opened and Hatter stepped into the room, uttering the words he'd often uttered at Talon's Point, though for very different reasons:

'We can't stay.'

♦ CHAPTER 16 ♣

It was not possible to gather a large number of imaginationists together without attracting the Club soldiers' suspicion, so Alyss, Dodge and Mr Dumphy went from tenement to tenement, systematically visiting every flat in the limbo coop.

'They broadcast the Lady of Clubs' speech here,' a lanky tinker explained to them as they settled in the centre of a narrow, humid flat so full of Wonderlanders that Dodge couldn't put a hand on his hip without knocking into one of them.

'Go on, Silas,' Mr Dumphy said, encouraging his friend.

Mr Dumphy had an impressive collection of friends. Whether this was due to the itinerant nature of his business or to his easy, optimistic nature, he frequently recognised someone in each of the visited flats. And his evident concern for the prisoners' well-being and that of their families, his general air of being privy to a happy secret he was about to reveal, helped lessen the shyness that overcame imaginationists when they discovered themselves so near the Queen.

'Go on,' Mr Dumphy coaxed again.

'Well,' said Silas, 'all of us here heard the Lady of Clubs' preaching, and even though I've made my livelihood by my wits, I think I agree with her – imagination causes more problems than it solves.'

'The burden of creating has always been a source of worry for me,' said a pouty-faced poet. 'Maybe it's better to be without imagination.'

'But how would any of you make a living without imagination?' Dodge asked. 'How would you feed and clothe your families?'

It had been the same in the flats Alyss, Dodge and Mr Dumphy previously visited: there were always imaginationists who felt as Silas and the poet did, who talked about the stress of their creative lives, the full brunt of which they had never realised until their imaginative gifts had been taken from them. But at least Silas and the poet weren't vowing outright to sign the Clubs' Pledge of the Unimaginative, as had prisoners before them. Alyss's task here – Dodge and Mr

Dumphy's task – shouldn't be as difficult as it had been in other flats.

'My friends,' Mr Dumphy asked, 'can we ever truly trust the Clubs, who have locked us up in this horrible place?'

'Regardless of what the Clubs wish,' Alyss said, speaking for the first time and addressing the entire room, 'imagination *is* returning to Wonderland. Very soon, if you haven't already, the lot of you will again begin to experience your own imaginations.'

A young girl raised her hand. She was sitting on her father's shoulders, the better to see the Queen over her flatmates' heads.

She looks just like Lorina Liddell. As she was when I first met her.

Alyss flashed on memories of the entire Liddell family: Lorina's hiccuping laughter, always easily provoked; Edith's exacting morning toilette, its primpings usually intended to attract some boy who may or may not have ever noticed her; the Reverend's breakfast grapefruit and his gentle voice; walking arm-in-arm along Oxford's High Street with Mrs Liddell. Alyss even had a sudden vision of Miss Prickett, the governess who'd tutored her and her 'sisters' in the dining room of Christ Church's deanery and had insisted she incorrectly spell her name 'A-L-I-C-E'.

It was strange to be thinking of these things now . . .

Inappropriate really, considering the circumstances.

. . . but the sight of the girl on her father's shoulders reminded Alyss of a promise she'd once made to herself – to never forget her life with the Liddells.

'Yes?' Alyss asked, because the girl's hand was still in the air.

'I have my imagination.'

'And I have mine,' the girl's father said.

'As do I,' a voice announced from another part of the room.

The admissions came more rapidly then, prisoners acknowledging the full or partial return of their imaginations, which they'd been too afraid to confide to anyone until now. Even Silas confessed that he'd again been getting ideas for products.

'And do you believe,' Alyss asked him, 'that the Lord and Lady of Clubs will be satisfied with any pledge you make to anti-imagination when they know you have imagination they themselves don't possess?'

'I won't tell them it's back,' Silas answered.

'I seriously doubt that'll keep them from finding out,'

said Dodge.

'What about imaginationists who refuse to sign their pledge?' Alyss pursued. 'Friends of yours perhaps, or members of your own family? What do you think will become of them if the Clubs gain absolute power?'

'We're imaginationists,' Mr Dumphy declared to the room. 'That's what we *are*. It's useless, our wishing to be what we're not.'

'We can all be free shortly,' Alyss said, 'and the Clubs' plot brought to ruin if we work together.'

'Work together how?' someone asked.

'Until I give word to the contrary, do nothing to reveal your imaginations even to the lowliest Club soldier. I've yet to feel the faintest glimmer of my own imagination, but when my gift returns, we'll take the Clubs by surprise.'

'We *can* defeat them,' Dodge said, 'but it's absolutely imperative for the return of imagination to be kept secret.'

Alyss agreed. 'Were the Clubs to discover it before I have my power and we're ready to act, there's no telling what they'll do to us, penned in as we are. The Heart decks are presently fighting to keep Wonderland out of foreign hands and won't be available to help us. Imagination is the only way.'

'I'm with you, my Queen,' Silas vowed.

One after another, every imaginationist in the flat swore to do as Alyss Heart instructed: imagination was the only way.

Mr Dumphy accompanied Alyss and Dodge from the tenement at the end of the limbo coop's main thoroughfare. They had canvassed both sides of the shoddy street, full of prisoners.

'All we can do now is wait,' he said.

'We're sure that's the last one?' Alyss asked. 'We didn't miss a single flat?'

'Not in *this* coop anyway,' Dodge said.

It was risky enough, implementing a counterplot dependent on so many keeping a secret, but they had no way of knowing how many imaginationists were imprisoned in limbo coops elsewhere.

That the Clubs *would* learn of imagination's return was a certainty. But before they did, Alyss tried to believe, she would regain her powers. She had to.

♥ CHAPTER 17 ♣

Had you walked the quartz-speckled pavements of Whiffling Heights or strolled the Turtledove Mews, had you window-shopped along Slithy Avenue or stopped to talk with sunflowers in the Brillig Street Gardens, you might not have realised Wondertropolis had just fallen to an invading army. Buildings gleamed as serenely as ever. Transit ways were clear of rubble and debris, wounded tribal warriors and dead card soldiers. Neighbourhoods might have been deserted, but nowhere within city limits would you have found the after-blast mayhem so common in war, with entire districts reduced to quarries of urban desolation. True, there *were* intersections in the Plattnerite and Cinnabar quadrants that evidenced recent violence – blown out shop windows, smouldering, overturned smail-transports – but most of Wonderland's resistance had happened on the capital's outskirts. And having no ambition to rule over a demolished city, Arch had instructed his troops to inflict as little damage as possible on Wondertropolis while still guaranteeing victory.

'It's beautiful,' the King said, admiring the skyline from the balcony of Heart Palace's upper salon – a balcony from which, in better times, Alyss Heart might have enjoyed the amusements of an Inventors' Parade passing below.

Defeated, lined up as if for inspection on the salon's threshold: Bibwit, General Doppelgänger, the white knight and the Lord and Lady of Spades. Behind them, Ripkins stood with his hands hanging loose at his sides, ready for whatever his King might command. Blister was in a corner, pinching the blush-pink petals of an orchid between thumb and forefinger and watching it die.

'You really don't know where Alyss is?' Arch asked, turning to the Wonderlanders.

'She went off before your attack,' Bibwit said. 'She didn't tell us where she was going and we haven't seen her since.'

'I can't believe that.'

'Whether you do or not doesn't change the fact that it is so, Your Highness.'

Arch glanced at his intel ministers grouped around a table in the centre of the salon. 'Without her imagination, your Queen must be a coward. What else explains why she escaped but left you all here to be conquered? Wait. Did I say "conquered"? I meant to say you've been left under my guidance, along with the rest of Wonderland's subjects.'

The intel ministers chuckled. Ripkins's mouth slanted upwards, approximating a smile. Expressionless as granite, Blister made his way to an arrangement of pansies and grass stalks.

'I'm not like Redd Heart,' Arch continued. 'I wish no damage to Wonderland and love it as much as any of you.'

General Doppelgänger snorted.

'I don't mean the intangible guff about imagination,' the King said, steely-voiced, stepping close to the General, 'but the actual, physical place – Wondertropolis's streets and architecture, the ice and rock of The Chessboard Desert, the jungles of Outerwilderbeastia, the greenery of The Everlasting Forest, even the scorched ground of The Volcanic Plains.'

'You honour us with insight into your thoughts, Your Highness,' Bibwit intoned. If he was being sarcastic, he gave no sign.

'As I'm aware,' Arch said. 'So long as you're all loyal to me, your lives are safe. General, you'll help me earn the respect and allegiance of the card soldiers. Knight, you're to help me earn the same from the chessmen. I expect the lord and ladyship's full cooperation in my taming of the Spade soldiery, and Bibwit, you and I will determine how I can best win the confidence of the populace. You'll all soon recognise the benefit of having me as your sovereign. But as I also have the Millinery to rule over . . . where is the Great Defector, Hatter Madigan?'

'I don't know, My Liege,' Bibwit answered.

Arch frowned for the first time. 'For a tutor, Mr Harte, you don't know much.'

'It isn't always the case.'

'Let's hope not. Leave me – all of you.'

Bibwit and the rest of the Wonderlanders left the salon.

'Have them watched,' the King ordered. 'And send in the Clubs.'

A minister hurried out to arrange surveillance while the walrus-butler ushered the Lord and Lady of Clubs into the salon. Arch was much pleased to see the ranking couple readily genuflect before him.

'Flugelberry wine?' he asked, dismissing the walrus with a flip of his hand and, without waiting for an answer, pouring the wine himself. He handed brimming goblets to the Clubs, raised his own in a toast. 'To the Kingdom of Wonderland!'

'To the Kingdom of Wonderland!' the Lord and Lady echoed, and emptied their goblets in a single swig.

'I hear the House of Clubs has been busy stirring up the population against the former Queen,' Arch said, pouring refills.

'The House of Clubs has done what it thought necessary for the betterment of Wonderland,' the Lady responded.

'I wouldn't have supposed otherwise.'

'Our house does *not* intend to continue its subversive activities,' the Lord promised.

'Oh?'

'No need. Wonderland's improvement, sire, has come with your being King.'

Arch's eyes widened and the corners of his lips dipped towards his chin, pulling his mouth into an upside-down crescent. 'And to what do I owe this prompt exercise of loyalty?'

'To our belief that you share our assessment of imagination's lack of worth,' said the Lady.

'And to your superior military,' added the Lord with a wink.

Arch laughed. His intel ministers laughed. Ripkins allowed himself another slanted smile. Blister abandoned the withered pansies and walked up to a pot of amaranths, pinching their blooms dead.

'My military *is* superior,' Arch agreed. 'As for what I think of imagination . . . I don't claim it's completely lacking in value, only that to me it's worth more when it's not around. More wine?'

The Lord and Lady of Clubs explained how their soldiers had forced imaginationists from their homes and corralled them in high-walled limbo coops they'd had constructed on their own lands. The lord mentioned The Pledge of the Unimaginative, to which he humbly hoped the King would add his name.

'Uncanny,' Arch said at length. 'It's as if you knew I was coming and had anticipated my intentions. I applaud the House of Clubs' treatment of imaginationists, who although without their powers now, have spent their entire lives making others feel inferior. For that, they should suffer.'

The Clubs, having their own views reflected back to them by so royal a highness, were about to express their devotion anew when a Doomsine warrior hurried in and –

'We found it, My Liege.'

'Boarderland's tribal leaders are in the banquet hall,' Arch said to the Lord and Lady. 'I doubt I'll grant them the privileges I intend to grant you in the future, but you should find them admirably lacking in imagination. Get them to sign your Pledge.'

With that, Arch strode from the room, Ripkins and Blister following in his wake.

Mute as a monk vowed to silence, the Doomsine warrior led them to the palace grounds, where the plantings were equally quiet as the King and his bodyguards were led along a path to a hedge indistinguishable from those around it. The Doomsine stepped in amid the hedge's branches; its roots shifted and a hatch camouflaged with furry groundcover retracted to reveal a subterranean chamber aglow with an uncertain light. Ripkins and Blister took up positions alongside the path. Alone, Arch descended through the hatch and down the bronzite steps to the platform halfway to the chamber floor.

He could reach out and nearly touch it: The Heart Crystal.

Glowing brightly one instant, dimly the next, even suffering the lingering effects of WILMA it was something to admire. Its light, in its fuller moments, as life-affirming as the suns', its warmth the comfort of a fire on a winter's evening: rarely was a source of so much power also so beautiful.

Arch spread out his arms as if to embrace it, to welcome its energy into his Kingdom.

'It's almost a shame,' he whispered.

Because to protect his reign from future threats, he was going to snuff out the Crystal forever.

♦ CHAPTER 18 ♦

Twice Redd had thought they would have a future together. She and Arch. The first time, she'd been the energetic, unconventional heir to Wonderland's crown ('wild', her father had called her; 'defiant', her mother had said). Impatient with princess protocol, lax in her studies with Bibwit, generally dismissive of the way things were done, she had enjoyed upsetting expectations of how she should and would behave. Her unruliness, defiance, rebelliousness, or whatever anybody wanted to call it, might have kept her in the crosshairs of her parents' disapproval, but it was also what initially intrigued Arch. Just twenty-two years old, he'd risen from obscurity to become king of a country that had never known a single overweening, over*arching* ruler. And despite his relentless ambition, his political and military genius, in his 'off-time' he too was wild and impulsive ('reckless', King Tyman had called him; 'immoral', Queen Theodora had accused). In Rose Heart, he found a partner.

They met at a gathering for some charitable cause, peopled with starched government officials and high-profile do-gooders, Arch invited because Queen Theodora understood the value of being on civil terms with her neighbours, especially those she didn't like. Redd had just rebuffed a prospective dance partner, and the King, looking as if the closest he ever personally came to dancing was in battle, made his way to her.

'I know who you are,' she said after he introduced himself.

'And I you, Princess. I've heard of what you consider fun.'

That's when she decided to test him. 'You know what'd be fun?' She motioned with her head at the ballroom of dancers. 'To send this boring bunch into a tizzy by inviting Wondertropolis reporters with me to a Black Imagination séance.'

'You know what'd send them into more of a tizzy?' he said, leaning close. 'If I went with you.'

So at the height of the festivities, when they were sure of attracting the most notice, they left the palace. The resulting gossip was, to Redd's mind, a satisfying tizzy, and after that she and Arch were constantly together – or were together as much as a Queen-in-waiting and the ruler of a neighbouring country inhabited by feuding nomadic tribes could be.

Often, without telling anyone, Redd would sneak over to Boarderland for a week at a time, and Arch, yet without any wives, exempted her from his notoriously dismissive attitude towards the female sex. She was the one genuinely strong female (the lone female) he seemed to respect.

'You haven't just strength of imagination,' he told her. 'You have strength of will. Imagination is nothing without that.'

She envisioned a future with him – cavorting as they pleased while she ruled Wonderland and he Boarderland, an enviable power couple if there ever was. Then it happened: her mother told her she would not be Queen and banished her to Mount Isolation. Arch promised to come to her but remained maddeningly vague as to when. Too flush with resentment to wait, Redd scouted Boarderland in her imagination's eye and spotted him camped with his tribe along a distant bend in The Bookie River. He wasn't making preparations to travel to her, and when she unexpectedly showed up at the encampment, he seemed more to wince than to smile in encouragement. She began to fume about her mother's nerve, exclaiming that Theodora had no right to remove the rightful heir from succession.

'This isn't a good time for me, Rose,' Arch said, stopping her. And with the manner of one casting off a worn-out mantle: 'You shouldn't have come. I've no use for a banished princess who has no prospects of ever being Queen.'

'You have . . . no use . . . for me?'

Sparkling clusters sizzled above her head. In the surrounding air: constellations of small explosions, countless miniature stars in their death spirals, but all of it harmless, her imagination directed not at Arch or anyone else because she was caught completely off guard by his rejection. She sulked back to Mount Isolation. And vowed never to be so weak again.

But, she recognised now, she'd been nearly as weak. Because after Arch dumped her, after she rid Wonderland of her mother and sister and installed herself on its throne; after ruling the Queendom for thirteen years, communicating occasionally with Arch's ministers but never with Arch himself; after losing Wonderland to her miraculously undead niece and jumping into The Heart Crystal to be birthed on Earth through some mediocre painter's imagination; after recruiting and organising a new army on Earth; after returning to Wonderland and navigating her Looking Glass Maze, thus increasing the strength of her imagination; after thinking herself beyond caring for anyone, impenetrable to the softer emotions, after all of this she had again paid Arch a surprise visit in his Doomsine encampment and – foolishly, idiotically – allowed herself to entertain thoughts of a future with him. She stripped him of his Kingdom, but she didn't kill him. Fearing that no matter how many assassins she surrounded herself with, no matter how many Cats she invented, she would always be alone, she had wanted a future with Arch, their mutual antagonism a game she envisioned them playing indefinitely. But he had swept his hand across the gameboard, knocking over the pieces. He had overturned the gameboard itself.

Sentimentality: the most dangerous weakness of all. It had brought her to this point, which she couldn't have imagined even at the height of her powers: being without crown or palace, without a formidable army and – since lacking imagination she had no chance of avenging herself on the world – without even the spur of revenge that had pricked her on since she was seventeen. Her imagination should have returned by now. The green caterpillar was toying with her. There would be no Everqueen. It was time to lie down and die, and she trekked across The Chessboard Desert, leading Vollrath, The Cat, Sacrenoir and the rest of her assassins towards the one place that had been her home more than any other: Mount Isolation, where she would ease into her old sleep pod and breathe her last breath.

♦ CHAPTER 19 ♣

♦

'You were right that I shouldn't have gone,' Alyss confessed, at the foot of the dolomite wall behind one of the limbo coop's tenements. Dodge was at her side, on the watch for guards while Mr Dumphy stood with his back to the wall, feigning nonchalance and with unseen hands working his Rearranger invention against the thick dolomite.

'Huh?' the guardsman said.

'The anti-imagination rally at the salvage lot. I shouldn't have gone. But I had to learn what I could first-hand.' *Yet I learned nothing.* 'I wanted to understand why they resented me and my family for our imaginations.' *I still understand nothing.*

Half listening, Dodge burrowed a hand through the seam of his jumpsuit and took hold of an AD52 holstered under his left arm; a Three of Clubs had stepped to the lookout of the nearby guard tower and was scanning the limbo coop with a nightscope. Despite the abundance of weaponry he wore concealed about him, guardsman Anders knew he was ill-equipped. Hemmed in by the dolomite walls, outnumbered and outgunned, any recourse to his weapons had to be a last resort. If pressed to expose his weapons, it meant it was too late.

'I've tried to use my imagination to do what was best for the Queendom,' Alyss said.

Her voice cracked, as it did whenever she was both offended and hurt: a lightning rod for Dodge's attention. He might save Alyss from external mortal threats, but what about the subtler ones that came from within her own head? Self-doubt, paralysing remorse – how could he save her from those?

'Maybe it has to do with your being the one who determines what's "best",' he said.

'But "best" means whatever does the most good for the greatest number of citizens.'

Dodge kept his hand on the AD52 even as the Three of Clubs in the tower shouldered his nightscope. 'You don't have to convince *me*,' he said. 'But Wonderlanders are not equal in their abilities and you know it. It's a fact you live with the same as the rest of us. All you can do is try to make it so we're equal in *rights* – subject to the same laws and afforded the same fundamental opportunities.'

No matter how kind or well-meaning you are, someone will always resent you.

'I didn't ask for the responsibility of being Queen,' Alyss said. 'I don't like to think I've been hated for having it.'

Mr Dumphy stepped abruptly from the wall. 'It's not working. The dolomite's too thick. My Rearranger's molecular chamber fills up before it's made anything more than a crater and it needs to be emptied to make a passage through the entire wall. Depending on the wall's thickness, it might need to be emptied several times.'

'So empty it,' Dodge said.

'I'm not sure you understand, Mr Anders. To empty it, I have to direct the molecules elsewhere, meaning that the portion of the wall I erase would have to be re-formed, and wherever I make that happen, it's sure to attract attention. It would also mean leaving a deepening crater in the wall, visible for any Club soldier to see.'

'Let's hold off a bit longer,' Alyss said. 'I should start feeling my imagination soon, shouldn't I?'

She hadn't meant this to be a question; it had none of

the assurance she'd intended, and Dodge was looking at her with a hint of –

Is that disappointment?

It felt as if she'd been frequently disappointing him these days – sometimes mildly, as now, other times poignantly, as with the salvage lot business. Did people in love always disappoint each other so much?

'Transmission,' Dodge said, and turned his back to the guard tower. He tapped his forearm keypad and a translucent image of Bibwit and General Doppelgänger formed before him.

'Unless you're planning the Queen's rescue, we're stuck here until Alyss gets her imagination back.'

'We don't have the power to effect anyone's rescue,' said the General.

'You mean he won?' Dodge was stunned. 'Arch *won*?'

The General directed his words at Alyss. 'My decks fought as hard as they could, my Queen. They gave everything they had.'

Alyss did her best to smile, the muscles in her face stubborn. *I was pressed into power too soon. Learning control of my imagination is one thing, gaining the knowledge needed to be Queen another.* 'Of course,' she said.

'We hope Arch's stay with us will be temporary,'

Bibwit said. 'Alyss, do you feel anything?'

'Right now, Bibwit, I feel many things, but my imagination isn't one of them.'

Somewhere in a tenement: arguing voices, a wailing child.

'Redd is alive,' General Doppelgänger said. 'Arch has sent packs of tribal warriors to hunt throughout Boarderland and the Queendom. When they find her, they're to dispose of her.'

'As yet,' said Bibwit, 'the King doesn't know of *your* whereabouts, Alyss, but that won't remain the case for long. In addition, Hatter believes, and I agree, that because he betrayed Arch by sabotaging WILMA, the King will be vindictive towards him – or rather, towards him and Molly. He's therefore taken his daughter into hiding, but vows to be of as much use as he can while seeing to her safety.'

The loss of the Queendom . . . my failure. I've disappointed so many.

'And how are the two of you managing?' Alyss asked. 'At least you're not imprisoned, which I assume since you've the freedom to make contact.'

The General glanced over his shoulder.

'Don't worry,' Bibwit said to him. 'If Arch's spies try to catch us unaware, I'll hear them beforehand. We're followed everywhere,' he explained to Alyss and Dodge. 'But I'm thankful Arch means to exploit us for his own benefit as much as possible. It's the reason we are, relatively speaking, free.'

'For your own continued well-being,' Alyss urged, 'cooperate with Arch.'

'We'll be careful not to appear *un*cooperative, but we'll not take initiative to aid him in his machinations.'

Dodge frowned. 'Arch has to know Alyss will get her imagination back and that he'll have serious trouble when she does, so he must have plans to prevent it.'

General Doppelgänger agreed. 'He's never without plans.'

It was the one thing Alyss and her advisors could know for sure.

She initially thought it was from a lack of nutrition – the prickling sensation similar to regaining feeling in a limb. She felt it in the sheath of skin covering her skull, radiating down from the top of her head to the back of her neck. Seven days and nights in a limbo coop will do that to you – leave you unsure of everything you feel except hunger and helplessness. Alyss was staring at the young imaginationist she'd seen sitting on her father's shoulders who reminded her of the Liddells. Huddled beneath the protective arm of her father, the girl was picking at a handful of dried squigberries, putting them in her mouth one at a time and sucking on them.

'What are you thinking?' Dodge asked.

Which was when Alyss realised what the prickling signified. Because Dodge couldn't see them. The girl and her father were nowhere in sight. They were in a crowded flat while she was here, outside, in a refuse-strewn galley between two tenements.

She had been remote viewing, watching the pair in her imagination's eye.

'It's coming back,' she said.

Mr Dumphy, who'd been dozing with his legs straight out in front of him, jerked awake and scrabbled to his feet as if to be of service in some capacity, *any* capacity.

'It is?' Dodge asked. 'How do you know? Can you conjure?'

Conjurings of the second order, phantasms born of imagination, having enough reality to deceive the eye but not the touch. Alyss started with the smallest first. Amid the litter at her feet: a pillow appeared, shortly followed by a mound of greasy, slithering Gwormmies.

'I've seen constructs before,' Mr Dumphy breathed. 'They were always ghostly, but these . . .'

He extended a hand towards the Gwormmies, but they

faded and a wooden chair took their place. He tried to lean on the back of the chair, but his hand passed through it and then he was faced with a gwynook, its wizened man's face observing him from atop its penguin-like body. The gwynook morphed into Alyss, then into a smail-transport and, briefly, a jabberwock.

'Finally!' Dodge said, ripping open his jumpsuit and exposing the weaponry that could easily arm three guardsmen. 'Let's get out of here!'

But Alyss wasn't done. Her imagination didn't feel as strong and clear as it used to; like an atrophied muscle, time and exercise would be needed for it to recover its former power.

Time is what we don't have.

Conjurings of the first order were not phantasms but the genuine articles – objects in all their bruising, sharp-cornered reality. Alyss concentrated on the weapons in her mind, her talent an intuitive knowledge of their arcane mechanics as –

A crystal shooter came into existence, leaning against a tenement. Then another and another and another until she'd created enough to outfit a full deck of Heart soldiers. A rack of AD52s had begun to solidify when she said, 'Mr Dumphy, please relay a message to your friends that our release from this prison is imminent. They should be alert for my signal.'

The tinker bowed. 'And what will that signal be, Your Highness?'

Alyss had finished with the AD52s, was imagining into actuality orb generators and cannonball spiders. 'They'll know it when they see it. Tell them to just be ready: the moment of our uprising is near.'

♦ CHAPTER 20 ♦

It wasn't in Hatter's nature to run, nor had his Millinery training instilled the impulse in him. He and Molly emerged from a looking glass in The Everlasting Forest and, despite knowing the importance of remaining inconspicuous, he couldn't keep himself from battle. Heart and Spade soldiers were exchanging fire with mercenaries positioned on their front and left flanks, the enemy darting behind protesting trees after each trigger-pull of their AD52s. Suddenly, from the card soldiers' right flank, an orb generator blazed through the forest.

Feeeeeeeeooooooshhhhkaaaghghgk!

The explosion took out two full hands of Hearts and Spades. The rest struggled to hold position and not let the mercenaries advance, but again from the right flank, the unexpected: mind-riders stabbing through the air towards them, indiscriminate of card number and suit, lodging into the foreheads of Twos and Fives and Sixes alike and injecting angst serum into the folds and crevices of their brains. The soldiers forgot the mercenaries and attacked those closest – one another. Maldoids stepped into the open on the soldiers' right flank and easily annihilated them.

Not ten spirit-dane lengths away from The Crystal Continuum's exit glass, Hatter activated his backpack with a shrug, reached quickly over one shoulder and then the other for the pack's protruding daggers, corkscrews, Hands of Tyman. With terrible accuracy, he flung them at the Maldoids, moving steadily forwards until he was in their midst and –

Fwap!

His top hat was off his head, flattened into rotary blades and sent punishingly into several tribesmen. He snapped both sets of wrist blades into action at once. Mercenaries' razor-cards ricocheted off spinning steel. Charging tribal warriors met their fate as if at the bottom of a blender.

Fffshaw!

Someone fired a gossamer shot. The web spread wide above Hatter's head and dropped down: the end of resistance for anyone not equipped with Millinery-grade weapons. Hatter held a set of wrist-blades horizontally over his head and they shredded a hole in the gossamer and the web fell harmlessly to the ground around him.

His top hat blades flew a single pass through the Maldoids, boomeranged back to him. He caught them, was about to let the weapon fly a second time when he glimpsed Molly standing beyond the violence – not trying to hide or join the fight, just standing there, a small figure between a pair of squalling cypresses as a mercenary, camouflaged by moss-covered growth at her back, released a spikejack tumbler in her direction, its spikes hurtling towards her.

'Molly!'

She turned her head to him, then to the spikejack coming up fast, but she didn't move. He would never reach her in time.

Fwingk, fwingk!

He pulled two scissoring V-blades from his backpack, sent one slicing into the mercenary. The other crashed into the spikejack and deflected it into a nearby Maldoid. Molly gazed at the fallen warrior, passionless, as if his fate had had nothing to do with her. Then, again, she looked at Hatter.

He had to keep running. Without his daughter, he never would have done it, never would have racked his brain for an adequate safehouse and decided there wasn't one – not in Wonderland. He would have stayed and fought, proudly owning his 'treason' of Arch – yes, *he'd* been integral in bringing WILMA down – and daring the King to reap vengeance. He would have fought in the Queendom's defence to the last spin of his Milliner blades and deemed death in such service honourable. But Molly changed everything. He *had* to run. If running was dishonourable . . . but how could protecting his daughter's life be dishonourable?

Maldoids surrounded him. Top hat still in hand, he moved his arms furiously, wrist-blades deflecting incoming razor-cards, crystal shot and the more primal swipes of sword-bearing warriors. By the light of discharging weapons, he caught sight of a mercenary aiming an orb launcher at him from the branches of a burnt-out tree.

Fi-fi-fi-fi-fith!

He sent his top hat slicing out over the tribesmen, ran straight at one of them. Flicking his wrist-blades shut and punching his belt buckle, he somersaulted over the warrior's head, the j-shaped sabres in his belt activated as –

'Agh!'

The mercenary in the tree dropped, a victim of the top hat blades.

Hatter landed behind the Maldoids at a run. His top

hat blades circled back to him, seemed to morph into their conventional shape and fix firmly on his head without his help. One set of blurring wrist-blades pushed out in front of him, he swooped past Molly and grabbed her hand and they ran. Thick clouds blotted out the moons; the more distance they put between themselves and the skirmish, the darker it became until Hatter couldn't even see a dozen Gwormmy lengths in front of him. Only the whispering trees all around told him he was still in the forest.

They were being chased. Probably by Maldoids. Hatter heard them speeding through the underbrush, snapping branches in headlong pursuit, almost exactly as he had heard, long ago, The Cat sprinting after him through these same coal-dark woods, he with seven-year-old Princess Alyss in his arms, having promised Queen Genevieve to keep her daughter safe, alive. This time, however, the promise he had made was to himself. And it had nothing to do with Alyss Heart.

The Whispering Woods opened on to a wide expanse, and father and daughter came breathless to the edge of a precipice – the cliff overlooking The Pool of Tears. They could hear the rough water below, just make out the occasional glint of the pool's crystal barrier.

'I don't want to go,' Molly said.

Hatter opened his mouth to say he didn't particularly want to leave Wonderland either when –

Fsoosh!

A slew of kill-quills arrowed out of the woods behind them. Hatter gripped Molly tight and pushed off from the cliff and together they plummeted towards the surface of the water.

♦ CHAPTER 21 ♣

Redd led her assassins through The Chessboard Desert to the square of black rock occupied by Mount Isolation. But when the fortress came into view on its promontory, it no longer looked like the place that had been her home more than any other, where she had so often breathed a bracing air, heard her footsteps echo in empty halls, and gazed out through the Observation Dome's telescoping glass at the wastes of the desert and beyond.

'Who are all those people?' she glowered.

'I don't know, Your Imperial Viciousness,' Vollrath answered.

She had expected to find the fortress abandoned or under heavy guard. She would not have been surprised to find it destroyed. But Mount Isolation resembled the centre of a fairground, Wonderlanders milling about and the squeals of happy youngsters punctuating music that piped out from who knew where.

Redd covered her head with cloth torn from Vollrath's robe. The tutor and The Cat would be too recognisable to bring with her. 'Sacrenoir, you come with me. The rest of you wait here.'

The long incline leading to Her Imperial Viciousness's former haunt was thronged with tourists and those who catered to them. She pushed past couples having holograms of themselves etched by entrepreneurial artists. She sidestepped vendors selling pennants, T-shirts and caps, all featuring a silhouette of the fortress and its name spelled in glittering, gothic letters. She strode through a thicket of Wonderlanders buying and selling Mount Isolation note crystals, writing scrolls, push pins, magnets, calendars, mugs, pot holders, tote bags, snowglobes, The Cat and Redd Heart action-figures.

'You'll have to get in line,' a doorman said.

She and Sacrenoir had arrived at Mount Isolation's front gate. 'What?'

'Back of the line if you want to get inside.'

Redd was caught between fury and humiliation and might have revealed herself if Sacrenoir hadn't given her arm a respectful tug.

'At least the line's moving,' the assassin offered when

they had progressed from the back of the line to the middle.

This did little to lighten his mistress's mood, but then they were again at the front gate, facing a booth that had not existed when Redd lived at the fortress.

'Admittance for two adults is ten-Gwormmy weight in gemstone,' the Wonderlander in the booth said.

'To get into my own home?' Redd snapped.

The attendant was tickled. 'You do play the part, don't you? I guess you don't want to hear then that your contribution goes towards promoting the principles of White Imagination throughout the Queendom.'

Sacrenoir drew Redd's attention to the time-battered sceptre she'd been using like a cane, which still had a number of unpolished stones clinging to it. Redd ripped off a pair and shoved them at the attendant in the booth.

The climate inside Mount Isolation had always been chilly. During Redd's occupancy, it had been impossible to generate enough heat to warm the place no matter how many fire crystals she added to the furnace. But now, with so many breathing bodies everywhere, the air was stuffy, oppressively warm. And so much for hearing her footsteps echo in empty halls. Her Imperial Viciousness and Sacrenoir drifted with the crowds . . .

145

The cavernous room she'd had carved from the land itself, in which hundreds of cages containing thousands of seekers – those hybrids of vulture and fly – used to hang from the ceiling, had been turned into a theatre. A sold-out musical revue, *Redd Heart's Blues*, was to begin in half a lunar hour.

'Who did this?' Redd rasped through tensed jaw. She had spent many comforting nights of self-pity in this room, serenaded by the screams of her aerial 'bloodhounds' with bird-of-prey bodies and the heads of blood-sucking insects.

The rest of the fortress was no better. The Invention Hall, in which Her Imperial Viciousness had displayed prototypes of her inventions in spot-lit alcoves – a Two card from The Cut; a Glass Eye with one long horizontal crystal for vision-intake instead of the more humanoid orbs – at first appeared the same. But then Redd noticed that someone had designated it The Museum of the Macabre.

'Nothing macabre about it,' she steamed.

Even the ballroom at the foot of the spiral hall, the site of her now legendary battle with Alyss Heart, had been desecrated, turned into a cafeteria. Behind the orb-blasted wall where she had stowed the genuine Heart Crystal: a graffiti-covered replica.

'Stupid Wonderlanders.'

But it was in The Observation Dome that Wonderlanders were most rampant, crowding five deep at the floor-to-ceiling windows to enjoy the view while others posed for photo crystals with the petrified wig-beast. The creature stood a metre taller than the tallest Wonderlander in the room, and was significantly hairier than the hairiest.

'It used to be so imposing in action,' Redd rued, recalling the moment she had imagined the thing into being from a curl of Jack of Diamonds' wig.

'What're those?' Sacrenoir asked.

A bank of mirrors Her Imperial Viciousness had never seen. In front of each glass, a Wonderlander stood making faces at his or her reflection, then pausing a Gwormmy-blink and laughing. Some asked their reflections simple questions such as 'How are you?' or offered trite observations – 'It's warm today' – then paused and laughed.

'Nonsense Mirrors,' Sacrenoir said, noting the sign as he and his mistress drew closer.

Redd scowled at each of them in turn – more so when she didn't see the Wonderlanders' reflections, which were visible only to those standing directly in front of the mirrors.

A young boy laughingly skipped away from his glass and

Redd took his place. Her expression was as unfriendly as usual, but the figure staring back at her looked nothing if not comical: protruding front teeth, ears sticking out from the sides of her head like underdeveloped wings, her eyes, nose and mouth scrambled into different positions all over her face.

'Is this supposed to be funny?' she whispered.

'Is this blahdeeblahdeebabooooo? Hunny funny hun hun!' her reflection said.

'Whoever's responsible for all of this . . .'

'Whoever booever responsibobbility-whee!' said her reflection.

'Your Imperial . . .' Sacrenoir said, but that's all he got out before the Wonderlanders at the other mirrors stepped back, gasping.

A black cloud had formed above Redd and crackled with jags of lightning. Glaring at her supposedly humorous reflection, she noticed none of it. She had let herself be insulted by doormen and booth attendants. She had waited in line (and paid!) to get into her own home, to see the rooms in which she'd spent years festering in enforced solitude despoiled by White Imagination losers.

'And now this!'

'Annow how this wow!' said her reflection.

The cloud above Her Imperial Viciousness's head roiled like water heated over a fire crystal. Believing it a surprise performance, part of the Mount Isolation experience, the tourists in the Dome gathered five-deep around *her*. Redd's dress began to move; the weave of its material squirmed, became serpentine vines blooming flesh-eating roses.

'I will *not* lie down and die! I'll have what's mine and kill *him*!'

Redd's reflection translated this into nonsense but she was no longer listening, completely engulfed by a cyclone of blood-hued energy. The surrounding tourists applauded, but then –

A thorny vine shot out, fast as a viper's tongue, from Redd's dress, and a rose blossom gnashed its teeth into the neck of a gleeful Wonderlander sporting his Mount Isolation T-shirt and cap.

'Aaaaghrrrr!'

In their rush to escape the Dome, the onslaught of panic, Wonderlanders shoved, kicked, kneed and trampled one another. More and more rose vines with teeth-clacking blooms stretched out from Redd's dress, grew to impossible lengths as they trailed the stampeding crowd down the spiral hall to the fortress's ground floor until –

The Wonderlanders burst out the front entrance, fled across the desert in every direction and –

In the Dome, Redd banged her sceptre against the floor and the vines of her dress shrank back, coiling close around her. The teeming cloud of imaginative energy vaporised. All was, for a moment, calm.

Redd Heart, Wonderland's supreme mistress of Black Imagination, was back.

♥ ♦ CHAPTER 22 ♣

Oxford, England. 1875.

Three in the morning. Most of the university's lecturers were tucked comfortably beneath their bedclothes, but Charles Lutwidge Dodgson, lecturer of mathematics at Christ Church College, sat awake in his bachelor's apartment in Tom Quad. At his desk with his journal open before him, he stared dumbly at the puzzle he had written a fortnight earlier:

> Two travellers spend from 3 o'clock till 9 in walking
> along a level road, up a hill, and home again: their
> pace on the level being 4 miles an hour, up hill 3,
> and down hill 6. Find the distance walked.

He had not been sleeping well of late, had in fact never been a sound sleeper, which accounted for these little maths puzzles scattered throughout the pages of his journals. Their twofold purpose: to serve as agreeable diversion, but also to drive out the blasphemous, unholy thoughts that tortured him in these small hours. Yet as Reverend Dodgson glanced at the clock – three-fifteen – he knew, as he'd known for the past hour, that this particular puzzle wasn't working. He was not agreeably diverted or kept from thoughts of a world he never heard mentioned at church but only by the once young Alice Liddell.

He bent to the puzzle again.

Two travellers spend from 3 o'clock till 9 in walking along a level road, up a hill, and home again: their pace on the level being 4 miles an hour, up hill 3, and down hill 6. Find the distance walked.

Had he truly composed this puzzle himself? It *was* in his journal, and the writing *did* appear to be his own. Why then did he have no inkling as to how to solve it? This inability to comprehend his own writings had been getting steadily worse, an inability all the more frightening as he didn't believe it the result of his recent trauma . . .

The authorities had found him on Sydenham Hill, in

The Crystal Palace's Greek Court, dirty and unshaven, dazed from hunger, and encaged by solid iron bars that blocked the court's every window and door. He'd heard approaching footsteps and thought it one of Her Imperial Viciousness's assassins bringing him food and water. He hadn't been given anything to eat or drink in days. Under such conditions, he could never have succeeded in what Her Imperial Viciousness had commanded of him – to write a book about her more enthralling than *Alice In Wonderland*, to immortalise her on Earth as he had immortalised Alyss Heart.

The approaching footsteps had belonged to a bobby, who informed Dodgson that Redd and her horde had vanished. The bars of his prison were demolished. He was questioned by Scotland Yard detectives, then returned to Oxford. But fearing The Cat would track him down, he still tried to resign himself to the task Her Imperial Viciousness had given him. He'd come up with no more than a title, *I, Redd*, when he began to suffer the creative lethargy that had since become a vacuum. He felt empty, unimaginative, unable to think creatively. It was more than a lack of inspiration. It was as if he were losing the capacity to *ever* be inspired.

What was worse: he didn't seem to be alone. He saw it in the lecture halls of the college. Once clever students had grown dim. And walking the streets of Oxford he noticed a lack of alertness on the faces of passersby, a curious clash in the garments each chose to wear, as if everyone had lost the ability to properly mix and match colours, patterns. He saw grocers unable to compute bills of sale, artists in Christ Church Meadow unable to complete the simplest sketch, people on park benches, blinking at their open books without ever turning a page, unable to comprehend what they read.

At his desk, he closed his journal. No point in torturing himself with a puzzle he couldn't hope to solve. Despite his reputation as a prissy, puttering, fastidious bachelor, the Reverend harboured a great affection for imagined worlds, though he had never confused imagined worlds for the real one.

Until now.

What other explanation could there be for the parade of characters from Alice Liddell's long ago story visiting him? The Milliner, The Cat, the woman claiming to be Alyss Heart's murderous aunt, they were either part of some elaborate conspiracy, actors employed in a hoax at his expense, or –

Thump thump thump.

Someone was at the door. Dodgson cast a furtive eye at

the clock – six in the morning. Much too early for visitors.

Thump thump thump.

What if it were The Cat? Or worse, Her Imperial Viciousness?

'I doubt either would knock,' Dodgson mused under his breath. Daring fate to do what it would, he stepped to the door, uncharacteristically yanked it open and –

In the hall stood a man and young girl, both dripping wet and dressed in identical knee-length coats of cracked leather. He did not know the girl. But he would never forget the man, the violence of whose previous visit had left him without an apartment door for a week: Hatter Madigan of Wonderland.

PART TWO

♥ ♦ CHAPTER 23 ♣ ♦

Good demarcation barriers make good neighbours, which matters not in the least when your neighbour is yourself. Arch no sooner conquered Wonderland than he ordered the barrier between his new realm and Boarderland permanently offline. Gone were the official immigration points, gone the soundwaves that fried would-be illegals from the inside out. All along what used to be the border, the soundwave-producing pylons were being dismantled.

Enticed by the novelty of the Wonderland landscape, Boarderland's everyday tribesfolk flowed into the former Queendom. The Awr and Gnobi and Scabbler persisted in their nomadic ways, camping everywhere from Outerwilderbeastia to The Snark Mountain foothills, while the Doomsines and Fel Creel opted for a sedentary way of life and took up permanent residence in Wondertropolis. The Maldoids, Astacans and remaining tribes found the initial flush of Wonderland's attractions already fading and were returning to the country of their birth to live as they always had – Wonderland, they judged, being a nice place to visit but not to live. And the last of the Astacans were still crossing back over what used to be the demarcation barrier when –

'Citizens of Wonderland, I introduce myself to you as your new king.' An image of Arch, in Heart Palace's public address studio, materialised on holo-screens throughout the Queendom. 'You may have heard that you now reside in a Kingdom. I congratulate you upon it and wish to invite you all to my festive coronation ceremony, which is to take place on Heart Boulevard, just outside the palace. Come see for yourselves what a well-intentioned sovereign I intend to be. Come celebrate the fact that you need not value imagination so highly, as you were forced to do during Alyss Heart's reign, nor live in fear, as you did during Redd's. I give you Minister Krill, who will inform you of the time of my coronation and the entertainment you'll find there.'

On screen, an intel minister stepped into view. Thanking His Majesty, he began to read from a long list of amusements, which included interactive cultural shows performed by Boarderland tribes and bobbing for dingy-pear contests, but even before he mentioned the spirit-dane stunt riders, His Majesty had left the public address studio. With Ripkins and Blister, he was entering one of the great halls, where Boarderland's twenty other tribal leaders waited for him around a table.

'We agreed to fight under your command for purely selfish reasons,' the Maldoid chief said once Arch was seated.

'I wouldn't believe anything else,' the King answered.

'Now that Wonderland's fallen, how will the Maldoids benefit from the increased mineral resource at our disposal?'

'Who are *you* to ask first for what you'll get?' the Fel Creel leader protested. 'My tribe lost more warriors than yours and we were far more brutal.'

'Lies!' cried the Maldoid chief. 'Propaganda!'

Arch allowed himself a faint smile. He would have no trouble controlling the tribes as he always had, antagonising them against one another to prevent their banding together against him. 'Friends,' he said, interrupting the Maldoid and Fel Creel leaders. 'I propose equal shares for every tribe, although of course I'll then have to take a bit more for administering the shares and for auditing output of the numerous mines.'

The Astacan leader started to protest, but –

'What I want to know,' the Scabbler burst out, 'is why the Awr are still encamped at the old Five Spires of Redd site when they know we're waiting for them to leave!'

The Awr chief accused the Scabbler of only wanting the site because his tribe occupied it and negotiations devolved into a general bickering. Arch pushed himself from his chair and went to a window at the far end of the room, staring out at the banners that fluttered from the roof of nearby Wondronia Grounds. He kept his back to the tribesmen. They were too easily manipulated for it to give him much pleasure any more. He wanted to let them fight, argue till they'd exhausted themselves of breath forever.

The leaders' voices abruptly ceased. Arch smelled moist earth. A tendril of smoke wafted up from behind him.

'I'm sure you know I've been expecting you,' the King said, still staring out the window. 'You offered to help Redd reclaim the crown.'

'And you took advantage of what I neglected to tell her.'

Arch turned to see the green caterpillar puffing at his pipe. 'As you knew I would. You wanted me to plot against Redd. You want the two of us striving against each other so that you'll get the best from both of us.'

'Let us not waste time discussing what we already know.'

The caterpillar twisted himself around, looking this way and that with a mixture of hope and disappointment. 'For such a plotting specimen, Your Majesty, I wish you'd plot to have a platter of tarty tarts around whenever I'm here.'

'We don't all have your ability to see into the future, caterpillar. I never know when you're going to visit.'

The tribal leaders hadn't moved from the table, watching as the King engaged with the oracle but not venturing closer. Arch spoke softly so they wouldn't hear.

'You told Redd that you scheme for the safety of The Heart Crystal, but you let me gain the crown, knowing, as I assume you must, what I intend to do with it. What's your real game?'

The caterpillar's hookah burbled, and as Arch waited for something more than smoke to emerge from the great worm's mouth, he was reminded not for the first time that he knew extremely little about Wonderland's oracles.

'My game?' Green smiled. 'I do not know that I have one, exactly. You of all people, Your Majesty, can have no idea how mind-numbingly boring it is, sitting on a giant mushroom for thousands of years, doing hardly more than watching others go about their active lives. The motive for my actions is simple: I am tired of being on the sidelines of history, an observer rather than a participant.'

'I was under the impression caterpillars were powerful enough to *make* history,' Arch commented.

'I have heard it said that we are powerful. But I have never felt it. I act merely to discover how much power I have.'

'What about The Heart Crystal?'

Again, the caterpillar smiled. 'When it amuses me to do so, I still claim I act only to ensure the Crystal's safety, but it is not true. I am, and have been, a prisoner to this great energy source. What little I have done these past millennia has centred on the Crystal. When it is gone, I foresee for myself futures not only of more action and less observation, but more *freedom*.'

'There are things you're not telling me,' Arch said.

'Are there?'

The King asked himself the same question. Did he truly believe the oracle was withholding vital information? Did it matter? 'I expect something from you,' he said at length, 'to prove to me we're working towards the same ends – the destruction of The Heart Crystal.'

'You need a fresh supply of silk from the six oracles,' said the caterpillar.

Arch nodded. 'I need a fresh supply of silk from the six oracles.'

Without another word, the caterpillar exhaled a tremendous lungful of smoke, which gathered underneath him and carried him out the open window and out over Wondertropolis.

Not sure a deal had been struck, Arch replayed the conversation in his head as he walked slowly back to the tribal leaders to conclude negotiations.

'Whatever you propose, we accept it,' the Maldoid leader said once His Majesty had regained his seat.

The other leaders promptly voiced their acceptance as well.

Being on familiar terms with a caterpillar, it seemed, had no end of advantages for a King.

♦ CHAPTER 24 ♣

'It's been confirmed by witnesses,' General Doppelgänger said. 'Redd caused the disturbance at Mount Isolation. She *has* her imagination.'

In the alley between the limbo coop's tenements, Alyss frowned at the static-laced faces of Bibwit and the General, which were being transmitted on to the air before her by Dodge's crystal communicator. 'Do we know when she got it back?' she asked. 'Because if Bibwit's theory is accurate and my imagination returned first . . .'

'Alyss,' Bibwit interrupted gently, 'I wouldn't worry whether you or your aunt recovered imagination first. I'm no longer sure that strength alone is enough to defeat you. Other attributes are equally important, perhaps more so if taken together – such as intelligence, discipline, maturity and patience. I may be just an overly pale tutor who's lived through his share of generations, but I've learned that Wonderlanders with tremendous powers often fail to achieve their ambitions if they don't know how best to control and direct those powers. I place Redd in this category, but not you.'

'Considering our current situation, Bibwit, I don't understand how you can think that,' Alyss said, her glance sliding to Dodge, who was being unusually quiet.

Indeed, since his initial outburst – opening his jumpsuit to reveal his weapons – Dodge had been growing more and more circumspect, withdrawing into himself and leaving Mr Dumphy to distribute the AD52s and crystal shooters to imaginationists as he deemed fit. Even now, the tinker was coming and going, stepping into the alley to hide weapons under his clothes and then shambling off again, visiting flats in a seemingly random fashion that had, so far at least, not attracted the Club soldiers' notice.

If Dodge is worried about me, about us, why doesn't he confide instead of –

'The military remains loyal to you, Queen Alyss,' General Doppelgänger said. 'I have your coordinates and will ready a battalion of chessmen to support your escape as soon as you give the command. But when you *do* command it, I hope your escape will be imminent, since any such move by the chessmen could alert the King of your whereabouts.'

An all-out escape, Alyss knew, would require immense strength and unblinking focus. The AD52s and crystal shooters she'd conjured were, at best, to be exploited only if she lacked the necessary concentration for success. The imprisoned imaginationists might be extraordinary citizens, but they were not soldiers. She could not expect them to perform like a trained military in the frenzy of battle, nor to witness the death of innocents with professional reserve. Notwithstanding the chessmen's help, a coop-wide escape depended largely on her imagination. She would be pushed to the utmost – imagining an attack on Club soldiers in every limbo coop she remote-viewed while simultaneously keeping imaginationists from harm with deflective energy shields. Her strength would be tested. Yet again.

'Listen,' Dodge said in the tone of a man tired of arguing a point in his own head. 'Everyone knows we want to get out of this place as soon as possible, but Arch has control of the Crystal, right? So why has he let Alyss and Redd recover their imaginations? If he figured out how to disrupt the Crystal's influence before, he can do it again. And he would've done it by now if he didn't have a reason for wanting Alyss and Redd to be imaginative . . . a reason that benefits *him*.'

The veins in Bibwit's head pulsed faster, his ears

alternately moved up and down as he considered the notion.

'Arch has revealed nothing to us,' General Doppelgänger said.

'I'm not surprised,' Dodge answered. 'But we have to think as he does. Several moves ahead.'

'Yes.' Bibwit noticed that the Queen had taken on the unfocused gaze of a remote viewer. 'What do you see, Alyss?' he asked.

What do I see? The eye of her imagination glimpsed the halls and suites and ballrooms of Heart Palace. *I see magnificently embroidered tapestries, plush floating sofas and chairs, glistening marble floors and onyx balustrades. I see luxury and opulence to such a degree I once couldn't believe I was to live surrounded by it. But now that it's all in the possession of an intruder, I want to scream, 'It's mine! It's ours! It belongs to Wonderland!'*

The muscles of Alyss's upper cheeks went suddenly lax, her mouth hung open; she had sighted the King. 'Arch is in the great hall with tribal leaders and . . .'

'And?' Bibwit prodded.

'. . . the green caterpillar. Arch is talking privately with the caterpillar, as if they have business that doesn't involve the tribes.'

169

'Arch and a caterpillar-oracle?' General Doppelgänger repeated, dividing into the worried figures of Doppel and Gänger.

Blue's conspicuous absence had, until now, seemed just another in a long line of the oracle's frustratingly mysterious behaviours. Could the true cause have been more menacing – that he had abandoned them?

'There must be a reasonable explanation,' Bibwit offered unconvincingly.

'Perhaps one of us should travel to The Valley of Mushrooms –' began General Doppel.

'– to confer with the caterpillar council?' finished General Gänger.

'If a caterpillar's meeting with *him*,' Dodge said, 'how do we know Blue or any of the oracles will meet with *us*?'

'It's worth the risk, isn't it?' the Generals said as one.

Alyss again took on the blank stare of a remote viewer, the eye of her imagination descending into The Valley of Mushrooms, scouting for the faintest wisp of hookah smoke, the slightest evidence of the caterpillar council's whereabouts. But it was no good. Wherever she trained her imaginative eye, she saw only the damp shade beneath mushroom caps and the many-coloured stalks so thick she wouldn't have been able to wrap her arms around them. She saw only the giant fungi that had given the valley its name.

'Dodge is right,' she decided. 'Our uprising against the Clubs should wait. Before I use my full power to free imaginationists, we should try to expose Arch's scheme against us. Whatever we decide, we cannot allow him to know where I am, nor my imagination to compromise our precarious position. We'll know better how to proceed if we learn his plan.'

Mr Dumphy, returned from his most recent errand, was preparing for his next, sliding a crystal shooter into each boot and tucking AD52s into his waistband beneath the hang of his coat. He didn't think it his place to eavesdrop on a meeting between his Queen and her advisors and he was humming to himself to drown out their voices until –

'Mr Dumphy,' Alyss said. 'I'm sorry to report, freedom for our fellow inmates will not be as imminent as I'd supposed. It *will* come, but in the meantime I hope they'll continue to keep their imaginations to themselves. And if others inform the Clubs of imagination's return, the prisoners might at least avoid harsher treatment by not showing it off.'

'My Queen,' Mr Dumphy said with one of his little bows, 'you are surrounded by friends and supporters here. I know you won't forget us and I'm confident we can unimaginatively tolerate incarceration a while longer if it will forever defeat those responsible for it.'

'I promise you, Mr Dumphy, I will effect your release, and that of every imaginationist, as soon as seems wise.'

Turning back to her advisors, Alyss made a point of including the tinker in further discussion. It was quickly settled: she would imagine a passage through the dolomite wall and she and Dodge would escape, after which she would immediately close the passage to avoid exciting other prisoners or alarming the Club soldiers. Mr Dumphy would remain behind and, by means of a conjured crystal communicator, periodically report on the imaginationists' morale.

'Redd might provoke Arch in a way that compromises us,' Generals Doppel and Gänger said.

'In a way that compromises Alyss,' Bibwit qualified.

The Generals nodded, but Dodge made a face. 'She can only do so much without an army.'

It was a reasonable assumption. But with Redd, one always knew: if Her Imperial Viciousness could be a problem, she would be.

♦ CHAPTER 25 ♣

Oxford, England. 1875.

The clock showed five after six. The fire in the hearth crackled and Dodgson busied himself with trifles – boiling water, warming the tea kettle, setting out cups and saucers, sugar and cream, to avoid thinking on the larger problems that had presented themselves at his door.

'Hatter M-Madigan is it?' he stuttered, though he of course remembered the name.

The Milliner inclined his head. 'And this is my daughter, Homburg Molly.'

Dodgson had already been introduced to the girl twice. The tea steeped. The fire in the hearth crackled.

'Th-this is highly unusual,' he said finally.

'I couldn't think of anywhere safer for my daughter,' Hatter returned.

Dodgson thought he saw Molly cringe slightly –

173

embarrassed or annoyed, he couldn't tell which.

'Do you i-i-intend to stay?' he asked, pouring the tea. 'B-Because, you see . . .'

He was about to say it was neither proper nor allowed, but he had experienced what Hatter and his blades could do. Would such a man care for the rules of a provincial college?

'. . . because, you see, I hope I have enough blankets.'

If Hatter was concerned about the Reverend's possible lack of blankets, he didn't say. He told Dodgson of King Arch, of WILMA and how even in her compromised state she had affected The Heart Crystal, virtually snuffing out imagination Queendom-wide. His tone remained even and unemotional, but the Wonderlander who epitomized the Millinery ethic of never uttering more than necessary had uncorked himself. From anyone else, the quantity of his words would have been unremarkable. But as Molly sat listening to a recitation of events she wished she didn't know, the guilt she felt all over again was tinged with something new; she had never heard her father speak so much.

'Queen Alyss and Redd Heart are both without their powers,' Hatter finished.

'Alice told me of The Heart Crystal,' Dodgson said, recalling that afternoon on the banks of the River Cherwell, young Alice excited but terribly serious as she described Wonderland while her sisters played in the river's shallows. 'She referred to it as a s-source, I believe. Wait a moment.' The Reverend dug in the cubbyhole above the desk for his old notes. 'Yes. Here.' In silence, he read over what he'd written. Then, to the room at large, in astonishment: 'No imagination in Wonderland m-means no imagination on Earth?'

It explained his recent creative drought, and what he'd been seeing in everyone around him. An outsized crystal in a parallel world that served as fountainhead of humankind's creativity? The logician in him thought it quite impossible. And yet the author in him, the part of him that had created worlds out of words, mere symbols on a page, had no doubt of it. He dropped into his chair.

'Not good.'

'The absence of imagination has been Arch's opportunity,' Hatter said. 'I don't know what's become of Queen Alyss under Arch's rule, but I fear the worst. When Molly and I jumped into The Pool of Tears, the Queen was confined in a prison-town with other imaginationists.'

'But w-why come to me?' Dodgson asked. 'Wouldn't anywhere on Earth be just as safe for your d-daughter?

Perhaps safer, since I have had some contact with . . . with a f-few characters in this drama.'

Hatter held his hat in hand, stared into the depths of its underside. 'I'm not sure. But when I was here before, of all the people I met, your glow was among the brightest.'

'My glow?' Dodgson glanced down at his hands. They looked like ordinary hands. A bit dry, but certainly not luminescent.

'To my eyes,' Hatter explained, 'almost everyone on Earth glows.'

'Mine too,' Molly said, hardly audible.

'Some darkly, others brightly,' Hatter elaborated. 'Some strongly, others faintly. I believe these glowings to be connected with imagination. The stronger the glow, the stronger the imagination.'

'Extraordinary,' the Reverend exclaimed.

'But unlike my last visit, all glows I've seen this time are faint to non-existent. Even yours. It's extremely faint right now.'

'Yes,' Molly whispered.

Dodgson wanted to add this alleged correlation between glow and imagination to his old notes on Wonderland. But welcome as this desire was, he made no move towards pen and ink. Wasn't it precisely this sort of obsessive note-taking that had led him to commit such violence on the memories of the young Alyss Heart/Alice Liddell?

He studied his visitors. Molly pouting at the dregs of her tea, as withdrawn as any teenager he'd ever known; Hatter tormented by uncertainties and parental worry: the pair might have been from another world, but they presently appeared nothing so much as Earth-bound, human.

'Now what?' he asked.

♦ CHAPTER 26 ♦

Familiar as the Gnobi were with various terrain from their nomadic life in Boarderland, able to trudge through The Swampy Woods of Chance as efficiently as they could scale The Glyph Cliffs, they had never experienced anything like Wonderland's Volcanic Plains. Wherever they went in the charred region, they inevitably found themselves at the base of an active volcano . . . or two. Their nostrils polluted with the stink of sulphur, their lungs scorched by the air, they were constantly having to avoid geysers of noxious gas, jets of flame shooting randomly from the rocky ground, pits and rivers of boiling lava.

Divided into groups and sent around the Queendom to hunt for Redd Heart, their instructions were simple: find Her Imperial Viciousness, kill her and present her body to King Arch as apology for letting her get away from them in Outerwilderbeastia.

'Listen,' a warrior said as the tribesmen avoided yet another spray of fire from underground.

Cutting through the low-pitched rumble of eruptions, coming from beyond a cluster of fossilised lava stalagmites that looked like an oversized bed of nails: the intermittent phlegm-rattling roar of beasts and the steady crack of a whip. Weapons drawn, the Gnobi weaved carefully through the stalagmites, peered out from behind the last of them.

There she was: Redd Heart, surrounded by eight jabberwocky while one of her assassins stood outside the circle of beasts, whipping their backsides. A short distance off, the remainder of Redd's assassins occupied a sort of natural terrace in the side of a volcano, their attention wholly on their mistress who gripped leashes of heavy chain in her fist, the other ends of which were fastened around the jabberwockys' necks.

Up on their hind legs, the beasts' small forearms – like those of a Tyrannosaurus Rex from Earth's prehistoric times – frantically paddled the air and their claws raked at nothing. They writhed to be free of their chains. They bellowed and tried to stomp Redd into the ground. But with atypical calm, and without dropping the sceptre she held in one hand, Her Imperial Viciousness avoided the slightest injury even as one of the jabberwocky opened its mouth wide enough to swallow her whole, the smallest of its teeth as large as The Cat's paw, and –

Chhhhooooooshhhhk!

The beast shot a fireball from the back of its throat.

Redd lifted her sceptre; the fireball hovered before her in midair. She blew at it as if to rid herself of a bothersome insect and it reversed directions, burning a comet's trail through the air and grazing the jabberwock on its way to smash into a distant volcano.

'You're of no use to me injured,' Redd said to the beast, 'otherwise you would have felt worse.'

The jabberwock roared and slobbered and swung its tail, hard. Redd jumped and let it whip past underneath her. Almost before she landed, she imagined a jabberwock tail on her own backside and, as if she'd been born with it, swatted the offending beast.

It lasted no longer than a Gwormmy-blink, but for the first time in Wonderland's history, a jabberwock wobbled in a daze, cowed. Then raged twice as brutally as before while –

Amid the stalagmites, the Gnobi aimed their orb cannons; with a synchronised release of the triggers, Redd and all of her assassins would be decimated.

'On my signal,' a Gnobi whispered, but a blanket of green smoke descended upon him and his fellow warriors, and they drooped, unconscious.

The green caterpillar and his hookah floated out from behind a stalagmite.

'You didn't have to do that!' Redd called to him. 'I knew they were there! Mr Van de Skulle!'

The dutchman took the jabberwockys' leashes from his mistress. Redd's conjured tail disintegrated. She approached the caterpillar, stood sneering down at the sleeping tribesmen.

'Call it a gesture of friendship,' the oracle said. 'I wanted to do something for you, however small.' He pulled and puffed at his hookah a moment. 'But you will say you have no need of friendship.'

Redd, on the contrary, said nothing. She was no longer sure what she needed. And she was trying to keep her mind empty, free of thoughts she didn't want the maddening worm to know.

'There are packs of warriors searching for you throughout the Queendom,' the oracle said.

'They'll soon find me at Heart Palace.'

'They search for your niece too.'

'Why do you talk to me of *her*?'

The caterpillar went on as if he hadn't heard: 'Tell me, now that your imagination has returned, how will you do away with Arch and gain control of The Heart Crystal?'

Descending from extraordinary imaginative power to utter barrenness, however temporary, had produced a change in Redd just now perceptible. Whereas the old Redd would have frothed, 'I don't know, slug! Why don't you tell me how I'll take control of the Crystal?' the new Redd felt a check to her rash arrogance and remained quiet. How *was* she going to get the Crystal? She'd yet to come up with an adequate plan.

'You told me my imagination would return and that what I chose to do then – *now* – would determine everything.'

'So you *do* listen,' the caterpillar said.

'You knew I'd get my imagination back. You know what I'll choose to do, even if I don't.'

'News to me,' the oracle said. And after indulging a moment with his hookah: 'I do not see the future so much as all possible futures. One-tenth of a lunar cycle from now, depending on what happens, there may be a wholly different set of possible futures for you. Be glad, Mistress Heart, you no longer have the futures that were yours if you'd not left

Mount Isolation before the tribal warriors arrived. For once Arch knows where you are –'

Redd guffawed. 'He thinks he knows where I am right now!' She banged her sceptre on the ground, smoke issued from its crippled heart, in the middle of which a lavish bedroom in Heart Palace became visible – Arch's bedroom, with gwynook skins and spirit-dane hides hanging from the walls. Knobkerrie in hand, the King was facing off against what he clearly supposed was Her Imperial Viciousness herself. The scene played out silently in the smoke while, far away in Heart Palace . . .

'You took a big risk coming here alone, Rose,' Arch said. 'Or is your feline with you? Not that it matters.'

He lunged, his knobkerrie swooping around to crack the construct in the skull, but the weapon came up short, clashing with a knobkerrie instantly conjured by Redd, and which she manipulated with her imagination, leaving the construct's hands free.

'I *did* expect this,' Arch said, swinging again, his knobkerrie clattering against Redd's, 'just not so soon.'

More knobkerries formed to pummel the King's arms and shoulders and gut while the construct watched, smug. Then, from nowhere Arch could see, a sword shot towards him, its point aimed for his heart and not a spirit-dane length away when –

Blister and Ripkins, hearing the commotion from the hallway, came rushing into the room. Blister jumped in front of the King, catching the sword in a gloved hand. Ripkins, his fingerprint sawteeth flashing, sprinted at the construct and –

Passed right through it. The bodyguards exchanged a surprised glance, but Arch only had eyes for the construct, which faded from sight, cackling at his gullibility.

In The Volcanic Plains, the smoke from Her Imperial Viciousness's sceptre thinned, drifted away. It had never been a good plan, Redd judged. A remote kill of Arch would have brought her satisfaction, but not necessarily closer to The Heart Crystal. There were too many unknowns. Who had been assigned to command in the event of Arch's premature death, before she and her remaining assassins could reach the palace and take possession of the Crystal? If no one assumed command and the tribes and Heart soldiers fell into civil war, would she have time to gather her former forces together – or enough of them, at least, to win the Crystal?

She sought the power source for the cosmos in her imagination's eye, might never have glimpsed its location if not for the extraordinary amount of activity around a certain shrub, the coming and going of intel ministers to and from its underground hiding place. It was, she knew, too much activity around The Heart Crystal to be innocent; Arch was up to something.

The caterpillar, intent on refilling the bowl of his hookah, did not confirm or deny these thoughts. He made no comment on what had just taken place in Heart Palace, and Redd was beginning to think the worm had forgotten her when he gestured with five of his right legs at the sleeping Gnobi.

'You should not be here when they wake.'

'They shouldn't wake at all,' Redd countered.

The caterpillar took to the air on a cloud from his hookah, rising higher and higher. 'To get what you want, Rose Heart, you must go towards that which you most despise.'

Redd watched the oracle until he vanished into great banks of geyser steam. She should go towards that which she most despised? She despised so many things: Alyss, White Imagination, happy, well-adjusted –

Raaaannghg!

She spun round to where Mr Van de Skulle was still taming the eight jabberwocky. When she'd been Queen, she had intended to train the beasts and use them in place of spirit-danes. It had amused her to picture herself charging through Wondertropolis on the back of such a ferocious creature, but now . . .

She might not yet know what despised thing she was to go towards, but whatever it was, however she proceeded, it *would* culminate in violence. Having jabberwocky at her disposal could not fail to be an advantage in the coming war.

♥ CHAPTER 27 ♣

♦

Although Alyss's imagination was again hers and she had strength and abilities he could never match, Dodge was unwilling to relax his vigilance for her safety. In case soldiers were lying in wait, he preceded her through the limbo coop's wall and out across land belonging to the House of Clubs. To prevent them being seen from above, Alyss conjured a canopy that took on aspects of the changing landscape over which they travelled, yet he insisted on leading the way, determined to take unto himself any enemy fire.

'You're on the northernmost rim of Outerwilderbeastia,' General Doppelgänger informed them via crystal communicator, 'in one of the Clubs' more remote land holdings.'

Dodge hacked a path into the jungle with his father's sword, cutting back vines thick as a spirit-dane's shin bone and rubbery fronds the size of tea platters. Pushing through the dank, heavy foliage, he tested each gwynook-length of spongy ground with his own body weight before letting Alyss follow. Infrequent communications with General Doppelgänger and Bibwit failed to settle them on a destination, and unsure how long it would take to manoeuvre through Outerwilderbeastia, they stopped to rest in a sort of enclave, an area surrounded on all sides by dense jungle and no larger than the table in the palace's briefing room.

'Why don't you get some sleep?' he suggested.

'What about you?'

'Don't worry about me.'

He knew he'd never be able to close his eyes. And so, with what passed for silence in Outerwilderbeastia as accompaniment to his ruminations – the whir of fist-sized insects, the caw and rattle of unseen creatures – he watched her sleep.

He'd been intending to propose – even before the Queendom's distant military outposts were attacked, before the need to figure out who or what was attacking them rendered the timing for highly personal questions inappropriate. And since then, there'd been one calamity after another, misfortunes contriving to prevent him from *ever* asking what his heart compelled him to ask. Couldn't he and Alyss manage so much as a quarter lunar hour together, which, if not romantic, might at least be free of invasions, rebellions, unlawful incarcerations, political and military subterfuge? Between Alyss's loss of imagination and the Clubs' uprising, the timing for a proposal perhaps hadn't been the absolute worst, since her loss of power had brought her closer to Dodge's level as an ordinary Wonderlander. Expecting a better opportunity, though, he hadn't acted. But what if a better opportunity never came? Maybe this was, in part, what it meant to love a Queen: where your personal life was concerned, you made what you could of unlikely times and places. There, in a tiny clearing in northern Outerwilderbeastia, watching his beloved sleep, Dodge made up his mind: he just had to do it – to not think but act. Their future survival was uncertain, but he would declaim his feelings for Alyss Heart, ask her to make him – despite all – the happiest man in Wonderland.

♥ ♦ CHAPTER 28 ♣ ♦

It was developing into a habit as firm as his chattiness had been previously – the royal tutor barely returning the greetings of the sunflowers, tulips and hollizaleas he passed as he hurried along a path in the palace grounds, not even murmuring to himself as he approached a hedge indistinguishable from those around it. His bald head glistening like a second moon in the evening's light, his ears pivoting as if to catch any sound made by nearby foes, Bibwit stepped into the thickest part of the hedge, his weight causing its roots to shift and a hatchway to open. A hand grabbed him and pulled him roughly back on to the path.

'Can't go down.'

The King's bodyguards: Ripkins and Blister. Where had they come from? How had he not heard them?

'I can't . . . go down?' Bibwit repeated. 'But . . .' What could he say? He had no official reason for being in The

Heart Chamber. He'd been overcome with a need to check on the Crystal, to confirm that its recovery from WILMA was continuing unabated, that he and Alyss, Wonderland and White Imaginationists everywhere, still had a chance.

'No one is to go down,' Ripkins said. 'King's orders.'

'Yes,' the tutor's ears belied surprise with a not-so-subtle flick, 'the King is down there. I have business with the King.' He struggled to think what that business might be, because once he descended the bronzite steps, Arch would demand to know the meaning of his intrusion.

'You're not going down,' Blister said.

'Your business with the King will wait until he ascends,' said Ripkins.

Unable to walk away without arousing distrust, Bibwit smiled weakly at the inexpressive bodyguards and resigned himself to waiting.

Arch didn't care how the green caterpillar did it – whether he lied to the other oracles to get them to give up their silk or somehow, despite their alleged omniscience, stole it from them without a word. Why should he care? The caterpillar had given him what he required. And if the story of the creature's boredom, of his need to test the extent of his power,

191

were a lie, he'd discover it in time. For now, he would press forwards with his scheme. He would figure out the rest as facts became known.

On the floor of The Heart Chamber, the waist-high spools of purple, blue, yellow, red, orange and green caterpillar silk were immediately before him, his intel ministers and their assistants working on what looked to be an enormous sock. The ministers consulted diagrams similar to the one Hatter Madigan was supposed to have followed when weaving WILMA's final thread into place over Heart Palace. Purple and yellow in a butterfly stitch *here*, the ministers instructed, more orange entwining the green *there*. The assistants wove the silks together accordingly, adding to the length and girth of the giant sock, and the repeated pattern made by the combined threads proved to be the exact one Hatter had purposely failed to weave into WILMA.

Arch reached down and teased out a bit of green silk from its spool. The caterpillar, plotting towards an end he had yet to fathom, might not have provided enough.

'You're positive the cocoon's measurements are correct?' the King asked a minister.

'We re-check constantly to be sure, Your Highness.'

The Heart Crystal, irksomely bright, pulsed like a vital

organ. The effects of WILMA would soon belong completely to the past.

'Get more men to help you,' Arch said. 'I want it ready as soon as possible. The Crystal's not to have its former power for longer than is absolutely necessary.'

'Yes, Your Highness.'

'There's been no word?'

'None that you would wish to hear, My Liege. Wherever Alyss and Redd are hiding, they continue to avoid discovery.'

There was something unsettled in the minister's tone.

'But?'

'But – my apologies, Your Majesty – a score of Gnobi were recently found dead in The Volcanic Plains. From the manner in which they were killed, we believe Redd is responsible. Warriors have scoured the area but discovered no further sign of her.'

It had to be Redd. It was not Alyss's style to leave twenty dead lying around for him to find. It wouldn't have been her style even if she'd known the Gnobi tribe was under orders to kill her and she'd exterminated them in self-defence. But she hadn't known. Arch had been careful not to divulge those orders to Bibwit or General Doppelgänger, in case they maintained secret contact with their former Queen.

'Neither Alyss nor Redd can hope to wrest the Crystal from me *and* remain in hiding,' he said. 'As soon as they're convinced imagination has returned to them just as powerfully as ever, they'll make a push for it – one or the other, both if I'm lucky. And that's when . . .' Arch let his voice trail off, nodded at the cocoon.

'Yes, Your Highness.'

'Get more men to help you,' he ordered.

Taking the bronzite steps two at a time, the King ascended to ground level, passed through the hatchway into open air and emerged from the hedge. The royal tutor, trying not to look discomfited, was standing on the path, flanked by Ripkins and Blister.

'Mr Harte. Just the Wonderlander I wanted to consult. Walk with me.'

Ripkins and Blister started to follow.

'No,' the King said to them. 'Stay and make note of every assistant the ministers employ, in case anything goes wrong.'

The bodyguards returned to their inconspicuous posts near the hedge.

'You were coming to see me?' Arch asked Bibwit, strolling along at a leisurely pace – so leisurely that the tutor, at his side, had to be careful not to get ahead of him.

'I was . . . out for a bit of air, My Liege,' the tutor answered.

The King looked unconvinced. They turned on to a path that led through hollizaleas and sunflowers, which bowed and greeted the King – some, Bibwit thought, more respectfully than others.

'You have everything you want?' the King asked. 'You're comfortable?'

'Yes, Your Highness.'

'No less comfortable than when Alyss was Queen?'

Bibwit preferred not to admit the truth. But perhaps, since he was so inept at lying, he should avoid it when he could. 'No less,' he said.

'Good. I can understand how the transition might be difficult for you, having tried to shape those fickle female minds for so many years and now you suddenly have to answer to a king. We wouldn't want lack of physical comfort to be an added strain.'

'There's another comfort I'd humbly request, Your Highness, if you'd deign to provide it.' And taking the King's silence as invitation to proceed, he asked, 'The Heart Crystal, how is it?'

'It's improving, Mr Harte. Comfort yourself with the

knowledge that it's greatly improved from what it was.'

Bibwit sifted through what he knew of Arch's connection to WILMA: the King had never directly taken responsibility for the weapon and, if not for Hatter, Alyss would not know of his guilt; to have actually produced a weapon of WILMA's power Arch had needed a wealth of caterpillar silk; only a few lunar hours before, Alyss had envisioned the King in talks with the green oracle.

'Does it not – forgive me for asking, My Liege – but doesn't it bother you that the Crystal's improving?'

'Why should it bother me, Mr Harte? Because I think Wonderland has for too long overestimated the Crystal's worth? I intend to change the citizenry's beliefs on that front. Or do you think I should be bothered for fear of Redd?'

'The latter, Your Highness. As to the Crystal's worth, I will humbly endeavour to change your mind.'

Arch cleared his throat, doubtful. 'I remind you, Mr Harte: Redd and her pittance of a following are on the run, she has no home and no military, nor can she get close to the Crystal to maximise her imaginative abilities. I'd say the odds are in my favour.'

The upper corners of Bibwit's ears folded once, then straightened – the tutor's version of a nod.

'And as for your dear Alyss, nothing convinces me more of her cowardice than her continuing failure to show herself.'

Bibwit, his eyes on the path, knew the King was watching him. He tried to slow his breathing and the throb of blood through his veins. He tried to give nothing away, to adopt the open expression of suspended judgement, as if he were reading a philosophical treatise and was still neither convinced nor unconvinced by its argument.

'Have you ever thought, Mr Harte, that Alyss might view my ascendance as an opportunity to unburden herself of regal authority? It seems to me the girl realised what the House of Hearts before her did not, that the throne is no place for a female.'

'I choose to believe, Your Highness, that Alyss's prolonged absence is caused by something else.'

'And what would *that* be?'

Bibwit shrugged, shook his head, weighed the air in his hands, shrugged again.

'Is this the tutor's infamous tongue?' Arch laughed. 'For your sake, I hope you're left speechless by the sudden benefits of residing within a Kingdom after years in a Queendom, because otherwise . . .' He shook his head, unimpressed.

'But speaking of years, for at least a score of them, I've been hearing of Wonderland's six oracles. The caterpillar council, I believe they're called?'

'They are,' Bibwit answered.

'Living as long as you have, I assume you and these oracles have had extensive dealings?'

'No one has had extensive dealings with them, Your Highness. They aren't sociable creatures. I would classify my dealings with them as occasional.'

'Hm.'

'A great many influential Wonderlanders believe them to be useless, a tiresome reminder of less developed times. Your friends the Clubs are among them.'

'But not you.'

Bibwit didn't answer.

'I want you to tutor me, Mr Harte.'

'You strike me as well-schooled, Your Highness. Particularly in the ways of people.'

'It's wise of you to flatter me, but I mean to study the oracles, not people.'

Bibwit had assumed they were following an aimless course through the palace grounds, but as they rounded a stand of gobbygrape trees, the King stopped outside the royal library;

this had apparently been their destination all along.

'I'd like you to gather every scroll,' Arch said to him, 'every document and encyclopedia crystal we have concerning the oracles, no matter how ancient the material. Bring these to me, I'll look them over, and then I'll no doubt come to you with questions.'

'That is what I'm here for, Your Highness.' Bibwit bowed, hoping that through such tutelage he might learn the nature of Arch's relationship with the green caterpillar.

It was nearly dawn, the sky still dark and star-filled as the tutor made his way along a path, gliding on silent feet past sleeping flowers and shrubs. He made no sound audible even to his super-sensitive ears, and this time no hand pulled him roughly from the hedge. He stepped in amid its branches and, without waiting for its roots to fully unlock, descended through the opening hatchway into The Heart Chamber.

Something was wrong.

Not that Ripkins and Blister hadn't been standing guard outside, nor that the chamber was deserted, with none of the customary ministers scuttling about. Not that the light wasn't as bright as it should have been, nor that the platform halfway to the floor seemed unmoored and the walls further apart than usual. It was none of these, yet explained them all: The Heart Crystal was gone.

❦ CHAPTER 29 ❦

Alyss gazed out over the Morgavian hinterlands – the thin, cone-shaped trees dusted with snow, the scattered ponds that, from her hilltop vantage, looked like artfully placed cobblestones in the gently thawing fields. She had never been to Morgavia before and would have preferred her first visit to the region to have a more pleasurable purpose.

'It's right for us to meet like this, without any attendants,' Redd sighed, the thorny vines of her dress slithering close to her body. 'If not for the strength of our imaginations, and that this picturesque view is making me nauseous, I could almost believe we were a common aunt and niece spending long-overdue quality time together.'

'If not for what you've wrought with your imagination, you mean,' Alyss said, and had to stop herself from adding 'murderer'.

Redd's permanent frown became more pronounced, the

parentheses-like folds in her cheeks deepening, filling with shadow. 'I'm not going to attack you. You don't need your shield.' Her sceptre feinted towards the nimbus of deflective energy Alyss had conjured around herself for protection. 'Did you tell anyone you were coming to meet me?'

The question rankled – as if Alyss should have told Dodge she'd agreed to meet the woman responsible for Sir Justice's death, for her own mother's death and her father's rapid decline into doddering imbecility. It was true that she'd thought of confiding in him, but every time she was about to, the sight of him demagnetising the ammo bay of an AD52, or brainstorming via crystal communicator with General Doppelgänger and ruling out any suggestion he deemed too risky to her safety – these had stopped her. He would have tried to talk her out of it. But the communication from Redd – dropped at her feet one night by a seeker with silent, outspread wings – had been unlike any she'd ever received from her aunt: urgent, solicitous, mentioning in roundabout, embarrassed fashion the need for once unthinkable alliances if imagination was to be saved. And she and her advisors had yet to decide on a course of action against Arch – a King who, it might be said, united aunt and niece by being their common enemy.

Not that any of this would have mattered to Dodge. He would have called Redd's interview request a ruse, a setup, perhaps even a plot to kidnap her and deliver her to Arch. He would have thought it his duty no less than his inclination to dissuade her from going. But Alyss hadn't wanted to be dissuaded. If she couldn't protect the entire Queendom from Redd, she could still protect herself. She was *not* afraid. And it wasn't a question of forgiveness. She would never forgive Redd for what she'd done to her family, her life. But contending with imagination's possible extinction, she was facing a concern so much larger than herself. The principles of White Imagination that had become so much a part of her – love, justice, duty – demanded that she explore all options.

Thoroughly scouting Morgavia's hinterlands in her imagination's eye, she'd seen no assassins lying in wait for her – just Redd, alone, on a wind-scourged hilltop. And since she couldn't have asked Bibwit for advice without alerting Dodge, she had told no one of her assignation with her aunt.

'We heard from Arch you were dead,' she said.

'He wishes!' The vines of Redd's dress serpentined out and the rose blossoms clacked their teeth. Redd took on what was supposed to be a calm expression, but it only made her look like a glaze-eyed corpse. 'I apologise for losing my temper,' she said, the vines of her dress recoiling. 'Notice that I can control myself when I must. But I swear to you, niece: between me and Arch, *he* will be the first to die.'

'Then why have you not attacked him?'

'For the same reason that you, with your imagination, have done nothing. I suspect a trap.'

'Why else would he let our powers return,' Alyss nodded.

'I see you're not as dumb as Wonderlanders claim.' Turning her back on the view, Redd spoke with face uplifted and eyes nearly closed, as if her words caused her pain. 'Arch cannot be secure in his reign until we're both dead. Let us suppose, for argument's sake, that you somehow amass enough of a military to clash with the self-proclaimed King of Wonderland.'

Enough of a military? 'The Heart soldiers and chessmen remain loyal to me,' Alyss said.

'How nice for you,' Redd glowered. 'Let us suppose, then, that you command this loyal military of yours against Arch's tribal forces, and with the benefit of your imaginative powers you're about to successfully knock Arch from the throne, but that's *exactly* when your imagination deserts you. Because

Arch, having control of the Crystal, makes sure of it. So there you are, powerless and exposed, your soldiers outnumbered. What do you think will happen then?'

'My troops would be doomed. *I* would be doomed.'

'To put it mildly. And I'd bet The Cat's last life I would suffer the same fate. If I showed myself during an attack, Arch would devise it so that I lost imagination when I needed it most, and that would be the end of me.'

'But he could do that even if –'

'– we joined together and attacked him with what support we can muster? Yes. But neither of us can rule without The Heart Crystal.' Redd yawned. 'I don't intend to start liking you, nor do I expect you to stop hating me. We both know Wonderland's crown is mine by right of succcession –'

Alyss tried to interrupt.

'Hold!' said Redd. 'As I say, we know the crown belongs to me, but so long as Arch controls the Crystal, he's a danger to us both equally. Worse, he's a danger to *imagination*. You and I don't agree on how best to use our gifts, but much as I loathe to admit, I think we can agree that a world with imagination is better than a world without it.'

Alyss eyed her aunt: the straw-and-wire hair, the stretched sinews and sickly skin of her neck. This was Genevieve's *sister*, the closest living reminder – however sullied in flesh and psyche – of her mother. 'What are you suggesting we do?' she asked.

'First, niece, we agree on what *not* to do. We remain out of sight. Neither of us, with or without our followers, makes a move against Arch until we're sure of toppling him or better – killing him. We vow to keep our imaginations as long as possible, preferably for the rest of our lives. Which, in my case, will be a while.'

Alyss nodded: they were agreed, aligned in purpose. *But I won't forget who I'm negotiating with. Can't forget. You will betray me as soon as it benefits you to do it.*

'As for what comes next,' Redd said, 'I haven't the faintest idea, but I think our chances better if we work together instead of on our own.'

'And if we survive and Arch is dealt with,' Alyss asked, 'then what?'

Redd sniggered. 'Then, my too-sweet niece, things can revert to the way they used to be, with me taking what's mine while you try to keep me from taking it.' Her Imperial Viciousness was about to leave, stood picking at the ground with the pointed end of her sceptre. 'You know, I can't see you without being reminded of my sister.

You have that same wounded look of naïve honesty.'

'I hope I have more of her than that in me,' Alyss replied.

'You *would*!'

Redd's dress flared from a sudden gust of wind, obscuring her niece's vision with blackness and –

Alyss awoke, sat up and stared at the branches and vines tremulous against the dawn sky. It took a Gwormmy-blink to remember where she was: Outerwilderbeastia, halfway between the Ganmede Province and The Snark Mountains, three-quarters of a night's journey from the limbo coop whose perimeter wall she and Dodge had walked through as effortlessly as if they'd been strolling the palace portico.

'What is it?' Dodge asked. He was seated on a rock, watching over her.

A dream, she should have said. But it felt too real to be a dream. *Could it be . . . is it possible I really communed with Redd?* Could the two most powerful imaginationists in Wonderland have met, conversed and come to an agreement telepathically? Had she experienced a sort of transmigration of her deeper self, made possible by her rare gift?

We summoned each other. Of necessity.

'You haven't slept,' she said to Dodge.

'If I sleep, who will watch over you?'

He came and knelt down beside her, took her hand in both of his and stroked her palm with delicate fingers. The increasing light silhouetted his long eyelashes, and with his head lowered and his unscarred cheek turned to her . . .

Could almost believe we're living what might have been: I'm still a Princess, with mother and father alive, he works at the palace under the guidance of Sir Justice, and we've sneaked away from everyone's expectations, just the two of us, shyly loving, and –

'I need to ask you something . . . personal,' he said. 'I've been meaning to for some time.'

Tell him.

'Dodge.'

But he was on his feet, an AD52 in each hand and aimed past her as a figure stepped from the brambles, a figure Alyss recognised as one of Redd's assassins by the spike-tipped whip coiled at his hip.

♠CHAPTER 30♣

Oxford, England. 1875.

On unseasonably warm, sunny days, streets from Longwell to Mill, Thames to St Giles, filled with open carriages bearing leisurely men and women, with bicyclists and strollers and window shoppers; the green expanses of Christ Church Meadow, Merton Field and Magellan Grove crowded with picnickers, footballers, cricket players and countless others. Revellers in nature, enthusiasts of every manner of outdoor activity – all emerged from the confines of four walls and a roof to partake of *al fresco* pleasures. But on one unseasonably fine day in 1875, along with this variegated lot, a certain trio were enticed to a certain sycamore tree on High Street between All Souls and Queen's College, though not by the sun and breeze, nor by the tree itself, however closely Reverend Dodgson seemed to study its bark.

'It's not that I doubt the validity of w-what you've told

me *in toto*,' the Reverend explained to Hatter and Molly, 'so much as . . . as there is a point or two that could use c-c-clarification, the foremost of which . . . if Alyss is in Wonderland, housed in a prison or some such, how do you explain *her*?'

Dodgson poked his head around the tree and with a darting bird-like jerk of the neck indicated a group of ladies congregating before a tea shop. The ladies were similarly dressed in ankle-length skirts, in flouncy blouses ruffling out at cuffs and collar from beneath short-waisted jackets, yet Hatter and Molly instantly recognised one of them as Wonderland's Queen.

'That's Alice Liddell,' Dodgson said, noting their reactions, 'the same young lady who told me of her Wonderland trials so many years ago.'

'Not the same,' Hatter said, catching his daughter's eye.

'It is, I t-tell you,' the Reverend sputtered. 'She's no longer as young as she was, of course. N-None of us is.'

How to explain to this timid, squeamish fellow the aftermath of Redd Heart's leap into The Heart Crystal? How to describe in believable detail the post-battle lull inside Mount Isolation, with Hatter, Molly, Bibwit, Dodge, General Doppelgänger, the white knight and the white rook as witnesses to Alyss's immediate assumption of Wonderland's crown? Could Reverend Dodgson, already beyond the limits of what he'd grown up believing, credit an account of Bibwit Harte suggesting that Alyss conjure a double of herself to occupy her place in the Liddell family – the place she'd rightly vacated to be Wonderland's sovereign? Would the Reverend empathise with Alyss's self-doubt as she questioned whether her powers were strong enough to birth a double even as she reached out to The Heart Crystal with both arms and – *popzzzzlllpipipopzzzx!* – caused the room to disappear in a wash of light?

It was an unprecedented feat – the conjuring of a live, independent being – but Hatter had never doubted the Queen's ability to perform it though he was only now seeing the result: a young woman in front of a High Street tea shop who'd never been anyone other than Alice Liddell. And if it was strange for the Milliner and his daughter to palpably confront the existence of this Alyss/not-Alyss, it was quadruply so for Charles Dodgson who, hearing from Hatter how this Alyss/not-Alyss had come to be, kept shaking his head and exclaiming, 'It's too much. Too much.' He was not, however, left to feel his dismay for long.

'It's my duty to return to Wonderland,' Hatter said. 'Molly will stay with you.'

The girl started.

'What?' the Reverend protested. 'N-No, please, it's highly improper she should stay with me. Highly improper. If people were to find out –'

'Don't let them. But I have to do all I can to help my Queen.'

Dodgson continued to plead. Silent, Molly glared at nothing. And Hatter didn't say what he was thinking: that if he gave his life in Alyss Heart's service, which he was prepared to do, he would not be back.

'Molly will stay with you,' he'd said, as if it was his decision and he could tell her what to do. She'd spent her whole life without a father and now he thought he could make up for the years he hadn't been around? What a joke. Did he really believe that in his absence she would answer to Dodgson? Because she didn't have to answer to *anybody*. She'd do whatever she wanted. No one could tell her what to do.

'I'm not abandoning you,' Hatter said, leading her several paces away from Dodgson for privacy.

'I don't have to do as you say. I didn't even want to come

here and now you think you can leave me with *him*,' Molly gestured at Dodgson, 'while you go back?'

'But you're not . . .' Hatter picked his words with care, '. . . yourself.'

'How would *you* know?'

The Milliner's hand twitched towards his top hat, as it would to ward off a physical threat, then fell to his side. 'You act as if you're the only one grieving the loss of your mother,' he said quietly. 'I've seen how you'd rather mope and feel sorry for yourself than wield Milliner blades with the skill I know you have. And since I don't know the extent of the dangers I face by returning to Wonderland, it's best you stay.'

There he went again, making pronouncements on what was allegedly best for her! She hated him twice over – for belatedly trying to play father and also for making her hate him, because to be overcome by any emotion, especially a negative one, was un-Milliner-like and reminded her that she was a halfer.

'Why don't you keep alert for anything you think will benefit Queen Alyss,' Hatter suggested, 'no matter how far-fetched it seems? When we don't know what's important, we should assume everything is.'

She wasn't dumb. He was trying to give her something to do, treating her as if she were a child playing at being an adult, and she felt the familiar sting of wounded pride. Which was weird, since she didn't want or believe she deserved any position of importance or responsibility – not as the Queen's bodyguard, a Milliner, whatever. Even weirder: she was starting to wonder if she might make up for the trauma she'd caused. Not erase her mistake from collective memory but balance it with a feat of immense good or –

Stupid, stupid, stupid. How could anything in Reverend Dodgson's world benefit Alyss Heart?

'I'll run off,' she said. 'I won't stay. You can't make me.'

Hatter's eyes grew moist. His chest rose and fell. 'No, Molly,' he said finally, 'I can't make you do anything you don't want to do. I'm *asking* you to stay with Mr Dodgson. When I come back – which will be soon, I promise – we'll return to Wonderland together and you can hear from Queen Alyss personally that she'll accept no one but you as her bodyguard.'

Molly folded her arms tightly against her chest, felt the unyielding bulk of her mother's notebooks in her coat's inside pocket. Her mother had loved this man. She would do it for her mother, would honour the ties of family and abide by

Hatter as a daughter should. At least for a little while.

She felt Hatter's kiss in retrospect, so preoccupied with her thoughts that she registered the brief press of his lips to her cheek only after he was disappearing into the High Street crowds.

Picking at the sycamore's bark, Dodgson glanced uneasily at her, as if to say, *Well, here we are.* He was no more than ten metres from her, though it might as well have been a hundred million for all Molly felt.

♦ CHAPTER 31 ♣

Mr Van de Skulle stepped from the brambles, his hands raised in surrender and his face impassive as Dodge's AD52s took aim and –

'No!' Alyss cried.

Razor-cards spun and sliced the air. *Fith-fith-fith-fith-fith!* Mr Van de Skulle made no move to avoid them, and just when he should have felt the stinging cut of steel –

The razor-cards parted to either side of him, shooting off into the jungle to his left and right, leaving him unharmed.

'What're you doing?' Dodge asked Alyss.

Mr Van de Skulle didn't reach for his whip, made no move of aggression whatsoever. Dodge again pressed the triggers of his AD52s but the weapons were jammed. His voice rose in frustration.

'Why're you doing this?'

Before Alyss could answer, Mr Van de Skulle said to her,

'As a show of faith, Her Imperial Viciousness has sent me to be of what service I can to you.'

Dodge whirled, his AD52s still trained on the assassin. 'Show of faith?'

I knew it couldn't have been a dream.

'Show of *what* faith? What's he talking about?'

'Redd and I have an agreement,' Alyss heard herself say.

Dodge's reaction pierced her as painfully as any blade: the AD52s lolled loose in his hands, too heavy to aim, and he kept shaking his head, the skin at the corners of his eyes tight with incomprehension, disbelief, mounting rage.

She hadn't even begun to explain but already it felt like a confession. Still, she *would* explain – the how and why of her pact with Redd, the tenuous bond created by a mutual enemy. She would explain and hope that Dodge's love for her was stronger than the resentment he would undoubtedly feel.

Dodge crouched on the opposite side of the clearing, as far from Alyss as he could be while still keeping an eye on the assassin who stood between them, waiting for something to happen.

It felt like duplicity – not just that Alyss had 'partnered'

217

with Redd, but that she hadn't discussed it with him first. A Queen didn't have to subject her doings to anyone for approval, let alone the head of her palace guard, but shouldn't she have *wanted* to talk it over with him? Wasn't that partly what it meant to be in love – that two people told each other everything, confiding without reserve or embarrassment their dreams, doubts, fears, plans, ambitions? Didn't being in love mean there was no need of secrets? Alyss had assumed the worst of him: that wanting to avenge his father's death, he wouldn't be able to clearly judge the strategic value of Redd's cooperation. And just when he'd made up his mind to propose!

He sensed Alyss's solicitous glances from across the clearing but stared into the jungle, pretending not to notice. If he couldn't fight Alyss, he could definitely fight Mr Skull or whatever the man's name was. He could send the lowlife limping back to Redd to let her know what *he* thought of her deal with Alyss. But . . . wait a Gwormmy-blink. Maybe he was thinking about this all wrong. He'd been counting on a larger battle against Redd Heart's army, a battle in which he would seek a one-on-one confrontation with The Cat, but that was no longer a possibility. Maybe this new connection with Redd was his best opportunity for revenge against his father's executioner. No matter how briefly or precariously Alyss and Redd were banded together, so long as they were in league to dethrone Arch, wasn't he more likely than not to have dealings with the slobbering feline?

Alyss had kept a secret from him, he would keep one from her.

He would pretend to accept the new arrangement between aunt and niece. No, he'd do more than that – he'd *encourage* ever greater cooperation between them, to better ensure himself of a run-in with The Cat. He'd continue to work towards overthrowing Arch and reinstating White Imagination to its supreme position in the Queendom, in the course of which he'd just happen to take The Cat's last life.

He rose to his feet and crossed the clearing. 'I don't like it but it's the right thing to do,' he said to Alyss. 'But you already knew that.'

'She's agreed not to risk imagination with an attack against Arch.'

Dodge turned a doubtful, appraising eye on Mr Van de Skulle. 'What makes Redd think you can be of service here with us instead of with her?'

'I know better than to answer for Her Imperial Viciousness,' the assassin said, 'but Wonderland is vast and filled with enemies. Imagination or not, there *are* just two of you.'

'And now there are three. I feel so much better.'

Alyss's hand fell lightly on his arm. 'Dodge,' she whispered.

If he was going to convince everyone that he accepted this new alliance, he had to stop trying to pick a fight with Redd's assassin. He had to act as if he trusted the man.

Feigning apology, he dipped his head first to Alyss, then to Mr Van de Skulle. 'We should inform Bibwit and General Doppelgänger,' he said, determined not to lose the best opportunity he had of slamming his father's sword hilt-deep into The Cat's guts.

◆ CHAPTER 32 ♣
◆

'Scrumptious!'

'Delicious!'

'So bold yet so subtle!'

'So pungent yet so delicately flavoured!'

'The perfect hint of cinnamon-minnamon and such a delightfully crumbly mouthfeel!'

Blue unstuck his lips from his hookah and grumbled: 'Ahem hum hem hem. I remind the council that the King's surprise delivery has not yet arrived.'

Sitting in a semi-circle deep within The Everlasting Forest, each oracle on a fungus as tall and wide as a three-room cottage and as intensely coloured as himself, Yellow, Purple and Red turned to one another, shocked, Orange and Green were horrified, but the antennae of all bent low to explore mouths woefully empty.

'I wish he'd hurry,' Purple moaned, 'I'm starving!'

As if in answer, Blue pushed a long funnel of smoke from his lungs – so long that it appeared never-ending, continuing to pour out his mouth even as its other end weaved off through the valley to some unseen rendezvous. Then he began to inhale, sucking the smoke funnel back into his lungs. Purple and the rest of the oracles twittered in anticipation, salivating outright when the funnel's end came into view, because moving towards them, following the trail of smoke, was one of Arch's intel ministers bearing what looked like a gigantic upside-down mushroom top filled with fragrant, steaming fresh –

'Tarty tarts!' the oracles cried at once.

Piled willy-nilly in the curious-shaped receptacle: enough tarty tarts to feed . . . well, six tarty tart-loving oracles. Caramel-stuffed tarts decorated with choco-nibblies. Tarts bursting with gobbygrabe goo and strawberry mash. Cream-filled tarts dusted with glittering sugar. Buttery tarts topped with vanilla icing, blueberry swirls, squigberry doilies, cinnamon-minnamon sprinkles. The minister had brought these and more, had in fact brought every variety of tarty tart known to Wonderland. Stepping before the council, he cleared his throat and –

'King Arch wishes to present us with a token of his esteem

and appreciation,' the orange and red caterpillars said.

Spooked at hearing the words he was about to utter, Arch's minister – acting by no means ministerial – stumbled off into the valley, where he would, the oracles knew, soon be lost.

Purple dropped from his mushroom and thrust his face into the cauldron of tarty tarts.

'Have some manners!' Yellow huffed.

Purple paused from his indiscriminate munching, lifted his head. 'I have *plenty* of manners,' he said, gobbygrape smears staining his cheeks and crumbs stippling the area around his mouth. 'There's the manner in which I puff on my hookah, the manner in which I move through dirt, and what you're presently witnessing is the manner in which I delight in tarty tarts!'

'*I'll* show *you* delight!' Yellow bellowed, and floated down next to Purple to shove his own face into the treats and munch indiscriminately.

The red caterpillar, meanwhile, had grabbed eight tarty tarts and was holding them in the eight feet closest to his mouth, taking a single bite of each in turn, over and over again. Blue was stacking tarty tart upon tarty tart to make a quintuple-decker tarty tart sandwich and Green was putting an end to the heretofore eternal question of just how many tarty tarts a caterpillar-oracle could fit in his mouth at one time.

'You proceed better than anticipated with the King,' Blue said.

'Aaanhaaah nanh nanh aanhing gah annnahghing,' Green answered, swallowing mightily so that a bulge of food visibly passed along the length of his body. 'Excuse me. Depends who was doing the anticipating, I meant to say.'

Blue and Green chuckled. Green chucked a raspberry-blast tart into Blue's eager maw, Blue tossed a dingy-pear tart into Green's. They chewed and swallowed.

'Homburg Molly is in place,' Blue noted between bites of his five-decker. 'But time grows short for getting Alyss to where Everqueen requires her to be.'

'Earth,' Green said knowingly.

The red caterpillar was now holding sixteen tarty tarts in the sixteen feet closest to his mouth, taking a bite of each in turn. 'You know what *I'm* going to say,' he announced, too busy attacking his baked goods to utter more.

'I know the many things you *might* say,' Blue prompted him. 'To which do you refer?'

'The third one.'

Purple lifted his head from the tarty tart cauldron, his front legs wagging in the air, his eyes wide and turned to the sky. 'Wait! I'm having a vision! Yes, I see . . . I see . . . that Arch *must* be the one to lure Alyss to Earth!'

'I see it too!' Red cried, lifting his sixteen tarty tarts heavenward. 'It will not accomplish what must be acccomplished to establish Everqueen if Blue directs Alyss to Earth without involving the King!'

Tipping the last of his tarty tart sandwich down his gullet, Blue addressed the council. 'Do we not see the past and all possible futures at every given moment?'

'I'm blind!' Yellow shouted; having removed his face from the pile of tarty tarts, gobs of the stuff were covering his eyes.

'Don't mind if I do,' said Green, plucking the gobs free and popping them into his mouth.

'Do we not,' Blue continued, 'alter all possible futures every time we intervene with lesser beings who vie for The Heart Crystal?'

'The possible futures of all beings change constantly,' Green pointed out.

'Every Gwormmy-blink of every lunar minute,' added the red caterpillar, 'every time a lesser being takes the slightest action. I find the role of an oracle exhausting even without this *flux*. Having to be aware of all the possible futures of every moment as well as the possible futures of *those* possible futures and –'

'It's enough to make my head hurt,' said Yellow.

'Tell me about it,' Purple agreed with a roll of his eyes.

Blue took a long pull of his hookah, grumbled: 'Ahum hem. If we again intervene, we create possibilities that will not exist otherwise. The most important of these, as we can see, represents the gravest risk to the Crystal and to ourselves.'

'He is, yes,' Green said.

'Who is, what?' asked Blue, as Yellow, Red, Orange and Purple looked to him for guidance.

'That is the answer to your next question. Yes, Arch is clever enough to discern the course of action that poses awful risk to us, but which Everqueen demands.'

'Yum,' Red said, gazing adoringly into the tarty tart cauldron.

'Don't we know that we *must* intervene?' Yellow quizzed the council. 'Do we not all see that? If we do not intervene, none of the possible futures for ourselves currently foreseen is, um . . . good?'

'It is decided then,' said Blue. 'Green shall prod the King

and I will do what must be done with regards to Alyss Heart.'

Red wiped his brow with a flugelberry cream tart as one wipes away sweat after much exertion. 'This reminds me of the time we were deciding whether to intervene when the Lady of Clubs tried to steal The Heart Crystal.'

'That's next month,' Yellow said.

'That *was* next month,' corrected Purple, 'now that you-know-who's done you-know-what.'

'Right!'

'Ugh. Now?' Green said, wrinkling his nose at Blue.

Blue exhaled a puff of hookah smoke that formed the sentence, 'Yes, now.'

'OK then, all right. Rush me, why don't you?' Green frantically tucked tarty tarts into the crevices between his annular muscles – horizontal crevices that acted like little pockets up and down his caterpillar belly. 'Let me just . . . I must have sustenance to fortify me on my journey. All right, off I go!'

Laden with his favourite foodstuff, Green stepped on to a carpet of hookah smoke and floated off through the valley to instigate events in which everything that mattered to Wonderland's oracles could be lost.

♥ CHAPTER 33 ♣

In Heart Palace's royal library, Bibwit Harte pulled scrolls from drawers and encyclopedia crystals from shelves, a charred codex and diaries of long-gone tutors from a glass display case in the centre of the room. With its numerous floor-to-ceiling shelves, its reading nooks and desks for study, the library was as accommodating as any place could be for the accumulation of knowledge, yet it didn't contain a tenth the number of volumes there had been in the former palace – so much of Wonderland's history, documented nowhere else, stolen by looters in the weeks following Queen Genevieve's downfall, or destroyed in the Redd-imagined collapse that ultimately rendered Genevieve's seat a mound of rubble.

'Oof!' the walrus-butler exclaimed, blowing on a scroll to clean it of dust and getting the dust all over his cheeks and whiskers. 'I'll have to make sure these are cleaned more frequently. Yes, they do need a good . . . a thorough cleaning and airing out, don't they, Mr Bibwit?'

Mr Bibwit would have preferred the volumes to remain as they'd been, collecting dust, rather than surrender them to Arch. He hadn't opened a single one of them since Queen Genevieve's last tutorial, but as he laid a milk white hand upon each, he saw their contents as clearly as if he and Genevieve were sitting down to a lesson. A Ten Card's chronicle of the early wars incited by discovery of The Heart Crystal; official transcripts of negotiations among the suit families prior to Wonderland's formation; the diary of a tutor Bibwit knew in his youth: these texts contained miscellaneous anecdotes relating to the oracles – a cryptic utterance by Blue ('Where did we come from? We have always been here. Waiting'); a vague reference to a Looking Glass Maze as the means to imaginative maturity for 'those gifted with imitation of The Heart Crystal's power'. What was known of the caterpillars had been culled from these and other volumes, distilled into brief entries found in the encyclopedia crystals.

'Despite the lunar hours of reading and viewing these volumes represent,' Bibwit said to the walrus, 'His Majesty isn't likely to come away with more knowledge of the oracles than he already possesses.'

'Ouff, goodness, this dust! – how is that possible, Mr Bibwit?'

Bibwit's ears softened. 'Gentle friend, I sometimes forget that although you and I are frequently together, you have little experience with the oracles.'

'None at all, Mr Bibwit, and I wish to . . . I do prefer to keep it that way. But if the oracles help Queen Alyss, our beloved distraught Queen, why, I *will* be extraordinarily grateful to them from afar.'

'I'm afraid the caterpillars' concern lies solely, as it always has, with The Heart Crystal as the generative force in the cosmos,' said Bibwit. 'They bother with kings and queens only to the extent that these impact the Crystal's welfare, and I have no evidence the oracles favour Alyss any more than they do, say, King Arch.'

The walrus's whiskers trembled, his tusks gnawed his lower lip. To think he might have to serve King Arch for the remainder of his days!

'But as I was saying,' Bibwit went on, 'these volumes contain no great information about the oracles. Many of the most reliable and informative – direct accounts recorded by others of my species – have been lost or destroyed. Even *In Queendom Speramus* has not yet been re-collated. What King

Arch will find here are unrelated quotes and rumours that span generations, the impression of which, taken together, present the oracles as frustrating, exasperating, often inexplicable and rarely or never easily intelligible. Just as they are in life. Excuse me.'

Bibwit abruptly reached under the sleeve of his scholar's robe and tapped the receiver node on his crystal communicator's keypad – before, to the walrus-butler's ear, the device even sounded. Projecting as if from the tutor's navel on to the air: an image of General Doppelgänger in the war room.

'Mr Harte,' the general whispered, 'I hope you aren't presently indisposed?'

'Since Arch has given me this assignment on the oracles, general, his spies have relaxed their guard somewhat – which is to say, a tad. I suspect Arch's belief in the inferiority of females is causing him to underestimate our Queen and any who'd plot on her behalf.'

Doppelgänger looked dubious and whispered, 'Spies haven't lessened their watch of *me*. But I've received a communication requesting our immediate attention.'

The general made some adjustments on the knobby slab of equipment before him and the vid nozzle of Bibwit's communicator shot forth a second projection: Alyss and Dodge in Outerwilderbeastia.

Alyss wasted no time with pleasantries. 'General, Bibwit, what I'm about to tell you is likely to be a shock, but in light of the extreme hardships we currently face, I believe we have more to gain from this new connection than to lose.'

'An assassin!' General Doppelgänger cried, splitting into the twin figures of Generals Doppel and Gänger as Mr Van de Skulle passed into view behind the Queen.

'Yes, General,' Alyss said without turning around, 'that's Mr Van de Skulle. He's here to help. Redd and I have agreed to work together against Arch.'

Flabbergasted, Generals Doppel and Gänger each split in two: a pair of Doppels and the like number of Gängers stared, loose-jawed, at Dodge. Bibwit, no less stunned, also stared open-mouthed at the guardsman.

'Why is everyone looking at me?' Dodge asked. 'I think cooperating with Redd is brilliant – hard to wrap the mind around at first, sure, but Arch won't expect it. And except for Alyss, I probably have the most reason to resent this affiliation, but I know my father wouldn't want me to sabotage our chances of winning back the Queendom by insisting on revenge against The Cat.'

He felt Alyss looking at him, turned and steadily returned her gaze.

'But certainly you don't –' the Doppels began to ask Alyss.

'– trust Redd?' the Gängers finished.

'I do not,' said the displaced Queen. 'Nor do I believe she trusts me, which is as it should be. The moment it is beneficial to her, she will betray me, and I'm prepared to betray her as soon as our strategy permits. But until then . . .'

'Allow me to query, my dear,' Bibwit's ears crimped and uncrimped worriedly, 'to what specific purpose is this alliance to be put? What do we gain that we don't already have on our own?'

'To my mind, Bibwit, it's less an alliance than an acknowledgment that, so far as imagination is concerned, what hurts me or Redd hurts us both equally, and remembering this we will consult each other when determining how to proceed against Arch.'

The four Generals shook their heads, rubbed sweaty palms down the front of their uniforms, then became two generals, then one – a singular Doppelgänger, apprehensive but resigned. 'If you think it best, my Queen,' he bowed.

Bibwit also bowed, albeit with wincing reluctance.

'General,' Alyss said, 'in the past you've mentioned a

certain scientist employed at the munitions factory in the flatlands outside Wondertropolis's Creedite Quadrant. I believe you've said he exhibits rare devotion to White Imagination?'

'Taegel,' said Doppelgänger. 'He was with the Alyssians during Redd's reign. It was he who devised the Wall of Deflection that hid our headquarters in The Everlasting Forest.'

'Do you think we might still consider him a friend, even if he hasn't suffered under Arch's rule?'

'As long as you live, my Queen, I'm convinced he would claim loyalty to you above all others.'

'Good. I want you to contact him and tell him to expect me and Dodge. Forwards his communication codes to us and we'll make arrangements with him once we're near the factory. Obviously, he can tell no one.'

Bibwit still wore his wincing, pained expression.

'We have to go where we can find food and shelter,' Alyss said as if answering his concerns. 'The munitions factory is close enough to Heart Palace to provide me with a better offensive position against Arch, and increased power from proximity to the Crystal, but it's not so close as to be suicidal.'

'And we'll benefit from whatever weapons Taegel can procure for the cause,' Dodge added.

'But my Queen,' said General Doppelgänger, 'to get to the factory, you'll have to pass close to The Creedite Quadrant, where there is a greater risk of your being discovered.'

'If anyone has a better suggestion, I'm prepared to hear it. But whatever I do will have its dangers.'

Bibwit finally spoke. 'Excuse me, my dear, but there is something else you should know. Arch has removed The Heart Crystal from its chamber and has not informed me of its location.'

'Nor me,' General Doppelgänger interrupted.

'Therefore,' said Bibwit, 'I assume he means to keep it hidden – whether because of extreme prudence or, what is perhaps more likely, because he suspects that you and I are in contact and I am thus untrustworthy.'

'How could he move it without anyone seeing?' Dodge asked.

'Your point,' Alyss said to Bibwit, 'is that if Arch has moved the Crystal out of Wondertropolis altogether, my journeying to the munitions factory is an unnecessary risk and the factory's location of doubtful benefit to our cause?'

Bibwit's ears flapped once, in concert with his shuttering

eyelids: this was indeed his point. 'You needn't attack Arch if you have the Crystal or know where it is,' he said. 'The Crystal is everything.'

'So Arch had a huge glowing gemstone of world-creating power moved without anyone seeing it?' Dodge asked. 'Didn't anyone *hear* it? Bibwit?'

Paying no attention to the tutor's answer, Alyss sought the Crystal with her imagination's eye, scanning the ballrooms of Heart Palace, its gardens and parks, Wondronia Grounds, the Aplu Theatre and every Wondertropolis landmark large enough to house the Crystal. She scanned what she knew of Boarderland. But wherever she focused her imaginative eye: no Heart Crystal.

At length, she said, 'I have to believe the munitions factory is our best option for now.' The projection of her and Dodge was already flickering to nothing when she signed off: 'General, Bibwit, if you soon hear reports of me leading an army against Arch's forces, I trust you'll know it's a decoy.'

The air of Heart Palace, from the war room to the library, transmitted perplexity, General Doppelgänger and Bibwit looking mutely at each other until the general murmured what neither of them was sure they'd heard:

'Decoys?'

♥ CHAPTER 34 ♦

I'm not abandoning you. The words rattled in Hatter's head as he walked briskly from Molly into the bustle of High Street. He hadn't wanted to leave Wonderland but now it required all of his mental strength to leave Oxford; he didn't trust himself to turn around for one more glance. Ready to give his life in service to his Queen though no less intent on returning to claim his daughter, he might not have been abandoning Molly, but it felt as if he were.

He turned off High Street, passed Radcliffe Square and rounded a corner on to Brasenose Lane, was in front of Lincoln College before he sighted one: a puddle where no puddle should be, in the middle of a sun-warmed pavement. He took his top hat from his head, flicked it into a stack of blades which he secured in an inner coat pocket and, without any change in stride, not caring if anyone noticed, he stepped into the puddle and –

Whoosh!

Sucked down and down and down, he struggled to keep his eyes open, to see what – if anything – there was to see, but the speed of his descent made everything a blur, the world outside his head a darkly shadowed blue murk. His pace slackened. He floated in the depths and then felt the upward tug, the reverse pull towards The Pool of Tears. He grabbed the ends of his Millinery coat and held them out wide, letting the garment act as a sort of inverted parachute, working against the water and slowing his ascent so that–

Perklop!

His head broke the water's surface long enough for him to take in breath. Dropping completely back underwater, he swam towards the crystal barrier and crawled over it on to dry land in less time than it required his wrist-blades to revolve. He didn't see any tribal guards, but that didn't mean they weren't somewhere, watching. ScorpSpitter-like, he moved to the lee side of the cliff overlooking the Pool and then along the rough, chalky rock until he reached foliage enough to provide cover.

He stopped to rest, to think.

He was without a crystal communicator, at least half a lunar hour away from the nearest hikers' cabin, from which he could send a transmission to Bibwit. He had to contact the tutor, but half a lunar hour's trek over land infiltrated by the enemy, where a confrontation with even the lowliest tribal warrior would alert Arch of his whereabouts and effectively end his chance of aiding Queen Alyss? It wasn't worth it. He might as well take the same risk and penetrate into Wondertropolis, cut and dice his way into Heart Palace where, if he was to lose his life, he would lose it while ensuring the end of King Arch.

He made it through The Everlasting Forest without being sighted and was about to step from the last cover its trees afforded. He had no way of knowing whether, under Arch's sovereignty, Milliners were branded as traitors or officially trusted and employed by the state, and the homes within view might have been commandeered to serve as monitoring stations by Arch's military. Which was why he kept his top hat in his coat pocket; on his head, it would make him conspicuous. But his coat too might make a target of him, so he slipped it off, balling it up to carry under an arm when –

He felt something. A watchful presence.

A patrol of two white pawns and five Catabrac warriors had fanned out along the street nearest the forest. They were combing the neighbourhood, passing up and back between the homes. One of the pawns, happening to glance at the forest, had spotted him and now they stared at each other, Hatter as still as any scuttling woodland creature in frozen alarm, his hand poised to snatch a blade from his backpack. If the pawn alerted his colleagues, Hatter would do what he had to do – grab and snatch at his backpack's array and put an end to the entire patrol. But the pawn didn't signal the others. He had recognised the famed Milliner. Discreetly, he removed a crystal shooter from its holster and unstrapped his communicator, dropped both behind a parked hovercycle and continued on his rounds. Hatter waited until he was sure the patrol had moved on, then sprinted to the hovercycle, took up the shooter and crystal communicator and, racing back to the forest, punched the code into the communicator's keypad that would put him in direct contact with Bibwit Harte.

♥ ♦ CHAPTER 35 ♣ ♦

It was Alyss's turn to wait, to be first to the Morgavian hilltop, standing solitary in a whipping wind. A mottled wet land stretched to the horizon, thawing in what passed for the hinterland's summer – the few weeks barely long enough for the spearheaded trees to shake off their winter coats.

The air bit into her skin, the ground crunched under her feet: the sensations as real as any she'd ever felt, yet . . .

I'm not here. I'm in Outerwilderbeastia, a dried scraggly patch of Outerwilderbeastia not a hectare's length from where the jungle gives way to the flatlands, the munitions factory.

Rhythmic stomping, tremors rippled the reflective pools of melting ice, and Alyss turned as –

A jabberwock reared up, almost trampling her. Redd was riding the beast bareback as she might a spirit-dane, pulling on reins of heavy chain-link.

'I trust you feel special,' Redd grimaced. 'I don't allow

myself to be summoned by just anyone.'

Flame jetted from the jabberwock's throat – close enough for Alyss to feel its heat.

'He likes you,' Her Imperial Viciousness said, yanking hard on the jabberwock's chain to keep the beast still. 'They're not the easiest things to tame, but that's why I like them.'

Say what I'm here to say. The sooner to be rid of this murderous company.

'Remember when you were Queen – ?' Alyss started.

'I never forget! How could I forget the only years I've exercised the authority that's rightfully mine?'

Alyss took a deep breath and tried again. 'Remember when you were Queen . . .'

She spoke of the time Her Imperial Viciousness had received reports of her rebel niece enjoying a gwynook kabob in Tyman Street, entering a tube station at Redd Square, roughing it on an Outerwilderbeastia safari. She asked her aunt to recall how The Glass Eyes and card soldiers despatched to these locations had found nothing, because the Alysses were decoys, constructs dispersed throughout the Queendom to confuse Redd's all-seeing imaginative eye.

'And this allowed me to reach The Chessboard

Desert and close in on The Heart Crystal unimpeded,'
Alyss said.

Her Imperial Viciousness's expression became more
and more steely as she listened to what she knew had
happened next: Alyss's feint of a full-on attack, she herself
in Mount Isolation, the sky brightening with day beyond
the Observation Dome's telescoping glass to reveal her
niece astride a spirit-dane at the head of a populous army;
she dealing the first hand of The Cut to engage in battle,
discovering in the initial explosions that Alyss's soldiers
were impervious to annihilation because the entire army was
a construct, a diversion that had allowed the real Alyss to
reach Mount Isolation undetected.

'You remind me of this oh-so-joyous time in my reign,
why?' Redd said in a clenched voice.

'I'm proposing we imagine decoys of ourselves and an
army to goad Arch into revealing his next move.'

'And what, my clumsily plotting niece, will that get us?'

Alyss had asked herself the same question many times,
beginning to feel that any attempt to provoke Arch
into exposing his scheme would be flawed. Only now
did she understand why. If Redd's hypothetical scenario
was correct – that Arch simply wanted to lull them into

believing their imaginations had returned for good, which in turn would cause them to reveal themselves in battle so that he could void their imaginations when they were most vulnerable – if this were true, then getting Arch to expose his scheme via decoys would render Alyss as powerless as if he'd *succeeded* with it. She would have accomplished nothing. She'd be stuck in hiding without imagination. Arch would still have the crown. Imaginationists would still be imprisoned.

'Too bad there's not someone close to Arch we could enlist in imagination's cause,' Alyss said.

Redd was intrigued, the vines of her dress squirming and squiggling with increased gusto. 'Yes. One of those bodyguards of his perhaps. They don't strike me as the selflessly loyal type.'

I'm not here. I'm in a self-induced trance, my actual body unmoving with my back against a stump in Outerwilderbeastia, Dodge watching over me and –

'I trust Mr Van de Skulle is behaving himself?' Redd asked as if the notion was distasteful.

'He does nothing offensive or inoffensive.'

Her Imperial Viciousness snorted. 'How boring. Though necessary, I'm sure. You haven't had occasion to use him, niece of mine. So far your trek to the weapons factory has been uneventful.'

Alyss showed no sign of surprise, expressed nothing at all.

'Where's the startled look?' Redd asked. 'None too long ago, it wouldn't have occurred to my ignorant niece that I might turn the eye of my imagination upon her to see what my new partner is up to.'

Nastiness is her civility. Arrange what I must. Get it done.

'You and your assassins,' Alyss said, her voice betraying no emotion, 'are in The Volcanic Plains, heading for The Whispering Woods so that I will be on one side of Heart Palace, you the other, and in a loose sense we'll have Arch surrounded.'

Redd's face cracked like a dried scab. 'Bravo! Oh, bravo, Alyss, for having turned your imaginative eye upon me as I turned mine upon you! But,' she lowered her voice, conspiratorial and sarcastic, 'doesn't it shock you to find we're thinking alike?'

I'm nothing like her. It's just ... with her I take precautions, knowing too well what she's capable of.

'What I think, niece of mine, is that the so-called adversities you've experienced have made you less stupidly trusting of others. I approve, but it's not very White Imagination of you.'

Ignoring this, Alyss said, 'So we're agreed? Instead of decoys, we'll try to turn one of Arch's guards to our cause?'

Redd sniffed in accord. 'And while I could stoop to tell you *my* methods for turning this disloyal guard, I'd much rather hear yours, seeing how like-minded we currently are.'

'We haunt him.'

Redd erupted with laughter that sounded like the pain-riddled screeches of a seeker. 'A haunting! I approve! Oh, niece of mine, we may have more in common than I ever supposed! But what else should I have expected? We *do* share some of the same blood!'

Her Imperial Viciousness's ear-stabbing cackle was taken up by the wind and she pulled at the jabberwock's reins she held in her swollen-knuckled fist. Screaming fire, the beast carried her galloping off, leaving Alyss alone on the hilltop once more, with Morgavia extending around her in all directions.

Does this land actually exist as it appears? Or is it a rendering of what Redd – and now me, borrowing from her – have imagined it to look like?

It was strange that she could summon Redd to a place she

might not physically be able to find. But it was strangeness short-lived: Alyss had summoned her aunt for the last time; they would never again meet in peace.

♦ CHAPTER 36 ♣

It was lovely when the family could be together, taking respite from their busy lives in one another's company – her father, Dean Liddell, surrendering himself to laughter as brother Harry, home for an unexpected visit, related a curious story involving a pheasant. It was hard for Alice to hear the story's details because across the table, Lorina – whom she thought too often moody – was teasing Edith about the attention the latter had lately been receiving from a young gentleman by the name of Harcourt.

'Oh, Edith, a daily visit from Mr Harcourt isn't much, not really, not when he could make three!'

Even her mother – whose ambitions for her children induced her to comment constantly upon the benefits of this or that connection – had been lulled into happy relaxation. For here was an opportunity to remind the table that Mr Harcourt was heir to Nuneham Park Estate, yet she surveyed all with contentment and said nothing! She merely bent her head towards Mr Skene, Lorina's husband.

'These strawberries,' he said.

'Not overripe, I hope?'

'Perfect, I'd judge.'

'Alice,' Mrs Liddell said, with a sudden turn of attention, 'why do you look so dreamy?'

'Do I? I'm sorry, mother. I don't mean to appear so. I assure you I'm very much present. I was just thinking that I used to consider these long family meals such a chore, but now . . . how I savour them!'

A man came suddenly through the wall next to the sideboard: Dodge Anders. 'What the – ?' he breathed.

Only Alice noticed him, Mr Skene and the rest of the Liddells enjoying their desserts as if he wasn't there. But before the guardsman could utter more, the dining room with its wainscoting and wallpaper, the sideboard and china cabinet and tea service, Edith, Lorina, Mr Skene, the dean and his wife – all began to dissolve. And Alyss Heart, the author of this elaborate construct, found herself no longer Alice Liddell. She was sitting on a tuft of dry grass in the flatlands instead of a handsome oak dining chair, her Oxfordian dress gone, replaced by the coarse maid's outfit and hooded cloak in which she'd been disguised for too long.

'What were you doing?' Dodge asked.

They had left Outerwilderbeastia behind and made camp for the night. Somewhere in front of them: the munitions factory and The Creedite Quadrant. To the east: The Whispering Woods and The Pool of Tears. Alyss was nearer the Pool than she'd been since her return from exile on Earth.

'I don't know . . . imagining,' she said.

The life that might have been mine for much longer than thirteen years. Not a carefree life by any means, but at least I didn't have the burden of securing an entire nation's welfare. Only my own happiness, and my family's, to consider.

Mr Van de Skulle was sitting at a respectful distance, greasing his whip with gryphon innards he kept in a pouch hanging from his belt. He must have seen the detailed construct she'd created, but he pretended as if he hadn't.

'Anything?' the assassin asked.

Dodge shook his head. He'd shown remarkable faith in the accord with Redd by leaving Alyss with Van de Skulle while he'd reconnoitred the vicinity. 'All clear,' he said.

There were probably a smail-load of questions he wanted to ask, Alyss thought. Why had she been imagining *that*? Why *now*? Questions she didn't know if she could answer. But he was trying hard to gloss over what he'd witnessed.

'Bibwit's patched through Hatter Madigan, who's asking what he can do to help us,' he said. He touched his communicator's keypad and a holographic image of the Milliner formed in the air.

'My Queen,' Hatter said, lowering his head. 'I apologise for the delay in being of service to you. For too long, I've not been doing as I should. I claim no excuse.'

'Save the love a father feels for his daughter, you mean. Bibwit informed me you were looking after Molly's safety.' It was momentary relief, to escape Dodge's accusing eye into the behaviour of a sovereign.

Hatter again lowered his head. 'And I trust I have secured it, my Queen.'

'As do I. How is she?'

The question gave Hatter pause. 'She didn't wish to stay where she is. But the feistiness with which she let me know leaves me confident she'll soon be capable of returning to her duties.'

251

All of us and our never-diminishing duties.

'I hope we'll be in a position to welcome her return to these duties,' Alyss said. 'Of course, Hatter, your service could never be more helpful than at present, but if you knew of a safehouse in Wonderland, we might have benefitted from knowing of it ourselves.'

'Understood, my Queen. But my daughter is not in Wonderland.'

'Not in Wonderland? Certainly she's not in *Boarderland*?'

'She's on Earth. With Dodgson.'

'Dodgson!'

It was so utterly unexpected, sent her mind reeling back to when she was a confused little girl hoping to find someone who believed the true story of how she'd wound up on Earth, unlooked-after and alone. A hope she'd all but given up when Reverend Dodgson urged her to confide in him. He didn't call her stories of man-cat murderers and living chessmen rubbish, as the Liddells and the children at Banbury Orphanage had. He seemed to understand and take her seriously, which in the end was what he most assiduously failed to do. He betrayed a trusting young girl for no increase in wealth or power, nothing but the pleasure of teasing her. The recollection of it pained her still.

And now Homburg Molly's been left with him?

She wanted to ask why the Milliner had thought of the Reverend, but Dodge was busy providing him details of her alliance with Redd, disclosing the reasons for their going to the munitions factory.

'I've already been in contact with Bibwit,' Hatter said. 'I know that he's to rendezvous with you and the scientist Taegel before the next rising of the moons. I'll meet you there. Unless the Queen has something else in mind for me?'

Alyss shook her head and the communication cut out before she could ask about Dodgson.

'Was it because of the prince, the man you almost married on Earth?' Dodge wanted to know, looking not at her but at the spot where Hatter's image had just been. 'Is that why you imagined yourself back?'

'What? No, how could you ask? Leopold wasn't even there. You saw.'

'Leopold,' Dodge said, and then, moving away from her: 'I'll dig a fire pit. It gets cold here at night.'

She was left to stare at Mr Van de Skulle. Finished greasing his whip, he was bending it this way and that to keep it supple.

'Been too long since I've gotten to use it on anything except jabberwocky,' he said to her, neither of them knowing that he wouldn't have to wait much longer.

♦ CHAPTER 37 ♣

Dodgson worried every time Molly left his rooms, not least because she refused to let him accompany her and the last thing he wanted was to answer to her father if she came to harm while in his care. Were he as strong in muscle as he was dexterous with pen, he would have physically tried to stop her going out, though he was unsure that a man even three times his size could succeed in preventing the girl from doing what she would. In Molly's most trivial actions, there was a suggestion of great power and ability. When she spooned sugar into a cup, he saw an unusual degree of athleticism, effortless hand–eye co-ordination. When she rearranged her legs as she sat on the floor reading, he saw an animalistic grace, a latent strength like that of a panther or lion at rest and in no way contingent on her ordinary size. So rather than force Molly to stay indoors, he tried to reason with her.

'By going out unchaperoned, you make yourself

conspicuous, and what if King Arch's soldiers have been sent to Earth and are searching for you?'

'It's bad enough I'm wearing the ugly clothes you found for me,' she answered, not looking up from her book. 'I don't need looking after.'

It was the most she'd said since they'd been together, having responded to his offers of food and tea with monosyllables, sometimes with no more than a nod or shake of the head.

'Anyway,' she finished, 'I'm as unchaperoned as any street urchin, the same as Queen Alyss once was.'

Difficult to say which made Dodgson more uncomfortable: the times she went out, leaving him alone with his anxiety, or the hours she spent on the rug, reading *Alice's Adventures in Wonderland*, which she'd pulled from its shelf above his desk.

'You were having a laugh at Queen Alyss and Wonderland,' Molly said, closing the book with a thump. It was the first time she'd commented on his writing.

'G-Good heavens, no! I believed I was happily elaborating on a young girl's f-fantasy world –'

'Whatever. I'm going out. Can I please have some money?'

This was the latest development: her requests for money

every time she left his rooms. 'How much do you need?' he asked.

'Enough for a cup.'

He didn't bother to point out that she hadn't finished the cup of tea he'd poured for her.

'Please at least remove your coat! What's the point of wearing the clothes I gave you if you insist on hiding them under *that*?'

She answered by holding out her hand for the money. He dutifully gave her a few pence and she left, stuffing *Alice's Adventures in Wonderland* into the pocket of her Millinery coat as she always did. And as he always did, he went to the window and watched her cross the quad towards the deanery.

The first time, it was a chance sighting – Miss Alice Liddell strolling in Magdalen's Deer Park with a woman Molly would soon know as Edith. She spied on them for a quarter hour and then – for no reason she could explain – followed them to the deanery's blue door. But the second time was no accident. Leaving Mr Dodgson's rooms, Molly waited outside the blue door, largely obscuring herself from its view behind a lamp post. She watched and waited, and again she could not explain what she was doing or why. She didn't even know if Miss Alice Liddell was at home. However, the lady at last emerged – again with Edith – and Molly followed them to the Water Walks, telling herself all the while that the person she saw was not Wonderland's Queen. Though why it mattered so much to her, she didn't know. Unless –

Unless she was punishing herself anew, letting this Alyss/not-Alyss serve as reminder of how much she had disappointed the Queen's hopes for her, and of how far she'd fallen from the standards she had set for herself. She didn't feel she deserved to be forgiven yet she wanted to ask forgiveness. And weirdest of all: she wanted to ask it of Alyss/not-Alyss.

Miss Liddell and her sister regularly visited a tea shop on St Aldate's. Wanting to observe her more closely, Molly had started to place herself in the shop so that she would be there before the ladies entered. Several tables usually separated them, but today Alice and Edith Liddell came in and sat at the table directly next to her.

'Excuse me,' Alice said to Molly after the waiter had taken her order. 'You were here yesterday, weren't you?'

The voice was *hers*, Alyss Heart's. Molly couldn't find words to answer and kept her eyes on the tea getting cold in her cup.

258

'I'm sorry,' Alice Liddell said, 'I don't mean to be intrusive. I simply wanted to tell you that I admire your coat. It's so . . . unique. I think I saw its kind in Amsterdam a few years ago. Wherever did you get it, if you don't mind my asking?'

The waiter returned with the sisters' tea. Alice Liddell's lightly pursed lips moved to the rim of the cup and Molly wanted to reach out and touch them, to confirm that they were genuine, *actual*.

'I don't mind your asking,' she finally managed.

'Oh, I'm so glad! But if you don't mind that, I don't suppose you'll object to our introducing ourselves. I'm Alice Liddell and this is my sister Edith.'

Both sisters held out their hands. Molly extended hers, felt cool flesh against the damp heat of her own. Alice Liddell was real. 'Molly.'

'Your accent isn't familiar to me,' Edith said. 'Are you visiting from somewhere?'

Awkward question, that. 'Uh huh. Far away.'

'Quite right!' Alice laughed, appreciative. 'Serves us right for asking so many questions in the first place. I hope you'll forgive us? Our unfortunate tendency to rudeness comes from living sheltered lives; we're so interested in others.

It does afford us vicarious adventures, but in addition – and I'm sure this sounds perfectly awful – it also gives us something to do.'

The Liddells had finished their tea and were preparing to leave.

'Well, Molly, we thank you for humouring our imposition, and apologise for now rushing off, but we've a family engagement. I hope we can see each other again soon.'

'Me too,' Molly said, sure that they would.

She took a tortuous way back to the quad. If she ran into Miss Liddell, she wanted it to seem a coincidence – the two of them living so close to each other. She found Dodgson in his rooms, bent over the desk. He'd been mumbling about feeling a return of his creative powers and was spending an increasing amount of time working in his notebooks. He turned to Molly when she entered but didn't ask where she'd been. He had learned by now: she would just rebuff him. But Molly was in the best mood she'd been in since before her mother died and, evincing an inclination not to be so incommunicative, she stepped up behind him and looked over his shoulder at his notebook:

5 sacks:

Nos. 1 & 2 weigh 12 lbs. Nos. 3 & 4 weigh 11½ lbs.

Nos. 2 & 3 weigh 13½ lbs. Nos. 4 & 5 weigh 8 lbs.

Nos. 1, 3 & 5 weight 16 lbs.

What is the weight of each sack?

'Five-and-a-half, six-and-a-half, seven, four-and-a-half, three-and-a-half,' she said.

It was, to Dodgson's astonishment, the correct answer.

♥ CHAPTER 38 ♦

Watching the Lord and Lady of Clubs partake of roasted gryphon wing in his dining room, Arch thought he should just call off his attempt to lure Redd and Alyss from hiding and do away with them for all time. Without further delay, he should bag The Heart Crystal, encase it in the cocoon of interwoven caterpillar silk he'd had made and thereby choke off its power – snuffing imagination forever. Why not let Redd and Alyss flounder in the underground like any pair of ineffective rebels? How could they ever be a threat to him without imagination?

'Honestly, Your Highness,' said the Lord of Clubs, 'I've never tasted anything like this before. Gryphon wing, roasted, you said it was?'

Arch nodded. 'A distinctive dish of Boarderland's Scabbler tribe. My chef was born a Scabbler, but obviously he became one of mine, a Doomsine.'

'Obviously,' agreed the Lady of Clubs.

Arch smiled at the space between his guests. It was never pleasant for him to share his table with a female, especially one harbouring pretensions to governing, but with an increase in land and subjects and power came certain compromises. At least until he wrung what use he could from the Clubs and was able to ignore them without harm to his interests.

'What I'm not sure I understand, Your Highness,' the lady said, continuing an earlier conversation, 'is why you don't just void The Heart Crystal now. My husband and I would very much applaud the action, as you know, and we've primed the citizens for it.'

'My good lady,' Arch replied, displeased that he and this creature had been thinking along similar lines, 'just a moment ago, I was asking myself the very same question. I believe I've told you that I need the Crystal to radiate for a short time yet, so as to do away with your two most recent Queens, Redd and Alyss Heart?'

'You have, sire,' said the lord. 'But you've not disclosed how leaving the Crystal functioning as it presently is will accomplish this.'

'Nor will I. But it isn't just Redd and Alyss I'm thinking

of. I need the Crystal to do away with their followers as well.'

'Ah,' the lord said, not understanding.

'I see,' said the lady, not seeing in the least.

Arch, a master of subterfuge coping with slow students, directed a humourous glance at Ripkins and Blister, who were standing against the wall. 'So long as Alyss and Redd live, or are believed to live, their followers will desire a regime change and be on the watch for opportunities to bring it about. They will remain loyal to Redd and Alyss whereas I want them loyal to yours truly. If I merely inform them that The Heart Crystal and imagination are no more and Redd and Alyss dead, they can too easily cling to hope that one of these former Queens might nonetheless lead a revolt. But let The Heart Crystal and imagination be *publicly* snuffed out, let Redd's and Alyss's deaths take place in full view of the citizenry, and what loyalists they boast will have a harder time of it. For these loyalists will then be witnesses to the truth: imagination, Black or White, can have no part in a regime change because not only has The Heart Crystal been eliminated, but so have the two Wonderlanders most gifted with its powers.'

'But Your Highness,' said the lord, 'I submit that a segment of the population may still remain unconvinced and choose to live in delusion.'

'Perhaps,' said Arch, 'but it will be a modest group, much more easily controllable than otherwise.'

'My Liege.' An intel minister had come into the room and was standing at the King's elbow. 'I beg pardon for the interruption, but you have a visitor. I believe he wishes to speak to you about a matter of considerable urgency.'

'I'm at a loss to know whose importance can justify excusing me from dinner with the eminent Lord and Lady of Clubs,' Arch said.

The minister bowed in understanding, then pressed his arms to his sides, thrust his head out on his neck and shuffled forwards in quick little steps. Receiving no royal reaction, he did it a second time – thrust out his head and shuffled forwards.

'What. Are. You. Doing?' the King asked.

The minister formed an 'O' with his mouth, motioned as if he were holding a hose to his lips and inhaled. He crossed his eyes and removed the invisible hose from his mouth and exhaled.

'I'm losing patience,' Arch said.

Ripkins and Blister stepped forwards. The minister gave up his charade and glanced at the Clubs, unsure.

'The green caterpillar,' he said quick and low.

Arch rose from his chair. 'Why didn't you say so, fool?'

'I didn't know if you wanted . . .' the minister tilted his head towards the ranking couple.

'I have no secrets from the House of Clubs.' Arch was already leaving the room with Ripkins and Blister in tow. 'Please excuse me, Milord and Milady. These large worms are a nuisance, but so early in my reign I think it prudent to humour them.'

The balcony doors of Arch's bedroom were open, the green caterpillar on the threshold, shoving the last of a tarty tart into his mouth while he admired the view of Wondertropolis's skyline, its sleek towers, moon-reflecting minarets and residential buildings with marbled quartz façades. Arch instructed Ripkins and Blister to wait in the hall, passed into his private rooms and –

'If the King believes he can woo Wonderland's oracles with treats,' Green said, not turning round, 'he is correct!' The oracle plucked three tarty tarts from the creases of his segmented belly and tossed them into his mouth.

'I'm glad to see you enjoy the tributes I sent,' Arch said, 'but –'

'No, I haven't,' Green snuffled.

The corner of Arch's mouth slanted up; he'd been about to say that he assumed the oracle hadn't come to thank him for the tarty tarts.

'You are having trouble luring Alyss and Redd Heart into the open,' Green observed.

'It's taking longer than I'd like, but I wouldn't call it troublesome.'

'And yet you're thinking of employing a different tactic.'

Arch stepped on to the balcony, where the city lights winked at him in the night air. He frequently came out here to ponder this new city of his. Depending on his mood, he sometimes thought the lights were winking *with* him, conspiratorial, as he secured his reign of Wonderland. But other times – now, for instance – the lights seemed to wink in mockery of his efforts, his vanity.

'Redd Heart will compromise herself from lack of self-discipline,' Green said. 'But Alyss Heart, she will need . . . assistance. It is known that Alyss Heart allows her softer emotions to get the better of her.'

'A fact I might put to good use, eh?'

'A fact you may put to good use.'

Green was puffing on a hookah he'd produced from nowhere Arch had seen. A fog of smoke gathered over the balcony, in which images of a couple and two young ladies flickered, all of whom were wearing old-fashioned clothes – coats and dresses and collared shirts so long out of date that Arch was only familiar with them because of the study materials recently provided to him by Bibwit, the chronicles of distant Wonderland history he'd read to educate himself about the Queendom's oracles.

'Those,' the caterpillar said, 'are the Liddells, with whom Alyss Heart lived for many years.'

'On Earth,' the King murmured.

The caterpillar nodded. 'Oxford, England, to be precise. Alyss Heart has strong feelings for the Liddells, the only family she has remaining anywhere.'

'And if something were to threaten them . . .' Arch said.

The caterpillar's face wrinkled with pleasure; Arch's brain worked with admirable speed. 'The King may not know where Alyss Heart *is*,' Green said, 'but were someone to threaten the Liddells, he can know where she *will be*.'

'You are trying to use me, caterpillar.'

'We use each other,' Green corrected.

Arch listened to the sound of the oracle's lips working at his pipe, the burbling water. 'And if someone endangered this Liddell family,' he asked, 'how would Alyss Heart know of it?'

'Oh, I wouldn't worry about that!'

Arch grabbed the caterpillar, a muscled hand tight around one of the legs closest to the oracle's mouth. 'Tell me where she is. Where they both are. Redd and Alyss. You *know*.'

Green giggled and slipped easily free of the King's grasp, went on giggling as he floated from the balcony and out over palace grounds. Arch stared after the worm a moment, then turned and went back inside to rejoin the Clubs in the dining room, where he sat distractedly slugging down his wine while Ripkins and Blister took up their positions against the wall.

'We hope the "oracle" didn't upset His Highness with any ridiculous prattle,' the lady said, noticing Arch's changed mood.

'I don't know how those things ever convinced Wonderlanders they were oracles to begin with,' huffed the lord.

To these, Arch said nothing. Whenever vital information was too easily granted him, he presumed he was being set up. Were he and the green oracle using each other? He was using the caterpillar, of course. But was the caterpillar truly using him? He might believe it if he knew what the worm gained by helping him to snuff the Crystal and rid the living world of Redd and Alyss Heart. All he knew was what he'd been told: the oracle was a bored prisoner of the Crystal and ached for freedom. But the more Arch considered this, the less he believed it. Why couldn't the caterpillar plot on his own to extinguish the Crystal? Why did he need anyone's help? More specifically, why did the worm require *his* help?

There was too much the oracle wasn't telling him. He determined to do nothing with the intel regarding Alyss Heart and her attachment to the Liddells. He would make use of it only if he had to, if he had no choice.

The Lord of Clubs cleared his throat. Arch was sick of looking at the Lord and Lady of Clubs.

'I trust you both enjoyed dinner,' he said, sliding a nub of agate into a slot in the console to the right of his chair, an action that brought the walrus-butler into the room. 'The walrus will show you out.'

Taken aback by their sudden dismissal, the ranking couple hardly had time to thank His Majesty as they were led out to the hall. Arch fitted an amoeba-shaped nodule into a slot on the console and his intel ministers swished into the room.

'Report,' he said.

'The Heart Crystal is no longer in transit, Your Highness,' one of the ministers answered. 'It has arrived safely and without complications.'

'No complications? You're sure?'

The head of every minister bobbed, affirmative.

Ripkins and Blister advanced to the table to forage among the leftovers, which caused the ministers some alarm since they generally tried to keep as much distance from the pair as possible. Striving for greater separation between himself and Blister, one of the ministers inadvertently knocked a goblet from the table. The bodyguard – a shred of meat poised in gloved hand before his mouth – eyed the clumsy minister with contempt while the fearful fellow and the rest of his kind stood hushed, expecting an outburst from the King. But the King remained silent, thoughtfully watching the mechanized vac that zoomed into the room and sucked the puddle of wine from the floor.

Perhaps he'd been too quick to dismiss the caterpillar's intel? Arch mused, his eyes on the vac as it zipped off to wherever it'd come from. Perhaps – and here he coded his thinking, letting random words and figures come to mind so that his thoughts would be incoherent to any caterpillars accessing them – there was a way to use what he knew of

Alyss's affection for the Liddells, to benefit from it without reducing himself to a larva's plaything. Yes, he might do something no one, not even the so-called oracles of Wonderland, would expect.

CHAPTER 39

'It takes a certain strength of mind to be bad.'

'Yes, Your Imperial Viciousness.'

'A vigorous mind, to always live according to the motto, Why put off till tomorrow the death I can bring about today?'

'And no one has lived it more forcefully than you have, Your Imperial Viciousness.'

Redd squinted round at The Whispering Woods, its trees annoying her no end by their silence. All arbourage whispering had ceased the moment she galloped into the woods on her jabberwock whose sulphurous breath torched a number of the more mature shade trees. Vollrath, The Cat, Sacrenoir, Alistaire Poole and Siren Hecht, each atop a jabberwock, had pulled up rein behind her. The quiet of the woods, while better than any nervous whispers of her presence, would nonetheless alert Arch of her whereabouts. If she stayed long enough.

'I'm no less vigorous or strong because I joined with Alyss,' Redd snarled.

Vollrath was having considerable trouble controlling his jabberwock. 'On the contrary, Your Imperial Viciousness,' he said, 'it shows how very strong-minded you are, being nasty and evil while thus aligned with one of such a pronounced beneficent persuasion.'

'Are we making camp?' Alistaire Poole asked.

'Don't be an idiot,' Redd scorned.

But in this instance, it could be argued, Alistaire Poole had every right to be an idiot. Because Redd had been extremely careful. Never knowing when Alyss might spy on her with imagination's eye, but assuming that her niece *would* spy, Her Imperial Viciousness had lied to Vollrath and her assassins, telling them their destination was The Whispering Woods when it was not. She withheld the truth because it *was* the truth and truth bored her, and because their actions were visible to Alyss at any time, she didn't want them to reveal her real destination by some bit of careless behaviour.

Since first sighting Arch's ninny ministers playing the busybodies around a specific hedge in the grounds of Heart Palace, she had kept her imagination's gaze steadily on the spot. And was rewarded. In the hours before dawn, vacant hours when even late-night revellers had succumbed to sleep, she had watched from The Volcanic Plains as Doomsines carted the heavily shrouded Heart Crystal from the palace. Adroit at such things from their nomadic ways, the tribesmen quickly worked their way out of Wondertropolis; before it was light, they were travelling with the Crystal out to the land beyond The Whispering Woods.

Redd's plan had always been to pass completely through the woods into the land beyond, where she now knew Arch was hiding The Heart Crystal in a prehistoric edifice that, at one time, may or may not have been the site of bloody sacrifices to unknown gods: The Iron Butterfly.

♦ CHAPTER 40 ♣

The munitions factory was secured by two networks of lightning-hot soundwaves, the networks separated by a track ten-metres wide and patrolled by pawns and Three Cards themselves closely monitored by Doomsine warriors. More easily accessible was the town that had formed to cater to factory employees and their families. Taegel, the Alyssian weapons genius, suggested the Queen – for so he continued to think of Alyss Heart – meet him at a certain café where the steady ebb and flow of diners would help ensure anonymity for Her Majesty.

Taegel arrived early, commandeering a table away from the windows, but much surprised when a Wonderlander with the skin of a newborn and a head of thick, curly brown hair joined him. Clearly, this was not Queen Alyss.

'Does Taegel not recognise an old friend?' the stranger asked.

The lips nearly as white as the surrounding skin, the mischievous play of the eyes.

'Bibwit!' Taegel said.

'As pale as ever though a little more hirsute,' the tutor acknowledged, pulling at his curls to show they were not part of a wig. 'Courtesy of Queen Alyss's imagination. Rather interesting – to have a bushel on one's head.' He glanced at the engineer's long grey hairs rising every which way in tremulous wisps, making it appear as if steam was emanating from the fellow's venerable skull. 'Don't take offence, dear Taegel, but I greatly hope – which is to say, it is my ardent wish – that my defection from Arch's authority won't require me to keep this hair for the remainder of my days.'

The engineer couldn't help laughing and even Bibwit allowed himself a brief chuckle. Which was how Alyss, Dodge and Mr Van de Skulle found them, basking in a lighthearted moment's afterglow. Seeing the Queen, Taegel started from his chair, intending to genuflect before her, but Dodge pressed a firm hand on his shoulder to keep him in his seat.

'Right,' Taegel said. 'Sorry.'

Alyss, Dodge and Mr Van de Skulle settled in around the table.

'Bibwit and General Doppelgänger have explained to me your reasons for being here,' Taegel told Alyss. 'I am humbled by their recommendations of me and honoured to do everything I can to help you.'

'You assume great risk by having us here, Mr Taegel,' Alyss answered. 'It's a reminder of what constitutes model service to White Imagination and it is *your* steadfastness in this service that humbles *me*.'

Taegel, embarrassed by the Queen's praise, busied himself with a satchel at his feet, pulled three smaller satchels from it and passed one each to Alyss, Dodge and Mr Van de Skulle. 'I didn't expect you,' he apologised to Bibwit, 'and still have to provide for you and the Milliner.' He explained that the satchels contained ID badges as well as subcutaneous ID chips, eyeglasses that presented to munitions factory security scanners a complete genetic makeup and 3-D image of eyeballs belonging to those with the highest clearance, and second-skin gloves with vetted fingerprints – all of which were needed to get the Queen into his lab at the munitions factory. 'I can take you tonight, if you wish,' he concluded.

Dodge and Bibwit were smiling at each other.

'Or tomorrow, if you prefer?'

This amused the tutor and guardsman even more.

'Or . . . the day following?' tried Taegel.

Still, Dodge and Bibwit grinned.

'What?' the weapons engineer asked. 'What is it?'

'Alyss's imaginative powers pretty much nullify the factory's security measures,' Dodge said.

'But we thank you for your trouble,' Alyss added.

'Speaking of trouble,' Bibwit patted the curls covering his head, 'it is probably best, my dear, not to tax your imagination with the inessential. Now that I'm free of Arch, I'll not trouble you any longer with my disguise – which is to say, I invite you to rid me of this most inessential hair as soon as we're somewhere more private.'

'You don't think Arch will have warriors searching for you?' Dodge asked. 'Because it wouldn't surprise me if he rounds up every member of the tutor species he can find.'

Alyss considered a Gwormmy-blink. 'I'd rather keep my tutor's hair than lose my tutor altogether,' she said, to the albino's obvious disappointment. 'Oh, you don't look *that* funny, Bibwit. Let's leave it be for now.' She stood. 'Is your home far from here, Mr Taegel?'

'Not very, Your Majesty. My transport is just outside.'

A factory-issue transport: missile-shaped, light as foil, all sleek, reflective surfaces. Seated in the vehicle's long, slender body, they shuttled along to their destination while Taegel – nervous, excited: the Queen would be in his flat! – chattered away as Bibwit often did, to no one and everyone.

'It was tough at work,' he said, unbidden, 'tough all around at the factory when imagination was blinkered, but I'd say things are back to normal. *I* think they are anyway. At least as far as my own work is concerned.'

Which was true enough since factory colleagues were once more finding the engineer busy at his lab in a nest of wire, relay switches, trigger mechanisms, nano-scanners, compression chambers, ammo cartridges, loading cylinders, docking bays from dismantled crystal shooters and AD52s – anything used in the manufacture of weaponry within arm's reach. Unfortunately for Alyss and her companions, Taegel's flat was just as messy as his lab. If, as Dodge did, you tried to sit in the lounge-pod, you felt the prick of springs and coils in your backside. If, as Bibwit did, you cautiously lowered yourself on to the arm of a floating chair, you wound up squashing the empty razor-card cartridges that had blended in with the chair's fabric. Better to remain standing, as Alyss and Mr Van de Skulle did – and not risk injury.

'Sorry,' Taegel muttered, scooping up armloads of weapons' parts and labouring into his bedroom. 'My apologies, sorry.'

'Hatter should be with us shortly,' Dodge noted.

'And General Doppelgänger told me he would establish contact as soon as . . . ah, there he is.' At the sound of his crystal communicator, Bibwit called up a projection of Wonderland's long-time commander of card soldiers and chessmen.

'Queen Alyss,' Doppelgänger said, seeing his sovereign, 'I'd like nothing more than to be there with you, but I hope to be of some value as your "man on the inside", as it were.' Then, splitting into two identical figures: 'We're your *men* on the inside!' Generals Doppel and Gänger said as one.

'And I, Generals,' Alyss responded, 'would prefer to have you near but believe you made the right decision. It's better for the stability of Wonderland's decks that you remain where you are.'

'Although we should hope,' said Bibwit, 'that my having left Arch doesn't endanger the General – pardon, the *generals* – further.'

Mr Van de Skulle stood quiet with his hand on his whip, and Taegel kept coming and going in his effort to clear the common room of lab debris, as Alyss informed Bibwit and the generals of her most recent 'meeting' with Redd Heart, of their decision to try and turn one of Arch's personal guards via remote constructs, and of Her Imperial Viciousness's being in The Whispering Woods to help surround Heart Palace.

'We, for two, are glad to hear of the attempt on the guard,' Generals Doppel and Gänger said in unison.

'Had you provoked Arch into battle with conjurings,' started General Doppel, 'as it seemed you were thinking of doing –'

'– we wouldn't have relished unshuffling the decks, even against an imaginative construct of our Queen!' finished Gänger.

Dodge was watching Taegel pick up what looked like junk – all of it, he knew, the scattered scraps of warfare technology that could help him protect Alyss, depose Arch, ruin Redd, and wreak vengeance upon The Cat.

'I'd definitely like to get hold of whatever new weapons are available at the factory,' he said, 'but we probably shouldn't chance a run on the place until we know how we're going to proceed.'

Bibwit's ears flapped. 'Now that you're here, Alyss,' he asked, 'do you feel Power of Proximity to the Crystal?'

Alyss shook her head.

'Perhaps if a guard's turned, he will disclose to us The Heart Crystal's location? But regardless . . .'

The tutor sniffed, his nostrils taking in a whiff of something curious, and in a moment they were all sniffing, breathing in the fragrance of leaves and soil after a downpour. Bibwit was the first to look up and see him: the blue caterpillar, hanging upside down from the ceiling, calmly puffing at his hookah as he would were he rightside up.

'About time,' Alyss murmured.

Indeed it was, particularly if one assumed that this long-overdue visitation from an oracle was a favourable sign. Generals Doppel and Gänger, to judge by their flurry of polite coughs and hair rakings, were unsure. And Bibwit felt too well the uncertainty of Alyss's role in maintaining the Crystal's future welfare. The caterpillars had kept aloof too long for him to optimistically interpret Blue's sudden visit. Like Dodge, he needed more, if he was going to be optimistic.

'Oh, wise, blue oracle,' the tutor began, 'your coming might be belated but is nonetheless –'

'Ahem hem hum,' Blue grumbled, and exhaled a miasma of hookah smoke, in the middle of which Alyss recognised the deanery's drawing room in Oxford. The dean and Mrs Liddell, Edith and Lorina were being roughly handled by –

Ripkins!

The guard shoved the family members down on to a sofa, where they huddled together, frightened. The serrated blades of Ripkins's fingerprints glinted, but as he moved towards the family, the scene and the hookah smoke dissipated.

Desperate eyes raised to the caterpillar, Alyss asked, 'Is this the past or the future you've shown me?'

'It is the present,' said the caterpillar.

Dodge stepped up close beside her. 'Alyss, it's a trap.'

'Yes, yes, a trap!' agreed Doppel and Gänger.

'To try and save them would be to reveal yourself to Arch,' Dodge warned. 'You'd be risking your life and imagination and everything we fight to achieve for Wonderland. There's nothing you can do for them.' He gestured to where the images of the Liddells had just been. 'Unfortunately.'

But it's the present I saw?! And there's nothing I can …?

She was, she realised with a jolt, wary of Dodge, the man she had believed would never give her the least cause to distrust. He'd reacted so jealously after he'd found her acting the part of Alice Liddell. Might he not say anything to keep from feeling that way again? Her doubt must have shown in her face because –

'As you know too well,' Dodge said, 'we've all sacrificed loved ones for the greater good. I say this for no reason except to see you back on Wonderland's throne and White Imagination again prominent in the Queendom: there's nothing you can do to save that family.'

'"That family"?' Alyss huffed. 'Their name is Liddell!'

'Ahem hum,' the oracle grumbled. 'What one sets as a trap, others know to be a release.'

'What's he talking about?' Dodge said, impatient, turning on Bibwit.

'Alyss Heart *must* go,' the oracle pronounced. 'Everqueen requires it.'

Everqueen?

The term, unknown to the Alyssians, left them temporarily silent. Mr Van de Skulle occupied himself with the braid of his whip. Taegel stood with a tumbleweed of wire in his arms, his eagle-eyes alternately alighting on Alyss, her advisors and the oracle.

'Who or what is the Everqueen, wise one?' Bibwit asked. 'Is Alyss the Everqueen?'

'She must go,' the oracle said again.

Has he ever been so forthright? Perhaps in one of his previous visitations, before she had passed through her Looking Glass Maze or –

'Please, Alyss,' Dodge said, his voice calm, petting. 'Why

should you listen to this oracle? Where has he been hiding? Why didn't he come to you before Arch took Wonderland or the Clubs were giving us so much trouble?'

'Yes,' said General Doppel, 'why does he come now?'

'He might not be on our side any more!' cried General Gänger.

But he visited Molly. He's on our side. I feel it.

The Queen's advisors burst out all at once, Dodge and the generals repeating why she shouldn't risk a journey to save the Liddells, Bibwit ruminating aloud whether she should risk the journey or not, the answer to which, he reasoned, depended on if the 'release' mentioned by the oracle was beneficial to both the Alyssians and The Heart Crystal, or to just the Crystal alone, though admittedly he couldn't see any benefit in it to either, not at the present moment at any rate, but –

Blue exhaled another mass of hookah smoke into the room, which sifted into four clouds – one each enveloping Dodge, Bibwit, Taegel and Mr Van de Skulle. In no more time than it took to breathe, the foursome were unconscious on the floor, and Generals Doppel and Gänger, their likenesses still projecting from Bibwit's crystal communicator, were left straining for sight of their Queen from beneath a footstool.

286

'Go,' Blue said to Alyss.

And she did.

After Green's visit, Arch acted quickly: consulted with his mechanics to make sure the siphons and tankers could do what he needed them to do; briefed the Doomsines and Fel Creel who would be operating the equipment on where they should wait for his command, which he said would be self-explanatory when he gave it. He sent a minister through The Pool of Tears dressed in a form-fitting undersuit whose sensor-fibres would monitor his vital signs, needing to make sure the data could be transmitted between worlds – heart rate, blood pressure and adrenaline levels relayed from Earth to the master board set up in the war room of the Wondertropolis palace. He told those involved no more than they needed to know to perform their given tasks, and he did all of this while running interference so as to obscure his scheme from the oracles, simultaneously despatching ministers to consult with tribal leaders and briefing Awr and Scabbler warriors on plans he might or might not execute; he didn't allow himself to decide even in the 'privacy' of his thoughts, lest he clued Green and the rest of the oracles in to what he was truly up to and they made moves to stop him.

'Once your undersuit transmits to me an increase in your heart rate and adrenaline indicative of a man in battle,' he told Ripkins, who had just been outfitted and was moving first one limb and then another while technicians confirmed that the suit functioned as it should, 'I'll know you've engaged with Alyss and may or may not then give my next command.'

There was a liquid *puuh* behind him, where Blister, moping ever since Ripkins had been chosen to go to Earth, was taking his feelings out on a potted sunflower left over from Alyss Heart's days. *Puuh*: the sound of blistered petals bursting, drowning in pus.

'I sent a minister through the Pool to be certain the suit works between worlds,' Arch told Ripkins. 'We received readings without a glitch, so I don't want to hear any lies about why yours didn't. There are no excuses for failing to engage Alyss.'

'I don't make excuses,' Ripkins said. 'I never fail.'

'You've been prepped as to where the Liddells are located and what they look like?'

'I have.'

Psssuuubsssshhhh!

Blister was pressing a naked finger against the skin of the sunflower's stalk, which had swelled up and down its entire length and popped, dribbling viscous green stuff and releasing trapped air like a body's expiring breath. Still flexing his arms and legs, Ripkins faced him. From the pair's deadpan expressions, one never would have known they had fought side by side in many successful battles. Then Ripkins bowed quickly to the King and left, and –

Though the sunflower was dead, Blister yanked it out of its soil and squeezed its drooping stalk in his fist as if to kill it all over again.

♦ CHAPTER 41 ♣

As she'd done years before – at age seven, leaping for her life under Hatter Madigan's protection, escaping the death of family and friends and the the only Queendom she'd ever known – Alyss fell towards The Pool of Tears, her feet pointed down and her arms held close to her body.

Kerplassshhhh!

She plunged through the water, down and down and down, then up and up and –

Prrrssshhhaw!

She shot out of a portal puddle on to the solid ground of Earth. But where? Because she was definitely not in Oxford, England. Snow-capped mountains. A village, its buildings with their white stucco and dark, rough-hewn timber: it was exactly like something she'd seen in the geography books given her by Miss Prickett, her governess when she'd lived with the Liddells.

'Switzerland!' she said, spinning round and throwing herself into the puddle portal, again plummeting to the depths but this time aiming her body slantwise so as not to drop straight down. Even after she reversed directions, torpedoing up, she held her body at a tilt until –

Prrrssshhhaw!

She splashed out into a large open square. People were muffled and bundled against the cold. At one end of the square: a many-coloured structure that resembled something made of gingerbread, its columns topped with striped dollops of cake icing. Next to this was a fortress: massive rectangular buildings surrounded by a stone wall complete with turrets and clock tower.

'The Kremlin!'

She dived back into the puddle portal, slanting her body to the left instead of the right as she had the last time and –

Prrrssshhhaw!

She was in a town, somewhere in France or Germany perhaps. She didn't stay long enough find out, dropped a fourth time into the puddle portal, aiming her body farther left as she went down and up and –

Prrrssshhhaw!

'The Houses of Parliament!'

She was in London. *Getting closer. One more time.* She again saw the inside of the puddle portal, again steered her body leftward and – *It worked!* – she came out practically at the foot of Oxford's Carfax Tower. Hoping to make up for the time she'd lost, she sprinted towards Christ Church, her feet barely touching the ground, as if her shoes had wings. Which, briefly, they did.

Finally!

The Deanery. She raced up the front walk, using her imagination to unlock the door and turn the latch. Inside the house, nothing had changed. The umbrella stand and hat rack, the family pictures hanging in the hall, even the gouge in the skirting board marking where she'd thrown her ice skates one winter afternoon: everything was exactly as it had been when she'd lived there.

'Please, what do you want?' the dean's voice reached her from the back of the house.

She sighted them in her imagination's eye: the dean and Mrs Liddell, Edith and Lorina. It was just as Blue had shown her. Their clothes a good deal ripped, the family huddled together on the drawing room sofa in fearful silence while Ripkins stood ominously before them, flexing his fingertips – deadly sawteeth pushing

292

up out of the skin in the pattern of his fingerprints.

'Please,' the dean said again.

Fingerprint blades flexed, Ripkins moved his hands fast in front of him, shredding air. Mrs Liddell flinched. The assassin took a step towards the dean, the sisters each let out a sob and –

'Hello?' Alyss called, walking directly into the room. She had imagined herself into Alice Liddell's long skirt and blouse, her hair in a tight bun. 'Excuse me, I didn't know there was company.'

She tried to look startled – eyes wide, mouth half open, head tilted apologetically – as she thought her double would. Wanting to catch Ripkins off guard, she pretended to be meek, cowed, and let him grab her and push her towards the Liddells.

Where he'd touched her, there was blood.

Ripkins's hands became a blur in front of him, churning air and moving in towards the dean's chest. Alyss had no choice but to expose her imaginative powers in front of the Liddells. With the slightest of movements, she conjured a deck of razor-cards and sent them cutting through the air.

Fiss! Fiss, fiss, fiss!

In a single swift motion, Ripkins spun clear and

unholstered a crystal shooter, firing a retaliatory cannonade. Alyss gestured as if wiping condensation off a looking glass and the shrapnel-like bullets of wulfenite and barite crystal clattered to the floor.

The Liddells sat dumbfounded, their fear muted in the shock of seeing their adopted daughter engage in combat, producing otherworldly missiles out of the air – flat blade-edged rectangles resembling playing cards, bursts of gleaming bullets. She conjured them as fast as she defended herself against them, what with the intruder making expert use of the strange guns and knives strapped to his belt, thighs, biceps and forearms.

'Father!'

A fistful of mind-riders rocketed towards the family.

Alyss threw out her hand and the weapons changed trajectory, shooting towards her. She annihilated them in midair with a pinch of her fingers, becoming like gravity itself, pulling whatever Ripkins hurled at the Liddells towards her until –

The wall pushed out a score of daggers. Ripkins, knocked backwards by a steel playing card as big as a man, slammed against them and slumped to the floor.

Silence, except for the ticking of a grandfather clock.

Alyss stood catching her breath, sensitive to the Liddells' awe and confusion but feeling relief above all: she had not been too slow to save the family, not this time.

♦ CHAPTER 42 ♣

At first he didn't see the tutor. On a table just inside the library was the reading matter the albino had gathered for the King's continuing study of the caterpillar-oracles, but not until Arch progressed deeper into the library did he sight Bibwit pacing as silently as a ghost before a collection of encyclopedia crystals.

'I have questions, Mr Harte.'

The King wanted a firmer understanding of the caterpillars' abilities. What did it mean that they 'saw' the future? How did the oracles define 'future'? Because he himself didn't believe the course of his life was already set out before him, as unyielding as The Glyph Cliffs. He refused to believe he had no power to direct the course of his own life. His future was open, changeable, and therefore unknowable. How then could the caterpillar-oracles foresee it? He would learn what he could from Bibwit Harte while being careful not to disclose his intentions regarding Alyss Heart.

But the King's questions apparently didn't interest the tutor. Because Bibwit went on perusing the encylopedia crystals, too enamoured with his thoughts to so much as acknowledge His Majesty.

'I said I have questions, tutor!'

Arch stepped closer, stopped. Bibwit Harte was translucent, an obvious construct of someone's imagination. The King did not doubt whose imagination it was.

'Gone to join your Queen, have you?' he frowned.

He had been right all along: Bibwit, loyal to Alyss Heart, had maintained contact with her. It would be the same with General Doppelgänger.

Beep, beep beep.

His crystal communicator alerted him of an incoming transmission and he reached to answer it just as –

The Bibwit construct blinked off once, twice, then was gone for good. As if Alyss had stopped focusing on it. Or had left Wonderland.

Beep, beep beep.

Arch punched his communicator's keypad, knowing it would be his lookout by the Pool contacting him to say that Alyss Heart had plunged into The Pool of Tears.

*

General Doppelgänger awoke in the war room, uncertain as to how he'd arrived there. Last he remembered, he was two – Doppel and Gänger, and they were abruptly ending communication with an unconscious Bibwit as four Doomsines stormed into his office to inform him that the King requested his presence.

He tried to stand. Immediately his vision warped as if he were looking out from behind a screen of falling water. His limbs were not his own. He dropped to the floor. Someone must have propped him back up, because after what could have been either a few Gwormmy-blinks or an entire lunar cycle for all he could tell, he was back in his chair.

'Drugs,' Arch said, standing before him.

On the other side of the conference table, Blister and an intel minister were at a mobile apparatus the general couldn't identify, its desk-like surface dotted with luminescent squares. Another minister stood before the room's crystal control panel.

'You're presently sporting high Boarderland fashion, general,' Arch said, 'a drug-delivery system that secretes through your skin a little knock-you-down concoction whenever you make a sudden, or too ambitious, move.'

General Doppelgänger carefully shifted his eyes downward to see what the King was talking about. Instead of his uniform, he was wearing a one-piece jumper made of an unfamiliar material that had no visible buttons or clasps by which to remove it. The collar fitted tight about his neck, the leggings tight around his ankles, and the cuffs of the long-sleeves pinched at his wrists.

'You're lucky,' Arch said. 'If I was convinced that killing you wouldn't compromise my control of the card soldiers and chessmen, you'd already be dead.'

'I don't feel lucky,' the general managed.

'The lucky rarely do. Now please direct your attention to the holo-screens. I've scheduled a bit of entertainment for us.'

Arch gave the nod, the minister at the control panel dialled in what was wanted, and the Wondertropolis thoroughfares and squares on the walls' holo-screens were replaced by the same scene: the stretch of land between The Whispering Woods and the cliff overlooking The Pool of Tears.

'This was recorded a short time ago,' Arch said.

Onscreen, nothing happened. General Doppelgänger heard the wind, the sound of lapping water in the distance. Gradually, the trees of the wood began to whisper, no more than a few of them at first, but then more and more until –

Alyss Heart broke from the wood and in a matter of a few impossibly long strides covered the distance to the cliff's edge. She jumped, plummeting down towards The Pool of Tears as –

The holo-screens went white. Views of Wondertropolis did not come back online.

General Doppelgänger seemed to be struggling with an unexpected onset of indigestion, his breathing short, his eyes narrowed and the bridge of his nose wrinkled with tension.

'You cannot divide into two or four or any number of little Doppels and Gängers while wearing *that*,' Arch said, nodding at the drug-delivery jumper. 'Why not sit still and try to enjoy the entertainment, since you have no other choice?'

At another signal from Arch, the minister at the control panel tweaked a dial and the room's holo-screens again showed The Pool of Tears, but this time from the vantage of the overhanging cliff.

'This is real time, general,' Arch said, 'the Pool of Tears at the present moment. Keep your eyes on it and be still. I don't want you to miss what's coming.'

Bleep.

The petulant noise chirped out from the unidentifiable

apparatus manned by Blister and the intel minister.

Bleep … bleep.

A staccato series of blips followed – *blip blip blip blip* – then a cacophony of bleeps and blips and buzzes coming fast one after another in an extended computerised warbling. Blister raised his eyes to the king.

'Now!' Arch shouted.

Onscreen, from camouflaged sites along the Pool's crystal barrier, Doomsine and Fel Creel warriors emerged burdened by tentacle-like conduits large enough for a grown Wonderlander standing at full height to enter. One end of each of the siphons was attached to a sanitation tanker, the vehicles that sucked refuse from streets to help keep Wondertropolis a resplendent city. There were two siphons to a tanker, four tankers in total. And as soon as the tribal warriors manoeuvred the siphons' open ends into the water, with the tankers humming and rumbling –

'Drain the Pool!' Arch shouted.

Sucked into the waiting tankers, the water lowered rapidly, and General Doppelgänger, trapped within himself, unable to move, believed everything was at an end: Alyss Heart would be exiled to Earth forever, the Alyssians and Wonderland and imagination doomed.

PART THREE

♥ ♦ CHAPTER 43 ♣ ♦

Oxford, England. 1875.

Ripkins slumped inert on the drawing room floor. Alyss – in the guise of the woman she had imagined into being to take her place in this world – stood over him while the dean and his wife, Edith and Lorina sat on the sofa silently mouthing disbelief at what they'd just seen: the conjuring of razor-cards, the trajectory of missiles altered by mental power alone.

'Oh!'

Alice Liddell and her gentleman friend, Reginald Hargreaves, stared from the doorway at the dead assassin and Wonderland's Queen. The dean, his wife and daughters looked from Alyss Heart to Alice Liddell and back again.

'I – ?' the dean started.

But that was all he managed before Alyss bolted from the room and out of the house, sprinting until she was well along St Aldate's Street. Certain the Liddells weren't following her, she walked briskly in the direction of Carfax Tower, towards the portal that would return her to Wonderland: a puddle where no puddle should be, in the middle of a sun-drenched pavement behind the Tower. But even from this distance she could see that something wasn't right. The portal was shrinking, its edges drying up fast. She started to run, her imagination's eye scanning the adjacent streets.

'How can it be?' she breathed, because all of the portals were shrinking, the Tower puddle already half its former size when she leapt for it, closing her eyes and sucking in her breath, anticipating the swift watery descent through portal waters, the reverse pull of The Pool of Tears, the –

Knees jarring, she landed on pavement. The portal had evaporated.

'How can it be?' she said aloud, already running, searching for another puddle where no puddle should be. *There!* Under a grocer's awning at Golden Cross, a splotch of water shrinking with every step she took towards it. She held her breath and leapt and –

She was in, felt herself dropping down through the wet. But the water was up to her chest when it all went wrong. She rose again, fast, the evaporating puddle pushing her up and out until –

No!

The force of it propelled her into the air, and by the time she landed, bystanders pointing in dismay, the puddle was gone.

She travelled the city with her imagination's eye: not a single puddle portal anywhere.

'How can it be?'

Dodge, Bibwit and the generals had been right: she'd forfeited any chance of saving imagination and the Queendom; the caterpillars' agenda held nothing good for Alyssians. Damp and exposed in crowded Golden Cross, she suddenly felt the staring Oxfordian faces surrounding her.

Not knowing where she was going, Alyss Heart ran.

♥ ◆ CHAPTER 44 ◆

♦

Reverend Dodgson was determined to discover how far Molly's mathematical ability extended – a determination that would have counted for nothing if Molly hadn't been amenable to his scrutiny, in a lighter mood on account of her recent acquaintance with Miss Alice Liddell. She glanced at the paper before her.

'Three,' she said.

Dodgson placed another of his Pillow Problems – the maths and logic puzzles with which he occupied himself in the small hours of restless nights – in front of Molly.

'Fourteen,' she said.

He presented the puzzles to her in order of increasing difficulty, though one wouldn't have known it from the effortlessness and speed with which she provided the correct answers. She had no need to work out the answers on paper and appeared to arrive at her answers by instinct.

Dodgson placed before her a puzzle he had not yet answered himself; nearly a page worth of scribblings had brought him no closer to its solution.

Bags H & K each contain two counters. Each counter is either black or white. A white counter is added to Bag H, the bag is shaken up, and one counter is transferred (without looking at it) to Bag K, where the process is repeated, a counter being transferred to Bag H. What is the chance of drawing a white counter from Bag H?

'Seventeen out of twenty-seven,' Molly said. She had taken perhaps a mere second longer to answer the problem than she had the previous ones. Dodgson didn't doubt that it would later prove to be the correct answer.

'How did you learn to do this?' he asked. 'Did someone teach you?'

'No, I don't know. It's common sense.'

'It is by no means c-c-common, I assure you. It is . . . remarkable.'

Dodgson's eager appreciation was having an effect on Molly.

309

'Maybe I got it from my mother,' she shrugged.

'What pedagog-og-og . . . methods did your mother use to teach –'

'That's not what I mean,' she said, and told him that her mother had been an alchemist at Wonderland's Millinery, a regular citizen except for her gift transmutating the elements of the physical world, which she'd done according to formulae kept in three private notebooks tied together with flugelberry vine. She pulled the notebooks from her inner coat pocket, showed them to him.

Alchemy? Were the girl's talents related to the incomprehensible symbols covering page after page of the notebooks? Could the girl's talents be related? Dodgson wasn't sure, though he knew someone who would be: the unorthodox Mr Rafters. He knew no one better to assess the girl, not even among the college's logicians and mathematicians.

'I'm a halfer,' Molly said.

'I'm sorry, a h-halfer? What's a halfer?'

She showed him the 'h' behind her ear. 'Half Milliner, half regular Wonderlander,' she said. 'You're either born a Milliner or you're not, but if you are, you're only supposed to be with other Milliners – to maintain the purity of the

Queendom's ultimate military force. But Hatter didn't. That's why I make too many mistakes. Big ones. It's what halfers *do*.'

In time, Dodgson would ask Molly about these mistakes, but right now, unable to ignore the self-laceration in Molly's tone, his softer emotions were piqued: no one should hate herself as much as this girl seemed to.

'You say halfer as if it's a terrible thing,' he said. 'But everyone I've ever known has been a halfer; if old enough t-to be called an adult, then ch-childish in their prejudices. All of us in this world really, I take to be h-halfers – half human, half divine, halfers of the best sort. I'd think the s-same must be true for the people of Wonderland, that there's . . . there is no such thing as s-someone who is *not* a halfer, or even a quarter-er, if you'll allow me the inelegant term.'

'Hatter's not a halfer!'

'I disagree,' said the Reverend. 'Hatter Madigan strikes me as *very much* a halfer. Has his devotion not been split in two, divided between w-w-what he owes to you as a father and what he owes to Alyss Heart and the Queendom as a M-Milliner? If he were not so divided, halved in this way, d-do you suppose you'd be here without him?'

Molly eyed Dodgson with such fixedness that some of

311

his old apprehension returned, his unease at being holed up with a Wonderlander whose abilities he'd hardly begun to comprehend. He called forth his easiest manner, arranged his note papers and put them away in his desk.

'Come,' he said, 'there is someone you should m-meet.' He was leading Molly to the door, out into the quad where the sky seemed wide enough to contain the heavens of both their worlds. 'Or perhaps I s-should say, there's a halfer who really must meet *you*.'

♦ CHAPTER 45 ♣

Blister stalked up and back in his shared quarters, touching everything of Ripkins's that he passed – the quilts of unicorn skin, the entertainment matrix, the virtual reality goggles, the game-controller body gear. Not for the first time, he cursed the fact that his touch didn't have its enflaming, pus-inducing effect on inanimate objects.

It wasn't that he despised Ripkins; he liked the Doomsine well enough, as much as he could like anybody, and he worked better with Ripkins than he had with any of Arch's previous lame recruits. But the King had chosen sawteeth fingerprints over instantaneous, fatal blistering: royal favour had been bestowed upon another. It didn't matter that the ministers said the King needed the blistering assassin close, because nothing they argued could convince him he hadn't been snubbed, forced to hang around, waiting to be given some scrap assignment the way the King's doggerels of war were thrown bones after a banquet.

'Ripkins,' Blister muttered.

He extended killing fingers towards his roommate's unkillable sleep-pod, felt movement behind him and spun.

'Redd Heart.'

'Miss your playmate?'

Fast as blood spraying from a wound, Blister hurled a pocket-sprocket at Her Imperial Viciousness, the fin-shaped blades a blur as the weapon rotated through the air like a ninja star of Earth, but –

Redd vanished before it reached her. The weapon clanked off the wall and on to the floor. Blister heard the grating hiccup of Her Imperial Viciousness's laugh, saw her standing under the archway that led to the public halls.

'All alone in the great big palace with nothing to do?' she asked.

He threw no weapon at her, made no move in her direction. Redd Heart, he knew, was both with him and not with him: a construct.

'Perhaps you've outgrown your usefulness to King Arch?' the phantom said. 'Perhaps you'd be better off with me and –'

Fzzzt!

The construct was gone: present one Gwormmy-blink, absent the next. As it would be if someone choked off the energy that had made its existence possible.

'I felt it! The Power of Proximity!' Redd spewed, stalking up and back in the hardscrabble dirt of the land beyond The Whispering Woods. The empty feeling she'd had when lacking imagination was back, the internal barrenness once more acute. 'I felt the infusion of energy I get whenever I'm close to The Heart Crystal!'

'But now?' Vollrath asked.

With her assassins holding the reins of their jabberwocky and looking on, Redd tried, and failed, to imagine a new construct of herself since the one she'd used to haunt Ripkins had somehow been taken from her. She attempted to conjure a flesh-swallowing rose blossom, but she couldn't manage that either. She stomped up to Vollrath as if he might be responsible for her inability.

'Now, tutor, I'm tired of trying to be clever. I'm tired of *strategy*. Now we fight for the Crystal. The old-fashioned way.'

'You mean without imagination?'

Redd scowled. 'Is that a problem for you, pale face?'

'If it isn't a problem for you, Your Imperial Viciousness,' Vollrath said, bowing. 'I wouldn't be so presumptuous as to claim that it's a problem for me.'

Not a hectare's length in front of them, The Iron Butterfly looked like some petrified primeval creature with its tail-end in the ground, its wings partly spread and its body slanted at a forty-five degree angle, antennae aimed at the sky. It wasn't made of iron but a kind of stone – of unknown origin and still not understood – that *resembled* iron ore: its hard surface a deep umber, spotted with corrosion and rust, seasoned by eons of weather. Even Wonderland's oldest tutors couldn't recall who had named the ancient megalith, nor when it had been named. It was believed to be as old as the land itself, constructed when the mountains, rivers, jungles, plains and desert had first formed, before there had been a Queendom or Boarderland, before there had been nations or 'civilisation'. And because the skills needed to build it were obviously beyond those possessed by the hulking Helmex of the earliest epochs, The Iron Butterfly had become the subject of a thousand rumours, some claiming it had been a temple, a shrine to stars, moons and sun, others that it'd been a house of sacrifice, where jabberwocky hearts throbbing with life were offered up to merciless gods, and still others that it'd been the site of duels, marriages, executions, births, coronations, regicides, crucifixions, resurrections, reanimations. Redd didn't care what it had been, only what it was: the current home of The Heart Crystal. She would make The Iron Butterfly the site of future history, the landmark in which she seized The Heart Crystal from the grasping hands of the undeserving.

'You don't feel the Power of Proximity any longer?' Vollrath mused. 'You *did* feel it but now you do *not*. We must conclude that Arch has devised a way of turning on and off the Crystal's power, as one, so to speak, turns on and off the light of a room.'

'My tutor,' Redd scoffed, 'well-schooled in the obvious.'

The Cat purred. Sacrenoir and the others grinned. The jabberwocky spat flame and strained against their chains.

Redd stroked her mount, its skin like volcanic crust. 'We'll be outnumbered,' she said, more to herself than her assassins. 'We'll be outgunned.'

'And your point is . . .?' Sacrenoir asked.

'That it will be a raucous good time so long as we annihilate them quickly! Before Arch's reinforcements arrive, I'd *better* be in possession of the Crystal.'

'You will be,' Sacrenoir promised.

'But Your Imperial Viciousness,' Vollrath asked, 'what if you're unable to revive its power?'

'Then we'll die, tutor. But if Arch can turn the Crystal's power on and off, so . . . can . . . I.'

'Of course. But perhaps since you and Alyss Heart are presently in cahoots –'

'"Cahoots"? Who's in "cahoots", tutor? I'll put *you* in cahoots, you intellectual!'

Vollrath again humbled himself before her. 'Please, Your Imperial Viciousness, I merely meant to suggest that since you and your niece are somewhat allied and we're outnumbered by Arch's forces, we might avail ourselves of the additional bodies – those of your niece, her guardsman and, of course, Mr Van de Skulle.'

The idea amused Redd, if anything could be said to amuse her; her nostrils flared as if at the foul odour of her pleasure. 'I suppose I *should* rue the misfortune that Alyss isn't here to fight alongside us. But what can I do? First to the Crystal, first to power. Too bad for her.'

Vollrath, The Cat, Sacrenoir and the others gathered round their mistress, her attention fixed on the looming edifice that held her future – either ultimate power or death, because she would accept nothing else.

'Here is how we'll attack . . .' she said.

♦ CHAPTER 46 ♦

The Doomsines and Fel Creel stared into the shadowy hole that had been The Pool of Tears, its water still sloshing in the tankers behind them. The siphons were put away and the warriors should have been proceeding back to the palace as King Arch had commanded them to do, but instead they stood in a religious silence, risking not only His Majesty's wrath but also – leaning as far over the cavity's edge as they could for a better view into the depths – their lives.

A Doomsine took a palm-sized medallion from his pocket and launched it into the air, where it briefly hovered, looking like a coin spinning fast on its edge. But unlike a coin, and emitting no sound louder than the rapid flutter of insect wings, the remote eye flew down into what had been The Pool of Tears, transmitting what it 'saw' directly to the Doomsine warrior's visual cortex.

'Well?' a Fel Creel asked.

'Nothing,' the Doomsine said. He did not speak again, but remained wide-eyed at what the others could not see: pure darkness.

'It's bottomless,' another Fel Creel eventually said.

This occasioned many grunts and nods, and several warriors were turning to leave when they all heard it: the echoing *womp* of the remote eye crashing to ground, just as –

The warrior who'd released the device jerked back, as if struck, from the abruptness with which its visual relay went offline.

They might have been taking longer than they should have to return to the palace, but the Doomsines and Fel Creel had something of importance to tell the King: the emptied Pool of Tears had a bottom.

Angry as he was, Blister didn't doubt what to do: he informed the King of Redd's visitation, of all that had happened between him and the imaginative construct. Arch laughed when he heard how the visit had ended.

'I'll bet Her Imperial Viciousness found that displeasing!'

Blister offered no opinion but didn't seem to share the royal enthusiasm. The pair were descending to the palace's nethermost level, three storeys underground, where Arch's ministers had found a storage cellar of suitable cold and damp and dark to serve as dungeon for his highest-ranking prisoner – General Doppelgänger.

'Did you know, Blister, the longer the Heart Crystal's cocooned, the more its power weakens until it becomes so faint it can never be revived, and then . . . nothing?'

'You knew I didn't, Your Majesty.'

'In other words, this Crystal – it's not a living being exactly, but it dies.'

'Death is not always a bad thing, sire.'

'For *others* – I agree with you. And since I was tired of waiting for Redd to show herself, why not render powerless the sole remaining Heart in Wonderland? The ministers have cocooned the Crystal in the neutralising caterpillar silk. I'm glad to know they managed it at the very moment Redd was in the middle of perpetrating a plot to steal *you*!'

The King was definitely starting to enjoy himself: all this bother with the House of Hearts would soon be over; before the next lunar cycle had passed, he would be able to luxuriate in his newly expanded authority. He would, until the next threat to his reign (there was always a next threat), be at peace.

'You do now see it's better that you're here and not on Earth?' he asked Blister.

'Alyss wouldn't have killed me as easily as she did Ripkins,' Blister said.

'Maybe not. But by keeping you here, I allow you to participate in significantly more than a single confrontation with an overvalued former Queen. You can have as large a role as you wish in the annihilation of Redd and her sad group. If I'm not mistaken, a certain feline among them didn't exactly fill you with warm feelings of friendship.'

Blister's eyes became heavy-lidded; his jaw tensed as if sutured shut: His Majesty was not mistaken.

'And that's in addition to the fun I've arranged for us now,' Arch said, bringing them to a stop outside a thick, wooden door reinforced with bars of uncut diamond and guarded by the two largest Doomsines in the tribe. 'Take off your gloves. It's time for us to conduct an interrogation.'

Blister – beginning to think he'd indeed been granted a better assignment than Ripkins – stuffed his gloves into a pocket, followed Arch past the guards and into the cellar. A single fire crystal glowed in the corner. He let his eyes adjust to the gloom. The stone floor and walls were bare. In the centre of the room was a figure, the silhouette of a male seated on a straight-backed chair: General Doppelgänger, imprisoned in his drug-delivery system.

The assassin took up position behind the military leader while Arch stood before him, frowning.

'It's useless to deny you've been in contact with Alyss Heart since my coronation,' Arch told the general. 'I had too much faith that civility – *kindness* – could win your allegiance. You wouldn't have suffered under my rule, Doppelgänger. You've been very stupid.'

'Was it kindness to have your spies trailing me about?'

'My *what*? You seem to be under a misapprehension, general. My spies, as you call them, were nothing more than Boarderlanders curious to know how you spent your days leading Wonderland's card soldiers. Besides, they didn't physically harm you, did they? If they did, I'll have them punished.'

General Doppelgänger wasn't fooled and said nothing, his eyes on the wall.

'It's strange that a tutor of Bibwit Harte's accumulated wisdom and intelligence should be so dumb as to choose the losing side,' Arch observed. 'Why didn't you go with the albino when you had the opportunity? Did you stay, by chance, because it was you who thought to spy on me?'

The military leader was given no time to respond; the King's hand swung round and slapped him on the cheek. Arch's hot face lowered to within a Gwormmy-length of his own.

'You know, Doppelgänger, I'd intended to ask you what excuse Alyss used to avoid war once her imagination had returned, but the sight of you is irritating me more than I care to let it.' Raising himself up, Arch addressed his assassin. 'Don't kill him yet. I'll soon give you that honour. For now, just come close.'

♦ CHAPTER 47 ♣

Hatter's arrival on a fraught scene often occasioned exclamations of relief, the sight of him enough to fortify Alyssians against what seemed insurmountable odds even to survive let alone retake the Queendom. But as the Milliner entered Taegel's home, neither Dodge nor Bibwit voiced any such feelings.

'Alyss has left us,' Bibwit explained, choosing not to use the word 'abandoned' and relating the details of Blue's visitation. 'When we regained consciousness after the caterpillar's waftings, she was gone.' And because Hatter kept glancing at his curly hair: 'Yes, I'm hairy! If you're compelled to stare at my bushy head, Mr Madigan, then stare and get it over with!'

Hatter apologised. 'I didn't realise I was staring.'

'We have no reason to suppose Alyss didn't do as the caterpillar wanted her to,' Dodge said.

Hatter responded to this intel with typical Milliner reserve. The tutor and guardsman, he judged, likely deemed Alyss's actions undisciplined, evidence of her disregard for her duty both as sovereign and as White Imagination's most powerful practitioner. There had been a time when he, too, wouldn't have understood the Queen's behaviour, but now he could relate to the need to temporarily shake off the responsibilities that had governed one's life if it was possible to save a beloved by doing so.

Mr Van de Skulle – standing erect, whip within easy reach of the hand hanging loose at his side – was watching him, scrutinising him in a way the Milliner found tediously familiar: the assassin had the doubting eye of a would-be challenger, a man wanting to test his own combat mettle against the touchstone of Hatter Madigan's renowned prowess. And Hatter was supposed to believe that he and Van de Skulle were working together? Easier to believe in Queen Alyss, no matter how unconventionally she went about her duties.

'A Queen with Alyss Heart's gifts understands things we cannot,' he said. 'She will not abandon us.' It felt awkward saying this to Bibwit and Dodge, two of the Queen's most intelligent, devoted advisors. 'You mentioned that General

Doppelgänger is still at the palace. If he can access the surveillance footage of The Pool of Tears, we'll know for sure if Queen Alyss has gone to Earth. We may be facing a more serious problem if her whereabouts are unknown and she didn't dive into the Pool.'

Bibwit was already pushing back the sleeve of his scholar's robe, entering Doppelgänger's code on his crystal communicator's keypad. 'Yes, of course. I was just about to think of that myself. The general doesn't need to answer his communicator if it isn't safe for him to do so on account of Arch's spies.'

It was evidently safe to answer: Bibwit's communicator beeped and its vid nozzle pushed out its light, projecting on to the air an image –

Not of General Doppelgänger, but King Arch.

'Bibwit Harte,' the King said.

The tutor's ears twitched every which way, like panicked creatures unable to flee a fire, and his hand shot to his communicator's keypad and cut transmission. But Milliner, tutor and guardsman knew the signal had been captured, traced, their location pinpointed for Arch's military.

'We can't stay here,' Dodge said.

'Take off your communicator,' Hatter told Bibwit. 'I'll

dispose of it somewhere. It won't keep Arch's forces from descending on the area, but at least it won't be signalling them precisely where we'll be.'

Bibwit removed his crystal communicator, handed its keypad, belt and shoulder straps to Hatter.

'Meet me at the bazaar on the corner,' Hatter said. But he was blocked at the door by Taegel, just coming in, whose wild, unkempt hair was at odds with the melancholy slope of his shoulders.

'It's over,' the engineer said. 'No work can be done at the factory. None of us is able to do anything.'

'What do you mean?' Bibwit asked.

'Conceptualising, problem-solving, technical analysis – it's all too much for us. Like the last time except worse.'

'The last time being WILMA?' Dodge said to Bibwit, whose ears dipped in confirmation.

Now it was Dodge's turn to enter a code on his communicator's keypad: an image of Mr Dumphy at the limbo coop crackled in the air.

'Mr Anders,' the tinker said sadly, 'in anticipation of your communication, my friends and I have been careful not to expose the return of our imaginations to the Club soldiers, but now that you and Queen Alyss are perhaps ready for our most creative support, the very reason for this communication –'

'You're without imagination again,' Dodge interrupted.

'We are, yes. Please inform Queen Alyss that as a group we're largely as loyal to her as always, but I should tell you, Mr Anders . . . some among us are finding it extremely hard this time around to maintain a positive attitude.'

'Understandable if undesirable. The Queen is indisposed at present, Mr Dumphy. I know you'll do your best to buoy up the others. You'll hear from us soon and the limbo coops *will* be destroyed. You *will* be free.' Dodge signed off. 'No Alyss, no imagination,' he said to no one in particular. 'Could our situation get any worse?'

They would wait until nightfall, avoiding Taegel's home and killing time in busy markets in order to avoid a confrontation with the tribal warriors out to kill them. Because trawling the shopping promenades, canvassing avenues in open-air smail-transports, searching, hunting: Arch's Doomsines were everywhere.

'By now, Arch has been informed of where Taegel's employed,' Hatter said, seated at a table in front of a brewmaster's stall, watching a patrol of Doomsines and

Two Cards move through the crowd.

If Taegel was concerned, he didn't show it. 'The factory's security is too cumbersome to be quickly taken off-line. It requires a concerted effort from a number of engineers with knowledge only of what they are required to do. No single Wonderlander has a mental picture of how the entire system is integrated and it will take time for Arch to gather those needed and orchestrate their efforts.'

The patrolling Doomsines and Two Cards were coming towards them. Hatter placed his hands flat on the table, ready to make use of his wrist-blades. Mr Van de Skulle surreptitiously gripped his whip. Dodge slid a hand under his jumpsuit to take hold of a crystal shooter.

Still, the Doomsines and card soldiers approached.

Bibwit turned his face to the ground, hoping the enemy might see only hair. But it was taking them a long time to pass, too long actually, and just when he was sure he'd been sighted –

The warriors and soldiers brushed past.

'We'll be safest at the factory,' Taegel said, 'at least for a while.'

Bibwit was trying to breathe easy. 'Arch can turn imagination on and off according to his moods. He'll undoubtedly solve the problem of the factory's security sooner than we'd like.'

'Yeah, but we could be all the army we're ever going to get,' Dodge said, 'and we need to arm ourselves accordingly.'

So it was, however reluctantly by Bibwit, agreed. After nightfall, using the second-skin gloves and other false identification paraphernalia provided by Taegel, they would raid the munitions factory and carry off all the weaponry they could handle.

♥ ♦ CHAPTER 48 ♣ ♣

'He's a man of the world – too much so for my taste, actually. But he is b-b-better prepared to plumb the depths of your talents than I am.'

'I'm not sure I want my depths plumbed,' Molly said.

She and Dodgson were climbing the stairs to the garret of a lodging house on Beaumont Street, in which lived one Mr Rafters – a man whose adopted name, the Reverend had explained, referred to the aerial heights at which he slept, washed and dressed.

'It isn't just that,' he said now, placing a hand on Molly's shoulder to stop her. 'Rafters is supremely intelligent and ingenious, but he also p-possesses esoteric knowledge of the kind that m-may tell us if your talents are related to your mother's.'

'He's an alchemist?'

'He's many things – a rather unorthodox g-gentleman, as

I say, not that I suppose his unorthodoxy will bother *you*. We will avoid visiting him on Sundays, and as to the d-discomfort he may cause me . . . your talent, Molly, wherever its origins lie, is worth it.'

If Rafters could teach her about alchemy, Molly thought, he could bring her that much closer to her mother, to understanding the woman Weaver had been; she'd try to be receptive. She followed Dodgson up yet another flight of stairs, could have sworn the lodging house had only three floors; it was so humble and rickety-looking from the street. Yet from the number of stairs they had climbed, they should have been well above the third landing.

'Here we are,' Dodgson said.

Molly was sure the garret door hadn't appeared until after he spoke. And not just that. There were more stairs. She gazed up the crooked flight that led further into darkness, about to ask what was *up there* when –

'Well, well, if it isn't the famous author, the great man.'

To Molly's eye, the fellow who answered Dodgson's knock at the door did not have a face suggestive of supreme intelligence. His misshapen nose revealed nothing of alchemy. The grey-splotched stubble of his cheeks communicated no analytical or mathematical genius. The rectangular brow overhanging his dull eyes seemed less a storehouse of arcana than a ruddy brick.

'I would not have called on you unexpectedly –' Dodgson started.

'At all,' corrected the man.

Dodgson forced a smile. 'I would not have c-called on you so unexpectedly, Mr Rafters, if I didn't be-believe you would want to meet this extraordinary person at my side, and were time not so p-pressing. Homburg Molly, Mr Rafters.'

The two greeted each other with scepticism, Mr Rafters apparently judging Molly's appearance to be no more indicative of extraordinary abilities than she had judged his. Dodgson produced a small leather-bound book from his pocket, opened it to a page on which he'd written one of his puzzles.

'Have you seen this before?' he asked Molly.

'No.'

He read aloud: "'Two travellers, starting at the same time, went opposite ways round a circular railway. Trains start each way every fifteen minutes, the easterly ones going round in three hours, the westerly in two. How many trains did each meet on the way, not counting trains met at the terminus itself?"'

'Nineteen,' Molly answered reflexively.

Rafters whistled mockingly, as if he thought their performance contrived, but he stepped aside to let them into his apartment. 'Mr Dodgson, you and your friend are welcome to my hospitality, unless of course you think your delicate sensibilities will be offended.'

The Reverend gestured for Molly to enter the garret and followed her over the threshold. Uncommon intelligence, a wealth of knowledge – these were as inevident in the apartment's shabby array as they were in Rafters's face. The dresser stood at a tilt, having but three legs. One side of the room was taken up with a pallet of straw covered with an old horse blanket. The grime on the lone window was too thick to see through and the dust on the floor so thick that Molly and Dodgson tracked footprints wherever they stepped. There were no books or pamphlets about, no scientific tools or writing instruments, nothing in the slightest to declare the garret's occupant an avid cultivator of his mind.

The occupant was speaking. Molly, trying not to touch anything, needed a second to realise he was addressing her, presenting her with a problem. It was a puzzle like the first ones Dodgson had shown her in his flat.

'Six,' she answered.

Rafters nodded: correct.

He asked her a few more, all of which she answered with similar ease. Then the puzzles changed, became games of symbols in differing combinations that required no outside knowledge to solve, just the ability to discern what effects the symbols were supposed to have upon one another when placed in various arrangements – coupled, de-coupled, adjacent to, on top of or below one another. These puzzles Molly also answered promptly, correctly and without effort. Rafters found a stub of pencil and a newspaper under his dresser. Transitioning from oral quiz to written, the puzzles grew more elaborate. Which was when Molly sensed a fog seep into her brain. She felt buffle-headed, taking longer and longer to correctly answer Rafters's puzzles, which should have given her no trouble. And Rafters himself seemed slower, as if formulating and writing out his puzzles had grown more difficult. By the time he finished composing one that Molly had no idea how to solve, she was pretty sure he didn't know its answer either. So they left off where they began: neither much impressed with the other.

'Show him your mother's notebooks,' Dodgson said.

Weaver's trio of notebooks tied with flugelberry vine, their contents as yet unfathomable to Molly though they were her dearest keepsakes. With reservation, she handed them to Rafters.

'Flugelberry,' he said, showing interest before he even untied the vine that bound them.

Molly almost missed it, worried about his handling of her mother's writings. He'd said 'flugelberry'? Did they have that on Earth? How could he have known about flugelberry unless –

'Come back tomorrow,' Rafters said, thumbing through one of the notebooks, his dull eyes as lively as Molly had ever seen. 'But only if you bring these.'

Once she and Dodgson were on the landing with the closed garret door separating them from Rafters, the Reverend asked, 'W-What happened in there? You've been s-successful with problems more difficult than any he posed.'

'I don't know,' Molly said. 'I feel . . . not right.'

'I feared so. I feel it as well.'

Out on Beaumont Street, everyone appeared to feel it. Some walked hesitantly, as if unsure where they were going. Others struggled to count out the money needed to pay carriage drivers or flower-mongers, while a not insignificant number acted as perfect layabouts – slack-jawed, glaze-eyed, doing nothing.

'It's n-nearly the same as the time p-p-previous,' Dodgson said, 'before you and your father showed up at my d-door. But this is worse. Do you suppose The Heart C-Crystal has been . . . is again shut down?'

Molly had no way of knowing and she didn't consider what such an event might mean for her, for Hatter, for Wonderland's Queen and the Alyssian effort. Not yet anyway, because –

Glimpsing a clock through a draper's window, she told the Reverend she would meet him back at his rooms and started quickly off: she had only a few minutes to make her rendezvous with Alice Liddell.

♦ CHAPTER 49 ♣

From the long tables cluttered with burners and tubing and glass vials to the white-boards covered with scribbled formulae to the chemical smells, Taegel's lab at the munitions factory looked no different from a science lab in any of Wonderland's schools. But it was here, as well as in the factory's surrounding workshops, that the prototypes of every weapon employed by Wonderland's decks and chessmen had been conceived, designed, built and tested – orb generators and cannonball spiders, AD52s and crystal shooters, porta-prison bombs and whipsnake grenades. The munitions factory: where theoretical physics and chemistry were wedded to practical application, the evolution of weapons' technology, and ingenuity was devoted to the instruments of death and destruction.

'How to begin,' Taegel was saying, 'when there's so much in the final stage of development?' On the wall behind him was an entertainment crystal tuned to a Wonderland news programme, the voices of its reporters constant background chatter. 'I always leave it on,' he explained, noticing Dodge's distraction. 'It gives the impression I've just stepped away and will return at any moment, which discourages idea-poaching by other engineers. It's quite competitive here. Now . . .' He picked up the nearest object at hand – an elongated fragment of glass with no sharp edges or corners, as if these had been rounded, smoothed, to prevent harm to its bearer. 'This is a splinterscape. It does . . . well, it's hard to explain really. Stand back.'

Taegel aimed one end of the weapon at a room that opened off the lab proper, the floor and walls of which were pock-marked with previous weapons' tests, its ceiling marred by scorch marks. He touched his thumb to a white crescent symbol on the weapon's side and finger-length glass splinters shot out, embedded at all angles in the floor and grew to over a metre in length.

'Cover the ground between you and an approaching enemy,' Taegel said, 'and unless the enemy's travelling by air, they can't get to you. Needs reloading only every 10,000 splinters.'

'We'll take five,' said Dodge.

Taegel set down the splinterscape and picked up what might have been the small limb of a cactus. 'This is a weapon in a similar vein: the shardstorm, which essentially creates what its name indicates. But while other bomb types detonate on impact with a hard surface, a shardstorm detonates when *impacting the air*, after a certain velocity has been maintained for four Gwormmy-blinks. This small delay is to allow the user a measure of safety and give him or her a chance to avoid the coming storm.'

Taegel tossed the shardstorm into the adjoining room and a tornado of wulfenite shrapnel formed. Two Wonderlanders high, its wulfenite whipped about and ripped at the walls and ceiling.

'We'll take as many of those as you've got,' Dodge said, before it had petered out, and not alone in his appreciation.

Bibwit was bending down before a pan containing what looked like spice to be sprinkled on someone's lunch. 'This smells tasty.'

'Don't!' Taegel warned.

But Bibwit had already brought a pinch of the stuff to his mouth. 'We're doomed!' he moaned. 'All is lost without Alyss! We might as well sit down and die right here!'

To prove that he didn't speak idly, the tutor plopped down on the floor, head in his hands. 'What's the point? What's the point of anything?'

'Dust of despair,' Taegel explained to the others. 'Takes away an enemy's will to fight.'

'To breathe is such a burden,' Bibwit complained to his lap.

'We'll take a few pouches of that,' Dodge said.

Taegel demonstrated the oozy, a rifle that sprayed out streams of foul-smelling mulch ('We'll take at least two,' said Dodge), and a dazzle dart, which upon hitting its target exploded with light bright enough to cause temporary blindness ('We'll take a couple of fistfuls,' said Dodge). The engineer might have gone on to demonstrate the rust-ruin, the tweedler and a host of other weapons not yet so complete if Hatter hadn't stopped him.

'I assume you have a supply of whipsnake grenades, cannonball spiders and AD52 ammo cartridges here?' the Milliner asked.

'Absolutely.'

To Dodge and Van de Skulle, Hatter said, 'We should load up.'

Which was what they were doing – securing the familiar

weapons about their persons – when Bibwit, still influenced by the dust of despair, cried out:

'We're dead already and don't know it! What hope is there for anyone? None! None at all! Just look! Feast your eyes on our demise!'

Pulling at his hair, the tutor directed everyone's attention to the entertainment crystal, which showed a crowd hundreds of Wonderlanders strong standing vigil at the edge of the empty Pool of Tears. An offscreen reporter was speaking of unprecedented events and the need for those whose loved ones had ever fallen or jumped into the Pool to grieve afresh, because with The Pool of Tears drained, there was positively no chance of seeing those loved ones again.

'How'd Arch . . .?' Taegel mumbled.

'Alyss,' Dodge whispered, his voice a mixture of anguish and alarm.

'She might not have gone in,' Hatter said. 'We need to leave. We've been here too long as it is.'

The Milliner helped Bibwit to his feet and Taegel led them back along the corridors the way they'd come, out on to factory grounds.

'Still online,' Taegel said as they passed through an unmanned checkpoint in the first soundwave barrier along the factory's perimeter. 'Which means Arch hasn't yet –'

Clickclicketyclacketyclick.

'Our end has come!' Bibwit moaned.

On the left and right of the Alyssians: too many Scorp-Spitters to count. Behind and in front of them: deadly walls of internal organ-charring soundwaves. Scorpion-like contraptions, the ScorpSpitters curled their 'tails' into a 'C', taking aim at the Alyssians, about to shoot bullets of deadly poison.

Fweppap! Fweppap!

Mr Van de Skulle brandished his whip, lashing Scorp-Spitter after ScorpSpitter on the left, while with one set of activated wrist-blades, Hatter deflected the poisonous gobs shot at them from the ScorpSpitters on the right.

Pzzzzzzzzzzzzztch!

Mr Van de Skulle's whip fell to the ground, the dutchman himself the lone casualty of a whipsnake grenade dropped from the sky. Dodge and Taegel glanced up at the gangways above the soundwave barriers; normally patrolled by Three Cards and white pawns, the gangways were crowded with Doomsine warriors and more senior chessmen. Among the latter: the knight and rook who'd fought next to Dodge in Alyssian battles during Redd's reign. Their weapons were trained on the intruders, but seeing the guardsman and Hatter and Bibwit, they hesitated. It was all the time Hatter needed to pull his folded top hat blades from his coat pocket and send them coptering into the enemy.

The rook and knight jumped clear, but the Doomsines, even as they gunned razor-cards and crystal shot at the trapped Alyssians, succumbed to the whirling blades.

The weapon boomeranged back to Hatter. Which was when Taegel saw a cannonball spider rocketing towards them from somewhere beyond the litter of ScorpSpitters, its legs unfolding midair, its pincers opening and closing. He barely got the shardstorm off in time. The cannonball spider slammed into the cyclone of wulfenite scraps and emerged with limbs severed at the joints, body dented and misshapen. It crashed to the ground and rolled to a stop at his feet.

'Yaah!' Dodge shouted, exchanging crystal shot with more Doomsines until –

Whooooosh!

A blinding light flared between the guardsman and his enemies: a dazzle dart's detonation. Eyes shut, Dodge ran into the light, his father's sword unsheathed and swinging. He felt one body fall, another and another. Then the flaring light burnt out and – *clank!* – steel met steel. Dodge found himself engaged in one-on-one combat with his old friend the white rook.

'We were told only there were traitors . . . didn't know it was you,' the rook said, stepping back to swing his sword, telegraphing his move so Dodge could easily defend against it. *Clink!* 'Where's the Queen?'

'Earth.'

Clank! Dodge's sword locked with the rook's. The white knight was above them on a gangway, armed with an oozy. He and the rook caught each other's eye, came to an immediate understanding as only two soldiers who'd survived innumerable firefights together could.

The Doomsines were being relentless, emptying AD52s and crystal shooters at the Alyssians, trying to spear them with sharpened knobkerries. Hatter cut and diced with his blades and Taegel tried to shelter Bibwit as –

'Meet us at the burial field near The Iron Butterfly,' the rook said to Dodge as the knight raised his oozy and took aim at them. 'But right now, you and I are going to jump to my left, and then you stab me in my shoulderplate. Not too hard, but make it believable.'

Dodge didn't have a chance to question; the knight fired and a thick stream of mulch missiled towards him. He and the rook jumped, tumbled clear as the mulch splat against one of the pylons that maintained the outermost wall of deadly soundwaves. The pylon's vents clogged, taking soundwaves off-line and creating a window of escape. The Alyssians barely made it out to open ground before the oozy's charred mulch fell from the vents and the soundwaves were again online.

The rook, a hand against his wounded shoulder, stood and watched his friends recede into the darkness, on the run from Doomsine fire determined not to let them live.

♦ CHAPTER 50 ♣

It was almost ten past the hour when Molly, preoccupied with thoughts of The Heart Crystal's doubtful well-being, realised that Alice was late. They had arranged to meet at the entrance to the Water Walk at two o'clock. Alice was never late.

'But you haven't known her long,' Molly said to herself.

She'd spent no more time with Alice than could fit in a single afternoon; despite the speed with which they'd become friends, for all Molly knew, the lady could have been frequently late to appointments. Still, Alice's tardiness made her uneasy.

'I'll check for her at the deanery.'

But Molly couldn't remember if Alice was supposed to be coming from home. What if she came from the opposite direction and she arrived while Molly sought her in Tom Quad? She had begun to notice this need she had to protect

Alice – indeed, would have been hard-pressed *not* to notice it after what had happened yesterday at the riverside . . .

'Look at that cute fellow!' Alice said, tossing a handful of seed in the direction of a plump duckling with black and grey feathers. 'It's a wonder his little legs can hold him up.'

'Won't be able to by the time we're done,' Molly said, and sprinkled seed on the ground for the drake and his fellow quackers. But then, at the upper edge of her vision, she caught sight of seekers dive-bombing towards Alice. Unthinking, she lurched in front of her friend, simultaneously whipping off her jacket and holding it spread out above her to catch one of the insect-birds before its beak could descend into Alice's neck. The rest of the seekers swooped momentarily away as she thrust her catch downward with the motion of one shaking dust from a blanket. She didn't watch the creature hit the ground but cartwheeled a circle around Alice, trapping the returning seekers one by one in her jacket and throwing them hard to the ground until the sky was clear, the threat gone and –

Alice and everyone else at the riverside stared at her in open-mouthed incredulity. Molly scoped the ground for seekers, because they probably weren't dead, but there were none to be seen, just wads of crumpled paper and splintered wood.

'Do you have something against kites?' Alice asked.

Homburg Molly: more like her father, who'd made a similar mistake years before, than she would ever know.

'Kites?' she repeated, only now understanding that what she'd thought seekers were nothing more than paper-and-wood constructions being flown by nearby schoolchildren whose leisure she had violently done away with.

'Where did you learn such acrobatics?' Alice asked.

Molly was at a loss to answer, but Alice yelped with laughter and took her hand and together they ran from the river and the children's accusatory faces.

Twenty-five past the hour.

'I'll give her a few more minutes,' Molly said.

Their second meeting had taken place at the tea shop on St Aldate's, where, over a pot of estate tea, Alice had spoken at length of her parents and siblings, and of a gentleman named Reginald Hargreaves, whom she was starting to fancy, and who, she was fairly certain, fancied her. With anyone else, Molly would have been bored – envious of Alice's close family bond probably, but bored. Except with Alice . . . to hear such mundane stuff from a lady who looked and sounded exactly like Queen Alyss Heart!

Whereas her own life had been marred by war and loss, with little of the solace offered by family, Alice's centred around her family and had been subjected to no combat whatsoever.

Half past the hour and still Alice hadn't . . . but here she was, running up from the direction of Tom Quad, agitated.

'Molly, you'll never guess what's . . . a man is dead! At the house! A man with . . . I hardly know how to . . . with knife-fingers who tried to harm mother and father and Lorina and Edith! The authorities are there, but my father has no idea who the man was! No one's ever seen him before! Why he would ever want to harm the gentlest, most caring people in the world, I can't . . . but that's not the strangest part! No, the strangest part is who saved them!'

'Who?' Molly asked. A man with 'knife-fingers'? She knew of only one.

'Me! Well, it wasn't *me*, of course, I wouldn't know the first thing about fighting anyone, let alone a devil like that! But it *was* me, a woman utterly like me in every way! It's all so, I don't know, impossible! I just came to tell you I can't spend the afternoon as we'd planned! I must get back, in case . . . oh, in case I don't know what! It's all so dreadful, so dreadfully impossible, so . . .'

Alice was already hurrying back to the quad, and Molly had fallen in step with her, alert for threats; if Ripkins had come to Earth, other assassins might be lurking. But why would Ripkins want to harm the Liddells? *A woman utterly like me in every way.* Wasn't that what she had said?

At the quad, Alice squeezed Molly's hand and left her, passing through the curious Oxfordians milling outside the Deanery, and now that Molly had a moment to herself –

A woman utterly like me in every way. She had definitely said it. Which meant . . . could it be . . .

'The Queen,' Molly breathed.

She would ask Dodgson. She would relate what had happened to Alice Liddell and ask him what he thought her words meant. But when she pushed open the door to his rooms, all intentions left her, because seated across from the Reverend –

Alyss Heart.

♦ CHAPTER 51 ♣

It hadn't been the easiest thing to do, to direct her steps
to Reverend Dodgson's door. Running from Carfax Tower,
the object of unwanted stares, Alyss slipped into an alley,
where she could be alone, invisible, while she subdued her
panic and waited for her clothes to dry, determining her
next move.

Something must have happened to The Pool of Tears.

Because puddle portals didn't just evaporate en masse like
that. She again tried to sight a portal with her imagination's
eye, discovered herself completely incapable of remote
viewing; she was without imagination. But unlike the first
time she'd been robbed of her power, she didn't feel even a
temporary release from responsibility, from duty. The most
– *the worst* – she had ever done, ever could do, was ignore
her responsibilities as Queen and White Imaginationist.
'Release', as she knew too well, was not possible. But her

next move? How could she make any move without The
Pool of Tears?

Am I never to see Dodge again?

She couldn't bear the idea; much less would she be able
to tolerate the reality. How could she live, not just without
Dodge, but without knowing what would become of Bibwit
and Doppelgänger, the walrus-butler, Mr Dumphy, and so
many others?

Don't give in to fear and despair. Think.

Yet if the oracles had had anything to do with the Pool's
disappearance, her situation could very well be hopeless. It
was the most probable explanation, wasn't it? The Pool of
Tears, like imagination, was gone. And how had Arch known
of the Liddells? There were, to be sure, a few possibilities as
to who could have told him of the family, but none made as
much sense as the caterpillars; they always knew everything.
Only the caterpillar-oracles had power and vision enough
to be behind it all. But even so, even supposing the oracles
were behind it all . . .

Blue my enemy? I can't . . . I don't accept it! Think.

She couldn't go back to the Liddells' without facing
questions from them and the police, the answering of which
which would accomplish nothing. Her answers wouldn't be

believed. What about Prince Leopold, the man who'd once almost become her husband? No, she'd gain nothing there: she'd have to get through too many royal attendants to reach him, and besides, he wouldn't recognize the committed Heart she currently was.

Then she remembered Dodgson.

If she had a list of people from whom she'd most like to seek aid, Reverend Charles Lutwidge Dodgson would not have been on it. She didn't know how he might help her, but Homburg Molly was supposed to be with him. And there was no one else.

Opening his door to her, the Reverend was not as taken aback as he would have been a fortnight earlier, the outfit of a Wonderland farmer's maid distinct enough to inform him that his visitor was not Alice Liddell but Queen Alyss Heart.

'I'm so sorry,' he said, after they'd stood several moments in silence.

Sorry, he said, for failing to acknowledge the truth of what she'd confided to him all those years ago. Sorry for taking a young girl's confidence in vain and turning her memories into absurd little books. He had never been sorrier in his life. He could never have known that her bloody tales of Wonderland hadn't been fiction – to believe such would have required a different man – but ignorance of his crime did not excuse it, and every hour he spent with Homburg Molly served as chastisement for how he'd betrayed her.

'And where is Molly?' Alyss asked, not quite able to keep regal authority from her tone or manner.

'S-She is . . . ah, well . . . she should b-be returning soon. Very soon, I'm sure.'

Sitting at his modest tea table, describing her predicament, her anger towards this nervous man broke. If she wasn't able to completely let her guard down with him, she could not allow past hurts and prejudices to get in the way of present necessities.

'Something's happened to The Pool of Tears,' she concluded.

'And The Heart Crystal?'

'I assume so, since I can imagine nothing.'

'Nor I. H-Has anything such as this ever happened to The Pool of Tears before?'

'Not to my knowledge.'

An awkward silence threatened, but Dodgson began to speak of Molly. His inhibitions fell away in his enthusiasm, and by the time the girl opened the front door, Alyss knew everything there was to know about her extraordinary talent in maths and logic, which Dodgson believed might rival the girl's Milliner skills.

'Molly,' Alyss said, standing.

The girl didn't move. She glanced from Dodgson to the hall and seemed on the verge of running away, but then a breath of resignation filled her. She stepped forwards and prostrated herself. 'My Queen,' she said.

'Please, Molly, get up. We don't need such ceremony between us, especially now.'

Alyss embraced her as she would a sister. Overwhelmed, Molly nearly sobbed: for the Queen to treat her like this after everything! She tried to explain how she'd wanted to be forgiven for contaminating The Crystal Continuum, for being weak-willed and doubtful of the trust that had been placed in her; she wanted to explain how she used to want this forgiveness even though she hadn't thought she deserved it, but that now, while she was no less regretful of her actions, she was willing to accept the burden of what she'd done. And yet she couldn't speak; her mouth wouldn't work.

'I know,' Alyss said. 'I know.'

Finally, Molly managed, 'You were at the Liddells'.'

'I was. But I wouldn't be here now if there were a portal

anywhere in the city. There is no way back to Wonderland.'

Molly felt an unmooring inside of her: No way back? But that meant her father could never return for her, that they could never –

'At least we have each other,' Alyss sighed.

Dodgson cleared his throat. 'And me.'

'Ah.' The Queen smiled with a sadness that might have reached back generations. 'Let's hope – no, let's *believe* – we are enough.'

♦ CHAPTER 52 ♣

Wonderland's oracles sat upon their respective fungi, the vibrant blue, green, red, orange, yellow and purple of their spongy mushroom thrones contrasting sharply with the faded colours of the wise, riddle-tongued creatures themselves. The oracles' colours had begun to fade with each passing lunar hour, their skin becoming ever more dried and shrivelled. Prophetic larvae of immodest proportions: they who had been ageless and suffered no debilitating physical change since before there was such a word or concept as 'Queendom' were at last showing the effects of ageing, victims of an accelerated process that kept time with the dying Heart Crystal.

Ignoring their hookahs, the caterpillars sat wearily, as if sitting were itself an exhausting enterprise. Forlorn, distrustful, they blinked milky eyes at the tarty tart cauldron before them – the third cauldron delivered to them by Arch's intel minister who had been ordered to regularly supply them with fresh treats.

'So tasty and yet so dangerous,' the once orange caterpillar said of the tarty tarts.

'You first,' the vaguely yellow caterpillar insisted to the formerly red caterpillar.

'I couldn't possibly think of partaking before Green,' the formerly red caterpillar demurred.

'It would be bad form to help myself before Blue has had a nibble,' said the barely-green-any-longer caterpillar.

The not-quite-blue caterpillar grumbled and said, 'I'm stuffed,' though he hadn't eaten a tarty tart in hours, his digestive system having lamentably grown tarty tart intolerant.

The more-ashen-than-purple caterpillar, in a painstaking, arthritic semblance of his earlier enthusiasm, betook himself to the cauldron, brought a squigberry tart to his mouth, bit into it and –

'Ow!'

Two of his teeth had fallen out, stuck in the tarty tart.

'What did I tell you?' the once orange caterpillar said. 'So tasty and yet so dangerous.'

'Obviously!' the vaguely yellow caterpillar said to the barely-green-any-longer caterpillar.

The barely-green-any-longer caterpillar crinkled his face. Not sure he understood what his fellow council member was about, he said questioningly, and in a single rush of breath, 'I was going to mention that the King has done what Everqueen requires but which we could not tell him to do outright because, wary as he is, he wouldn't have done it, and so we arranged circumstances in hopes that he might figure it out on his own, which he has since done, thinking he is catching us unaware with his doings?'

'Obviously!' said the vaguely yellow caterpillar. 'He believes himself to be a strategist without equal!'

'The risk to ourselves was necessary,' the not-quite-blue caterpillar reminded them. 'Although there are possible futures that hold the worst for the Crystal and this council, the only path towards establishing Everqueen is through the events we have put into motion and on account of which we currently suffer.'

'And now it is up to Alyss Heart.'

'And the girl.'

'Yes, the girl! Homburg Molly!' said the others.

'And one other,' the not-quite-blue caterpillar corrected. 'The council forgets a possible future that now appears imminent as a result of our intervention.'

'I see so many futures, I can't keep them straight!' complained the once orange caterpillar.

'Welcome to old age,' said the barely-green-any-longer caterpillar.

'You *never* could keep them straight,' the formerly red caterpillar said to the once orange caterpillar.

The more-ashen-than-purple caterpillar, not knowing what else to do with his two broken teeth, returned them loose to his mouth, after which the eyes of every council member went wide as they all envisioned the imminent future scenario to which not-quite-blue had referred, and which involved none other than –

'Redd Heart!' the oracles cried simultaneously.

♠ CHAPTER 53 ♣

They had manoeuvred nearer The Iron Butterfly, as close as Redd thought they could get without being betrayed by the unsubtle tread of their jabberwocky, obscured from sight by burial mounds made in earliest time.

'You have a quarter lunar hour to get in position,' Redd said.

Without a word, Alistaire Poole and Sacrenoir galloped on their jabberwocky to opposite flanks of The Iron Butterfly. For the next quarter lunar hour not a word was spoken, though Vollrath several times opened his mouth, on the verge of speech, only to shut it again at the sight of Redd's unwelcoming demeanor, her unrelenting focus on the Butterfly. She was, the crosshatched creases around her downturned mouth declared, not to be distracted with trifles, and Vollrath's fear for his life was a trifle.

'It's time,' Redd said, just as –

Booooshhhhkrrrchhchchchk!

An orb generator exploded on the sunrise side of the Butterfly, which Sacrenoir, positioned behind a burial mound in the area, had set off. A knot of Astacans on the Butterfly's sunrise side started towards the explosion site.

Raaaarghghgh!

On the Butterfly's sunset side, a jabberwock bucked and roared and spewed flame. The beast had been prodded into the open by Alistaire Poole and was supposed to tramp towards the megalith, though it was evincing more interest in the burial mound the assassin was hunkered behind.

'Idiot beast,' Redd muttered, watching from her hidden vantage.

She scratched two scabs of skin from her jabberwock's back and stuck them in her ears. Vollrath and The Cat did likewise. Redd pointed her sceptre at Siren Hecht and the assassin unhinged her jaw and let out a head-splitting scream as –

She and her murdering cohorts spurred their jabberwocky into a run behind their mistress, stampeding towards The Iron Butterfly. Doomsines, Awr and Astacans fell to the ground in pain. Some covered their ears with dirt, ammo cartridges, whatever was near, trying to block out the wretched peal of Siren's voice. Others pounded the ground or thrashed in agony. Redd and her assassins weren't without pain themselves since jabberwock skin did not completely prevent Siren's scream from penetrating their skulls. Which was why the assassins went round to every writhing tribal warrior and did away with them as quickly as possible. Within the Iron Butterfly, they split off in every direction, eager to rid the place of Arch's followers and leaving no one alive, while Redd herself stalked the cobwebbed corridors, stabbing the sharp end of her sceptre into every Doomsine warrior and intel minister unfortunate enough to fall in her path. By the time she passed into The Iron Butterfly's innermost sanctum, Siren had stopped screaming. One by one the assassins entered the cavernous room to find Redd surrounded by the dead and dying, staring with disgust at a giant knitted thing taking up the centre of the floor.

'I'm right next to it but feel no stronger, no Power of Proximity,' Her Imperial Viciousness said.

The assassins didn't understand, but Vollrath stepped up to the knitting and started to pull at it.

'Help him!' Redd scolded.

Before she could grow more impatient, Vollrath and the assassins had the cocoon of caterpillar silk bunched on the floor. With The Heart Crystal freed, Redd extended her arms and lifted her face to its glow, absorbing its energy through every pore. And so she remained, her assassins in silent awe until –

'Pardon, Your Imperial Viciousness,' Vollrath braved, 'but don't you think it likely that a distress signal might have been sent to Arch?'

'And do you not suppose, tutor, that I shunted any such signal to oblivion with the first flush of imagination returned to me?'

Vollrath showed his mistress the top of his head. 'With one as clever as you, Your Imperial Viciousness, my job is ever more redundant.'

'Which is no doubt why you perform it so admirably.'

'Although it's possible, is it not,' the tutor's ears bent flat against his skull, 'that a distress signal may have reached Arch before you were reinvigorated with imagination?'

Redd fixed her annoyance on the tutor. The rose vines of her dress snaked close to his exposed skin. 'I'm prepared,' she said at length, and then, using her sceptre, poked at the cocoon on the floor. 'Caterpillar silk.'

'Everqueen!' a disembodied voice echoed throughout The Iron Butterfly. 'Ev-er-queeeeeeeen!'

To Her Imperial Viciousness's ear, it sounded like the green caterpillar trying to be ominous. 'Show yourself, worm!'

'Everrrrrqueeeeeeeeeeen!'

'The Everqueen is here!' Redd shouted. 'I've come! Now it's time to reclaim my throne!'

'Everrrrrqueeeeen!' the voice repeated one last time before fading to silence.

Redd turned on her assassins. 'What is it I always say?'

The Cat, Sacrenoir and the others bandied uncertain glances about.

'Don't be stupid?' ventured Alistaire.

'I should kill you now?' offered The Cat.

'Do I have to murder everyone myself?' tried Siren.

'No, idiots! When in doubt, go for the head. *That's* what I always say.'

'I never heard . . .' Sacrenoir started, but one look from his mistress shut him up.

'Arch is Wonderland's Head of State,' Redd intoned, her sceptre thrust skyward, The Heart Crystal turning crimson and shooting sparks and jags of energy everywhere. 'And so . . . off with Wonderland's head!'

♦ CHAPTER 54 ♣

In the grounds of Arch's Wondertropolis palace, in the subterranean chamber that once housed the power source for the cosmos, a cadre of intel ministers tended the fire crystals being used to evaporate the water drained from The Pool of Tears. There were a thousand such crystals, and the moment one no longer burnt as bright as when first cracked open, it was doused and replaced, which required the ministers to clamber constantly about, exchanging crystals in the grate that had been laid out across the flooded chamber near the water's surface. Siphons hung through the chamber's open hatchway, reaching like gargantuan tendrils to the submerged floor, and whenever the water level fell more than a spirit-dane length from the fire crystals, more was pumped in from the tankers parked above – in the formerly well-kept garden now marred by swaths of destruction, those outsized vehicles having trundled over hollizalea and sunflower and daphnedews.

The King observed the evaporation process from the bronzite platform on which Alyss Heart had once stood to coax The Heart Crystal's weakened energy into her. 'So they're even uglier than they were the last time?'

'The caterpillars will surely be dead soon, Your Majesty,' confirmed the minister returned from delivering tarty tarts to the oracles.

'Not soon enough.' Arch shouted at those working on the grate below: 'More fire crystals! The evaporation is taking too long!'

'My Liege.' An intel minister was at the control desk so often manned by General Doppelgänger in the past. 'We have . . . an issue.'

The desk's viewing screens were broadcasting images of tribal chiefs encamped with their warriors on the outskirts of Wondertropolis, all reporting the same thing.

'Repeat,' the Awr chief said. 'We're facing a full-on attack by Redd Heart and her army.'

Two of the viewing screens revealed what the chiefs were seeing: Redd, riding a jabberwock at the head of a massive mercenary force.

'Impossible,' Arch said.

Not one to wait for an enemy to strike first, the Awr chief

ordered the launch of orb generators, which lobbed through the air, on target to wipe out Redd's front line, but –

Baaaklaaghboooooooshhch! Baarghchkssssh!

Redd and her army were unharmed, still positioned for attack.

'A construct?' the minister at the control desk gasped.

'Not possible,' Arch said.

But the other tribal leaders confirmed it: their weapons had no effect on the enemy. Redd's army was a well-wrought illusion, the product of unsurpassed imagination. Arch tapped a finger quick on his crystal communicator's keypad, contacting his ministers at The Iron Butterfly. A hologram of one of them, bowing in reverence, projected from the communicator's vid nozzle:

'What's happening there?' Arch asked.

'Nothing, My Liege. Everything is as it should be, according to your last commands.'

'The Heart Crystal?'

The hologram expanded to take in the cocooned Crystal behind the minister.

'Rap your hand against it,' Arch ordered.

The minister did so; it appeared solid. Arch cut communication.

'Something's wrong.'

Blister, who'd been at the King's side for some time, stepped to attention, awaiting orders.

'Take the fiercest Doomsines,' Arch instructed him, 'take the Clubs' soldiery and anyone else you need to The Iron Butterfly. I'll follow when we're done here.'

Blister had hardly hustled from the chamber when –

'Something wrong, Archy?'

On the platform, not a boulder's throw from Arch: Redd Heart. But the King wasn't going to be taken in by *that trick* a second time. What he saw, he knew, was a construct. And instead of showing anger, he fell into the flattery he employed whenever wooing another wife.

'You *are* an impressive specimen, Rose. If I was going to underestimate a female, it should never have been you. Remember when we used to visit those Black Imagination dens together? You were, what, seventeen years old but you insisted on ingesting as much artificial crystal as any man.'

'More.'

'Yes, more.'

Redd's face contorted, looked about to break into many pieces – a grimace born of happy reminiscence, but she checked it. 'I no longer have the intention of letting you be my weakness, Archy. And in the interest of preventing future temptation . . .'

A Hand of Tyman materialised and its five spikes flew at the King. A lesser warrior wouldn't have had the speed to pull a knobkerrie from his sash, but Arch managed to raise his weapon in time. *Clongk!* The Hand of Tyman crashed against it, missing Arch's carotid artery but its outer spikes still grating across the side of his head. He stumbled to the rail of the platform, pressing a hand hard against his wound to staunch the bleeding as best as he could, hot liquid life cascading over his fingers as –

Chaw-chaw-chaw-chaw!

The intel minister blasted at the Redd construct with a mauler rifle. But you can't kill what isn't there, even if what isn't there can kill you. Which knowledge the Boarderlander came to as he dropped dead to the floor, skewered by a spear that hadn't existed a moment earlier.

On the grate below, ministers stopped tending the fire crystals to stare up at their dead brethren, at their troubled King and the spurned, vindictive Black Imaginationist of supreme ability having her revenge.

'Back to your orders!' Arch yelled at them.

Knobkerries of a size and heft never wielded by any

Doomsine formed in the air, batting His Highness this way and that. He broke his own knobkerrie in half trying to defend himself from a blow.

'I'm stronger than I've ever been!' Redd boasted through her construct.

In addition to the pummelling knobkerries, Arch had blades of all kinds to contend with: cutlasses swished past his ear; sickles swooshed before his eyes; daggers, razor-cards, swords, javelins, so many skin-shredding weapons threatened him, it was as if he were losing a fight against several Milliners at once. He didn't know how many times he'd been stabbed, couldn't have said how many bleeding cuts riddled his body. Something was wrong with his left arm; it flapped useless at his side.

'Ugh!'

He felt a blade drive into his chest below his right collarbone, fell face down on the platform and blinked past its girders at the ministers on the grate beneath him, the ministers who were trying to ignore the violence and keep to their fire crystal work as he'd ordered. But any lunar minute they'd have no work to keep to, because the last of The Pool of Tears was evaporating – a puddle no larger than a Boarderland wash tub being all that remained and getting smaller with every Gwormmy-blink.

The Redd construct, laughing, was suddenly quiet. It turned its head, as if becoming aware of something. 'Ah, company's arriving at The Butterfly.'

Arch started to drag himself towards the edge of the platform with his one good arm.

'Do you think, Archy, that your bodyguard and his band of toy soldiers can defeat me when they CAN'T EVEN CHALLENGE ME? My mercenaries are flocking to me again now that I can exercise my full power! My *true* power!'

Arch was almost to the platform's edge. He pulled himself closer, closer as –

'I do thank you for ridding Wonderland of my niece,' Redd said. 'There'll never be another like you, Archy. Which is just as well.'

Blender blades large enough to mince a grown Boarderlander formed on both sides of the King. Whirring, they pushed in fast towards him just as –

He heaved himself over the edge of the platform. Falling, he crashed down into the grate of fire crystals and knocked a section of it loose, continued falling past the busted grate towards what remained from The Pool of Tears, which was now no more than could fit in a bucket, and –

Kersplash!

He dropped into the water, was sucked out of sight.

The subterranean chamber became exceptionally still: no sound but the pop and crackle of fire crystals. The ministers on the grate stared down in disbelief: The Pool of Tears was gone, completely evaporated, and their King gone with it. When they dared to look up, there was no sign of Redd; they were alone.

❤ ◆ CHAPTER 55 ◆ ◆

The burial field in the land beyond The Whispering Woods: hundreds of mounds spaced evenly in rows, each mound signifying the resting place of one who'd belonged to the ancient Helmex race. In the near distance, from nowhere the Alyssians could see, came adrenaline-spiked cries of battle, the whistle of air-splitting missiles.

'Where precisely are we to meet them?' Bibwit asked. Recovered from the dust of despair, the tutor was armed with an oozy. In his nervousness, he had more than once mistaken a weed trembling in the wind for an enemy, spraying it with the weapon's mulch.

Dodge noticed a winking light at the burial field's northern perimeter. 'There,' he said.

A few lunar minutes later, when the Alyssians met up with the white knight and rook, the knight directed the Alyssians' attention to The Iron Butterfly, which was glowing with a reddish nimbus out beyond the burial field.

'Arch has converged his most aggressive forces on it,' the chessman said. 'It's a battle for The Heart Crystal.'

Dodge, Hatter, Bibwit and Taegel gazed off at the mysterious edifice, around which Doomsines and Club soldiers were hacking it out against Redd's troops. Here and there – in the deflective energy shield surrounding mercenaries, in the sudden materialisation of orb cannons – Redd's wrathful imaginative doings were fully evident.

'Has anyone seen or heard from General Doppelgänger?' Bibwit asked.

The chessmen answered that they had not, and in the ensuing silence, Hatter checked the spin of his wrist blades.

Dodge nodded towards the battle. 'There are too few of us.'

'Are there?' the rook asked with something of his usual gallantry.

As if on cue, chessmen stepped from behind every nearby burial mound: the entire set of Wonderland's chessmen. And then – *fwi-fwi-fwi-fwish!* – there was the sound of decks unshuffling and five decks of Heart Cards stood with the chessmen, ready to fight.

'For General Doppelgänger,' a Ten Card said.

Dodge took his father's sword in one hand, a splinterscape in the other. 'Well then, I guess we should do this,' he said, with a last look at the surrounding faces before –

'Wooooohoooooooo!'

He sprinted out from the shelter of the burial field, leading the Alyssian charge, slashing through enemy soldiers with glinting sword and without concern for his own well-being, an orb's explosion highlighting the four parallel scars on his rugged cheek. Using the splinterscape to keep enemies at a distance, he worked his way through scrums of hand-to-hand fighting, and crossed dangerous terrain over which Doomsines and mercenaries exchanged fire. The Cat was nowhere to be seen. He would fight his way towards The Iron Butterfly's entrance: wherever Redd was, The Cat would be nearby. But Redd's military was still relatively small and Her Imperial Viciousness was, imaginatively speaking, everywhere. To make the most of the Power of Proximity, she physically remained inside the Butterfly, within arm's reach of The Heart Crystal, but in her imagination's eye she was outside fighting next to Alistaire Poole and Siren Hecht, killing no fewer Club cards than either; she was riding her jabberwock along the flank of a sword-bearing Sacrenoir as he drove pawns and Heart cards towards his ravenous, flesh-chomping skeletons; she was conjuring replicas of Hatter Madigan's top hat blades and launching them straight at the Milliner as he fought a pair of Doomsines and a Five of Clubs.

Fsssssssst!

His top hat a blur of spinning death, wrist-blades activated, Hatter knocked the replicas to the ground without letting up on his adversaries for even a Gwormmy-blink. Meanwhile –

Dodge caught sight of The Cat, who had squared off against Blister just outside The Iron Butterfly. No hot surge of vengeance filled him. Cold, matter-of-fact, he would do what had to be done, and he annihilated tribal warriors and Club cards with an ease rivaled by very few as he fought his way towards the feline.

He might have failed at everything that mattered – at helping to restore White Imagination to prominence, at saving the Queendom from tyrants; he might have failed most of all at keeping Alyss safe – but if he was to die, he would take The Cat with him.

♦ CHAPTER 56 ♣

Molly didn't want to keep her appointment with Rafters, but Alyss insisted.

'You said you believed he's from Wonderland?'

Molly nodded. She'd told the Queen how Rafters had recognised the flugelberry vine that bound her mother's notebooks together when no such thing grew on Earth.

'Then keep your appointment,' Alyss said, thinking of Blue's visitation to the girl. 'We don't know where an opportunity to return to Wonderland will come from. Or when.'

So Molly reluctantly brought herself to Beaumont Street, climbed the lodging house stairs that seemed to continue up without end until, frustrated –

'Here I am,' she said, and the garret door appeared where a moment before there had been none.

Rafters said nothing as he let her into the flat, acted

as disinterested as he'd been at the start of their previous meeting. But he had readied the room for the appointment. The window was still fogged with grime, the floor still a gathering place for dust mites, and the pallet of straw looked as rough and prickly as ever beneath the horse blanket. But the three-legged dresser was now a multi-tiered workbench that supported scopes and tumblers and pestles and a host of implements unfamiliar to Molly. Weren't those the outlines of the drawers and drawer pulls she saw in the table's surface? Somehow the dresser had been transformed into a properly functioning four-legged table as solid as oak.

'How are you feeling?' Rafters asked.

She knew what he meant. Her imagination was back. She would not be slow in solving his puzzles today. 'Fine,' she said.

Yet he tested her with a number of puzzles, and not till he was satisfied by the speed and ease of her answers did he ask to see her mother's notebooks.

'The formulae these books contain,' he said, untying the flugelberry vine, 'are comprised of symbols which, in their proximal and implied interactions, represent the play of physical substances. Everything that seems to the sight and touch to be perfectly solid is, at its most fundamental level,

382

a swamp of animated particles. Your mother's art is simply a matter of redirecting the movement of these particles.'

Eternal flux, malleability, atomic collision – Molly tried to take it all in, to not let a single word escape her understanding. For herself. For Weaver.

'We'll start with something basic,' Rafters said.

Within five minutes Molly had turned a pennny into a shiny gold piece. Using the formulae in her mother's notebooks, she was soon transmutating stalks of straw from Rafters's bed into Millinery-grade steel. And the more she transformed, under Rafters's impressed eye, the everyday objects of Earth into Millinery gear, the more she felt she was not in an Oxford garret but in her mother's laboratory, being allowed to help as a child might help her parent prepare dinner in the kitchen. She saw Weaver shaping the blades to be used by Hatter in battle, struggled to imagine their lives before her birth – her mother and father and a love too strong to be held in check by Millinery codes, societal considerations. Tears formed in the corners of her eyes.

'One more ingredient,' Rafters said.

She was standing over an experiment in progress, the aim of which he had not divulged. She looked at the formula in her mother's notebook:

v/ [( )]   (/) //

She looked at the incomplete experiment on the table in front of her – the shallow bowl which had once contained a collection of solid metal pieces and gems and which had turned first into a gelatinous mass but was now more akin to slush.

'One last ingredient and you'll have done it,' Rafters said.

So why didn't he tell her what the ingredient was? Because no way could she guess, not when the symbols in her mother's notebook were gauzily unclear on account of her tears and she was ready to give up on all this schooling and cry out for –

Ploink!

A tear fell from her cheek into the experiment's bowl; the slush frothed and fizzed, liquified.

'Do you know what just happened?' Rafters asked.

Molly sniffled, wiped at her face. 'Yeah, I ruined it.'

Rafters said nothing, dropped a leftover pebble of quartz into the water and watched it speed down and out of sight.

'Now do you understand?' he asked.

Molly, still unfocused by thoughts of her mother, shook

her head. Rafters upended the bowl, spilling its contents on to the desk top and making –

'A puddle where no puddle should be, a means of transport,' he said, though the wet splotch was not large enough for anyone but a baby to enter.

Molly glanced from him to the puddle and back. 'A means of transport,' she said. And then: 'You worked at the Millinery.'

The saddest expression the girl had ever seen marred Rafters's face. 'I did. Before your mother's time. Hatter Madigan wasn't even the age you are now.' As a young alchemist, he said, he'd made a mistake. 'The exact nature of the mistake isn't important for you to know. But I recognised it too late. My self-inflicted punishment was to follow the Wonderlanders whose actions earned The Pool of Tears its name – those who'd also made mistakes in their personal or professional lives and had stood on the cliff overlooking Tove Pond, as it was called, letting their tears fall into the water before they jumped, never to be seen by friends or family again. I've lived with my mistake for more years than I care to count.'

'But you could've gone back,' Molly said. 'You can go back now.'

He shook his head. 'I'm not yet brave enough to face those I left behind who are, I pray, still living. But I've related all of this Molly, only so you'll understand when I tell you that I have cried myself out long before today. More tears are needed to enlarge this portal if you're to return to Wonderland. *You* must provide the tears – genuine, heartfelt tears they must be. I will give you privacy.'

He was out the door before she realised it. But left alone in the garret, with everything – the end of Queen Alyss's second exile, her own reunion with her father – dependent on her own grief-loosened tears, her eyes remained dry. Only when she gazed round at the trappings of a Millinery alchemist and let her mind drift back to Weaver and the father she was afraid to let herself love, only then did the tears come.

'I can't decide if it bodes well or ill that I'm without imagination one hour but possessed of it again a few hours later,' Alyss said. 'It's so strange, with regards to imagination, to be at the mercy of what happens in Wonderland.'

'It may be,' Dodgson responded, sifting through the letters on his desk, 'that it boded ill when imagination was n-nowhere to be found, but bodes well now that imagination's returned to us.'

Alyss was sceptical. 'Mine is not of much value without The Pool of Tears.'

'You've confessed what you find s-strange,' Dodgson said, ignoring his letters, 'and so I will c-confess the same. I think it at least as strange that a source of power as great as The H-Heart Crystal can be possessed or c-controlled by a single individual. By any group of individuals. W-We are each of us born with our own talents, that much remains clear. But to th-think, to *know*, that to the extent each of us is able to utilise the imaginative ability with which we're born . . . to know that this d-depends upon who possesses The Heart Crystal and w-what he or she does with it . . .' the Reverend shook his head. 'Possession of so much power will always lead to c-c-corruption. If not in the person who controls the object, then in those around her.'

Alyss did not deny it, having for a while now considered that being sovereign of any state meant constantly guarding against corruption in one form or another. She was about to say as much when the door banged open, as if kicked, and Molly burst in, as excited as in days of old.

'I've made another Pool of Tears!'

♠ CHAPTER 57 ♣

They had no more than half an hour – the most Alice Liddell was willing to spare apart from her family – and so they didn't venture far, sitting in Christ Church Meadow and absently watching the people come and go as if it were any other day, any other hour, not the last time two friends would ever meet.

'Father is about his work at the college again,' Alice Liddell said, 'but mother and I spend much of our time comforting Edith, who's been the slowest to recover. I made her laugh earlier today.'

Only Molly knew it was to be their final meeting. Queen Alyss had thought it best not to expose the Liddells to more trauma or confusion. But it was harder than Molly had anticipated, to sit here and say nothing.

'The authorities refuse to tell us about the man who was killed,' Alice went on. 'I don't mind, really. What does it matter who he was or how he contrived to make it seem as though knives came from his fingers? I doubt knowing either would explain why he did such a thing to my family.'

'What about, you know, the other you?' Molly asked.

Alice shrugged, her hands worrying in her lap. When she spoke, she was too adamant, as if trying to convince herself of what she thought others wanted her to believe though she didn't, couldn't believe it. 'I think my parents and sisters mistaken as to the extent of the similarity between us. I saw the lady but briefly and am sure I overstated our resemblance. I *would* like to know if she'd been the man's accomplice and had second thoughts, since how else could she have known he was threatening our family? In any case, I'd like to thank her for saving them, but I don't expect to have that privilege.'

A boy ran giggling past, chased by a shaggy terrier.

'I should get back. I promised to read to Edith. Perhaps we can meet for tea next Tuesday, if my sister's improved by then.'

'Yeah,' Molly said, saddened to know Tuesday tea would never happen; Miss Liddell wasn't the only one who had to get home. 'Yeah, maybe I'll see you then.'

*

Alyss and Dodgson were waiting for her at Rafters's garret: the bed of straw, the dresser turned into a workbench, the puddle where no puddle should be. Molly pocketed the Milliner blades she and Rafters had produced with the help of her mother's notebooks – C- and S-shaped blades, daggers and folding knives, skin-boring tools that looked like mini tridents, all weapons that might have come from Hatter's backpack.

'You're sure you don't want to come?' Alyss asked Rafters.

He bent from the waist. 'I thank you. But it's not as if you're returning to a paradise. Though, who knows? One day I might have the courage . . . and you'll see me again in Wondertropolis.'

'I look forwards to it,' Alyss said. There was nothing more to do but leave. She looked around and added, 'Well . . .'

'Well . . .' said Dodgson, and suddenly bowed: 'May we never meet again, Your Majesty.'

Never meet again? After I thought we'd made amends and –

'F-For if we don't meet again,' the Reverend explained, 'I will know you've s-succeeded in retaking the crown and, of course, that imagination for both our w-worlds is safe. I do trust, however, that if we're never more to meet, I may then be free of your aunt and her followers as well.'

'Oh. I see,' Alyss said benignly. 'Then may we never meet again, Mr Dodgson.'

The Reverend turned his attentions to the Queen's travelling companion. 'Good day to you, Homburg Molly.'

Difficult to say who seemed more uncomfortable, Dodgson with his starched pose or the fidgeting Molly, though it was the girl who braved demonstrativeness. She stepped forwards and, without looking at the Reverend, gave him a quick hug, after which, without a glance for anyone, embarrassed, she hopped on to the workbench, next to the puddle where no puddle should be. Alyss climbed up beside her, and without further ado, they jumped one after the other into the portal, neither of them fighting against its steady downward pull, its deepwater lull, its upward push: the question about to be answered, of whether they would emerge into a recognisable Wonderland or an alien place in which friends and beloved were forever absent.

Even amidst the bloody free-for-all outside The Iron Butterfly, The Cat and Blister were left to themselves, as if in hopes they would do away with each other.

Dodge had, for the present, manoeuvred as close to The Cat as he wished to be. He hadn't waited this long for vengeance, suffered this long, to shoot the humanoid freak in the back. He wanted the assassin's full attention, and so he occupied himself with any enemy who confronted him – tribal warriors, Club soldiers, he didn't care. He fought whoever came at him.

'Hguuunh!'

Dodge turned, saw The Cat standing with his legs firmly planted and his body positioned as far from Blister's reach as he could, keeping one arm extended and a pawful of claws rammed up into the bodyguard's stomach.

'Ghuuuh,' Blister drooled, hands fumbling at the assassin's arm, blistering it repeatedly.

The Cat rammed his claws deeper into the bodyguard before spitting and flinging him to the ground. Dodge stepped forwards.

'Sir Justice's spawn!' The Cat hissed.

The assassin was badly blistered on his thighs and back, blood seeped from his shoulder and arms, but if he felt pain, he didn't show it. He sprang at the guardsman, morphing into a kitten while airborne so that Dodge swung his sword too high, and returning to humanoid form as he landed. He swatted the guardsman in the back and sent him reeling. Dodge regained his footing and charged; sword clattered against claw and fell from his grasp. The Cat kicked the blade away and Dodge reached under his jumpsuit for a whipsnake grenade. Within moments he had recourse to every weapon he was carrying. Whipsnake grenade, AD52, shardstorm: not a single one went untried, but The Cat's speed and agility were more impressive than the guardsman remembered.

Too impressive.

After failing at everything else, he, Dodge Anders, was going to fail at this too. He would not outlive Sir Justice's murderer. While The Cat bobbed and weaved to avoid shardstorm shrapnel, Dodge made his father a whispered apology for his failure. He apologised to Alyss and offered her his undying love. His clothes were tattered, shredded – his flesh, too, in many places. He'd exhausted his arsenal except for a single dagger. He ripped a strip of cloth from his jumpsuit and flapped it at The Cat, who abruptly fell still, as if mesmerised. Dodge again flapped the shred of cloth.

'Stop it,' The Cat said, unable to move, fixated on the cloth.

'What's the matter, kitty?' Dodge teased, waving the string-like cloth, moving closer. 'Infatuated by the string, kitty?'

'Stop it!'

But Dodge didn't stop it, at least not until he was close

enough to press the point of his dagger against the hollow of The Cat's throat. Unfortunately, The Cat at the same time managed to lift a claw to Dodge's chest, where his heart was.

'So it will end for both of us,' The Cat said. 'Do it.'

Dodge stared into The Cat's pulsing eyes, the moist nostrils, the slobbery fangs. He was not afraid to die, but . . . revenge? It had never been the way to honour his father's memory. He'd always known it, but now, for the first time, he *felt* it. His hesitation lasted no more than a whisker twitch, but The Cat sensed it.

'Time to join your father,' the assassin mocked.

Dodge suffered the pop of skin as The Cat's claw penetrated his chest. Revenge might not have been the best way to honour a father's memory, but what good were such considerations now? He put pressure on the dagger against The Cat's throat.

'Mreeeooooooow!'

The Cat leapt away, staggered, an entire deck of razor-cards lodged in his back. And there was Blister, barely able to stand, a forearm pressed against his stomach, loosely aiming an AD52 at the feline.

Dodge let his dagger fly – *wi-wi-wi-thimp!*– and even

before it pierced Blister, killing him instantly, The Cat had disappeared.

Prrrsssshhhaw!

They splashed from the water and landed on the floor of a vast well – all that remained of The Pool of Tears. Far above: a circle of sky no larger than the mouth of a wine bottle. Alyss immediately tingled with the increase of imagination that came from being in the same world as The Heart Crystal.

'Sit back and hold tight to the rail,' she told Molly.

'Sit back and – ?'

Something bumped the girl behind the knees, knocked her to a sitting position. She was next to Alyss in a flying machine for two. A silver rail ran the width of the seats, securing her and the Queen in place. Behind them, a shaft rose up, supporting the coptering blades that carried them swiftly out of the crater and into the Wonderland sunshine.

'Look!'

'It's Alyss Heart!'

The cliff overlooking the crater was still lined with Wonderlanders feeling the loss of loved ones who, without a Pool of Tears, could never return to Wonderland. Alyss landed the flying machine a little way from the cliff's edge.

'Where did you come from?' some asked.

'How did you . . .?' asked others, pointing at Alyss and then into the crater.

'Is there really a Pool of Tears?' still others asked.

'There is,' Alyss said in answer to the last.

The news caused the Wonderlanders to cry afresh, not in sadness but joy. Because if The Pool of Tears existed, if inter-world travel was possible, then they might see their loved ones again after all. The Wonderlanders' happy tears rained down into the crater even as one of them, an admirer of the House of Hearts, expressed dismay that Alyss was not at The Iron Butterfly.

'The Iron . . .?' Alyss said, directly casting her imaginative eye to that oldest of Wonderland structures, where she saw chessmen and Heart Cards among the welter of clashing soldiers – *Dodge! Bibwit!* – surrounding it. And inside the Butterfly: Redd Heart, Vollrath, The Heart Crystal. She scanned for Arch but couldn't locate him.

She had an idea, wouldn't know if it was brilliance or suicide until after she'd brought it to fruition. *If it's even possible.* She couldn't allow herself to be seen again. Not yet. Which meant that she couldn't protect Dodge as he fought at The Iron Butterfly, couldn't add the strength of her imagination in support of the Alyssians.

The hardest part. Hurry.

Arriving at the land beyond The Whispering Woods with Molly, Alyss imagined her conjured flying machine back into millions of microscopic particles. She needed the Power of Proximity as much as possible and crouched behind a hobblebush, a grenade's toss from The Iron Butterfly. About to make use of all the imagination she possessed, she noticed Molly's restlessness. Looking out through drooping branches, the girl's eyes were skittering from one pocket of fighting to another, her hands active with shadow-moves, hinting of what she'd do were she amid the violence.

'I have something for you,' Alyss said and held out her hand, in which a homburg took shape, solidified.

Molly grabbed it as if it were a long lost friend, gave it a flick; it flattened into a knife-edged shield.

'You could probably also use . . .' Alyss said, and Molly found herself outfitted with a Millinery backpack.

In front of the hobblebush: a Three of Hearts about to make the ultimate submission to a Four of Clubs' mauler rifle. Molly sidearmed her homburg shield at the Club soldier and, running after it, shrugged the corkscrews and blades of her backpack to the ready. Alyss watched as the girl saved the Three of Hearts, watched her spin, kick, somersault, tumble, punch and wing her Millinery weapons at the lesser-skilled, so very like her father in every move she made.

Her father, Hatter Madigan: who'd sighted Molly while twirling with activated belt sabres through a gauntlet of Doomsine warriors. How had she come to be there? his expression seemed to ask. Where had she found her homburg? He and Molly battled their way towards each other, and then – spinning, kicking, somersaulting, tumbling – more than held their own against a too-numerous enemy force.

Seeing father and daughter together, up against this too-numerous enemy, Alyss was reminded of something and . . .

At the limbo coop situated in the remotest of the Clubs' land holdings, where Mutty P. Dumphy walked through a dirty lane, an Alyss construct appeared.

'Now, Mr Dumphy,' the Queen's proxy said. 'Now is the time for imaginationists to rise up!'

The tinker didn't need to be told again. Protected in a bubble of deflective energy, he ran from tenement to tenement, calling all imaginationists to take up their arms against imprisonment.

'Rise up and imagine again!' he shouted. 'Fight! Live!'

Word spread, and in limbo coops throughout the territories belonging to the House of Clubs, a similar scene played out: Alyss constructs urged the prisoners to rise up, and Club cards not diverted to The Iron Butterfly were overwhelmed by imaginationists fighting their way to freedom.

Alyss, in the land beyond The Whispering Woods, had meanwhile started to concentrate, focusing her thoughts on a pair of objects and devoting all of her power to their creation: high above The Iron Butterfly, obscured by a layer of clouds, two orb generators came into being – generators ten times the size of ordinary ones but imbued with the strength of a hundred. Fully formed, they dropped in a vertical line like falling suns, dropped towards The Iron Butterfly's inner sanctum, where Redd, carried away with the annihilation of petty beings, wouldn't have guessed what was coming even if she'd known her niece was in Wonderland. That Her Imperial Viciousness used her imagination to keep Arch's forces and Alyssians from raiding the Butterfly was a given. That she used it to protect herself and her proximity to the Crystal was also a given. But that she should have been shielding the source of her power itself . . .? She would not have dreamed that any imaginationist, let alone one as powerful as Alyss, would direct violence at *it*.

Booooooooooooooooooooshhhhhhhhhchchchchchkkckck!

The first of Alyss's generators detonated against The Iron Butterfly's roof. The second generator, directly behind the first, plummeted through the hole made by the explosion and crashed into The Heart Crystal, but –

No second explosion. While Redd was frantic, yelling at Vollrath for an explanation, her coveted source of imagination began to throb violently, each throb causing the Crystal to grow in size and increase in brightness.

'Your Imperial . . . hurry!' Vollrath urged, yanking at a rose vine of Redd's dress, cutting his hands on its thorns. 'We must leave at once!'

'NEVER! THE CRYSTAL IS MINE!'

But no sooner did she utter the words, holding out her arms to the Crystal, than it swelled and filled the sanctum, consuming her and Vollrath entire, while –

Outside, where a number of card soldiers and tribal warriors had already been distracted by the massive orbs falling from the sky, all fighting stopped. Alyssians and Heart Cards, Doomsines and Club soldiers, assassins and mercenaries, all held off bashing and shooting at one another to stare.

It was like nothing anyone had ever seen: where The

Heart Crystal had been, a great font of kaleidoscopic energy shooting up through The Iron Butterfly's demolished roof; a geyser of natural power, both frightening and beautiful, pushing up to the heavens, its rainbow-colours and lightning-works roiling out across every Gwormmy-length of visible sky.

♦ CHAPTER 58 ♣

The initial burst from The Heart Crystal dimmed, calmed to a steady up- and outflow, a fluid column rising from The Iron Butterfly and then spreading out to blanket the clouds, extending to unknown ethereal regions, revealing –

Wonderland's entire caterpillar council. Restored to their rich shades of blue, green, red, purple, yellow and orange, the larvae of notable girth floated on clouds of hookah smoke, their mouths unstuck from their pipes as they stared wide-eyed at the glittering heavens.

'Everqueen,' they said as one.

A disturbance rippled through the witnesses – the remaining legions of Wonderlanders and Boarderlanders, the mercenaries recruited from Earth, Redd's assassins. Alyss Heart had emerged from the hobblebush and was approaching The Iron Butterfly, the caterpillar council, Dodge. Bibwit scurried out from somewhere and walked along with her.

'Alyss! We thought . . . we didn't know if . . . something's happened to The Heart Crystal. As yet we don't know how bad it is, which is to – '

'The Crystal's destroyed,' Alyss said in a tone that caused the tutor's ears to jerk back, startled, then lean tentatively forwards.

'You?' he asked.

'Me,' she said.

This did little to tame Bibwit's ears, which seemed to be trying to separate from his head as he and Alyss stopped beside Dodge, in the shadow of the caterpillar council. The guardsman turned his battle-weathered eyes from the miraculous sight of dispersing energy and smiled at Alyss. 'Not looking my best, am I?'

'But you're alive.'

She reached out her hand. He took it, interlaced his fingers with hers.

Skittish, Bibwit glanced at Alyss and the caterpillar-oracles. With an uncharacteristic lack of confidence, he began, 'Wisest council, while Alyss Heart's mistake is I assume the impetus – which is to say, cause – for this, your unprecedented appearance – '

'You have done what was required for the establishment

403

of Everqueen,' Blue interrupted, addressing Alyss. He motioned with his two frontmost legs at the rest of the council, the legs behind echoing the gesture. 'We've *all* done what has been required.'

'Yes, all done what was required,' the other caterpillars said, bobbing their heads.

Bibwit was stunned to silence.

Alyss looked to the sparkling sky. '*That* is Everqueen?'

The oracles again bobbed their heads.

'Imagination has been established forever,' said Blue. 'You and others with imagination will have the gifts with which you were born. For those of future generations, it will be the same. Some shall be born with much imagination, others little. As it is now. But Everqueen can never be destroyed, nor the inspiration she provides lessened.'

'Possession of the Crystal corrupts,' Alyss said under her breath, remembering what Dodgson had said.

Blue puffed on his hookah and exhaled in short bursts, the smoke spelling out a single word: I-N-D-E-E-D. 'Everqueen is imagination,' he said. 'Imagination is Black and White. There is both or neither. Rose Heart has become part of Everqueen.'

'We pledged to help reclaim the throne!' Green exclaimed.

'And so we did!' put in Orange.

'If Rose Heart assumed we were reclaiming it for *her* – ' Purple elaborated.

'– that was her business!' finished Yellow.

'But we reclaimed the throne for *imagination*!' Red clarified.

'Mr Anders?'

It was a Two of Hearts, standing over something just inside The Iron Butterfly's entrance. Dodge limped over and found –

A golden-haired kitten, curled up, dead, its back ravaged by razor-card slashes. He stood staring down at the creature and said nothing. Most of his life had been lived for this moment. The motivation for taking air into his lungs day after day . . . there it was, its last life gone.

He felt Alyss at his side. He didn't much want to hear what she was going to say – that The Cat's death wouldn't counterbalance his father's murder; he would get no relief or sense of closure from it. But she did the perfect thing, uttered not a word, hooked her arm under his and seemed content to stand with him as long as he wished. It was good, he thought, good and right that the vengeful part of him was dead. He had better things to live for.

Hatter and Molly approached.

'Remember that promise you made a while back to Queen Genevieve, the one about seeing to Alyss's care and protection?' Dodge asked.

The Milliner nodded.

'Maybe you shouldn't worry about it so much, since I *have* been unofficially trying to handle it anyway. And you've a lot to occupy your attention, what with the re-established Millinery and your daughter . . .'

'I plan to spend as much time with my daughter as she'll allow,' Hatter said, his eyes on Molly.

'As our *duties* allow,' the girl corrected, returning his look.

Behind them, Bibwit was regaling the white rook and white knight with his plentiful thoughts:

'Well, well, I don't know that I shouldn't chronicle this extraordinary adventure for the public archives – which is to say, in order that future Queens might learn from it. I realise I'm nothing more than a venerable member of the tutor species with an unruly head of hair, but what, I ask you, is imagination if not the potential for betterment? Forever losing the chance to improve, both ourselves and Wonderland – why, in some ways that would've been worse than losing everything! Excuse me.'

Bibwit reached under the sleeve of his scholar's robe

and tapped the receiver node on his crystal communicator's keypad – before, to anyone else's ear, the device even sounded. Projecting as if from the tutor's navel on to the air: an image of General Doppelgänger in Heart Palace.

'General, sir!' the knight and rook cried. Their commander, with the wounds he'd received at Blister's hands visible, had looked better.

General Doppelgänger smiled in greeting. 'Bibwit. Chessmen.'

'We were beginning to fear we'd lost you, general,' said Bibwit.

'Not yet, Mr Harte. Not yet. I intend to fully recover and serve Queen Alyss as long as she'll have me.'

'Ahem hem hum,' Blue grumbled loudly, to get everyone's attention. 'We oracles have been in Wonderland these many, many, many, many, many, many, many, many, many, many, many, many, many, many, many, many years, waiting for the time of Everqueen. Now that she's come . . .' the oracles shone beatific faces to the sky, '. . . we are no longer needed.'

Upon which, with astonishing speed and dexterity, each oracle wrapped himself in a chrysalis spun of his own silk. And as Redd's surviving assassins – Siren Hecht, Alistaire

Poole and Sacrenoir – slipped away into the surrounding country, as Club cards of high number and earth mercenaries escaped to cause trouble another day, the cocoons broke open and the largest butterflies ever seen in the Queendom emerged, flitted up and away into the streaming energy of Everqueen as –

Alyss and Dodge, Hatter and Molly, Bibwit and General Doppelgänger, the Heart soldiery and white chessmen, all joined together in huzzahs.

CODA

Reverend Dodgson sat at his desk with only the ticking clock and crackling fire for company. His imagination hadn't failed him once in the fortnight since he'd last seen Alyss Heart and Homburg Molly and, with notebook open before him, he reasoned out the answers to his maths puzzles as fluently and creatively as ever. The more time that passed without harm to his creative powers, he believed, the more it signified Alyss's victory in the war for imagination and the less chance there was of his again being accosted by Redd Heart or The Cat. Although he couldn't know for sure. Which was why he wouldn't throw his false starts to I, Redd into the fire. Not yet.

> Still she haunts me, phantomwise.
> Alice moving under skies
> Never seen by waking eyes.

It was a stanza from the poem he'd published at the conclusion *of* Through the Looking-Glass. *He had perhaps never written anything so true; for whatever else was to happen, Alyss Heart would remain a phantom in his life, a presence he thought of from time to time, but particularly whenever he crossed paths with Miss Alice Liddell. Musing thus, Oxford's most famous bachelor closed his notebook and set down his pen for the night as –*

Half a world away, a man who'd appeared out of nowhere was allowing himself to be nursed back to health by the nuns of St Mark's church in New York City; a man who had once been a conquering King – at present one of Earth's anonymous multitudes but who, with his outsized ambition, his skills of manipulation and self-promotion, would one day be as recognisable to millions of Americans as he was to Alyss Heart.

And where was Wonderland's Queen? Sharing a pot of tea with Dodge in Heart Palace's ancestral chamber, with Bibwit Harte before her, chattering on and on and on, while the walrus-butler bumbled about the room's perimeter, trying to be inconspicuous.

'*I'm told that if one stands at the edge of The Pool of Tears and looks closely,*' *the tutor reported,* '*it's now possible to see the water, which continues to rise as Wonderlanders refill it with tears of happpiness.*'

'Happiness?' *queried Dodge.*

Bibwit's ears folded once, then straightened. '*Over the*

possibility of seeing long-lost loved ones again. I should also report, my dear, that The Clubs' trial is set to begin next quarter-moon and Boarderland's tribal leaders are back in their own country, hashing things out among themselves and apparently not the least concerned as to what's become of Arch. However, I can't help saying that no one's quite been able to explain to my satisfaction what's become of the King, and if he's living ...'

The tutor chose not to finish his thought: a rare occurrence.

She hadn't returned to a paradise, Alyss reminded herself. As much as she hoped otherwise, she knew that in years to come the Pool would be refilled by more than a few tears of sadness. And regardless of what happened to the Lord and Lady of Clubs at their trial, there would still be anti-imaginationists in Wonderland, as there would always be Black Imagination devotees.

'What are you thinking?' Dodge asked her.

'Just that I'll never give up on the principles of White Imagination, never stop working to secure the greatest good for the greatest number of Wonderlanders, no matter the obstacles or enemy.'

'I have tutored you exceedingly well, haven't I?' Bibwit beamed.

'So well, Bibwit,' returned the Queen, 'that I won't be remiss and ask you to stay while I attend to a personal matter of great importance.'

'Of course you won't,' Bibwit said without moving.

The walrus-butler waddled over and put a gentle flipper to the tutor's back, to urge him towards the door. But the learned albino didn't budge.

'Walrus, Bibwit, would you please leave us a moment?'

The tutor glanced at the butler, who was trying to tell him something with his eyes. Baffled, not understanding, he said, 'Yes, of course. I believe I have to powder my head,' and allowed the walrus to lead him from the chamber.

'A private matter?' Dodge asked.

Alyss went to him, took his hands in hers. She said his name softly, almost to herself, and then –

'I know we haven't always agreed, and that I've disappointed you in some of my actions, especially recently.'

'No more than I've disappointed you.'

'I will always try and live up to your generous belief in me, Dodge. I'd ask for a reciprocal vow if I didn't know the standards you set for yourself are higher than any I could request from a friend and . . . husband.' She paused, let him take in the word. 'Despite my faults, will you be my husband, Mr Dodge Anders?'

The guardsman remained silent for a maddeningly long time, then –

'Will I become your husband, the happiest man in the Queendom? Yes, Alyss. Yes.'

He leaned close and kissed her — each too lost in the other's touch to notice the figures of Queen Genevieve and King Nolan watching them from the wall's looking glass, witnesses to a love that could only add to the wonder of Wonderland.

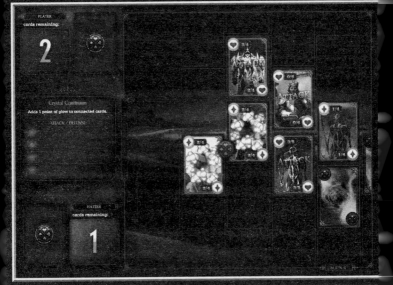

Also by
Frank Beddor

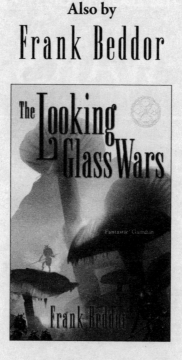

You think you know the true story of Alice in
Wonderland? Well think again.

Alyss is destined to become Queen of Wonderland . . .
until her parents are murdered. She flees to safety in
our world, but one day she must return to take the
crown that is rightfully hers.

Step into a dazzling new world. Dare to enter the
Looking Glass Maze. Because this is Wonderland
as you have never seen it before!

Also by
Frank Beddor

Return to the dazzling world of
The Looking Glass Wars®

Alyss of Wonderland's rule has only just begun, but the Queendom is already under threat. Someone is using the brutal Glass Eyes and attacking Wonderland on all sides.

It can only mean one thing: the evil Redd Heart has returned . . .

EGMONT PRESS: ETHICAL PUBLISHING

Egmont Press is about turning writers into successful authors and children into passionate readers – producing books that enrich and entertain. As a responsible children's publisher, we go even further, considering the world in which our consumers are growing up.

Safety First
Naturally, all of our books meet legal safety requirements. But we go further than this; every book with play value is tested to the highest standards – if it fails, it's back to the drawing-board.

Made Fairly
We are working to ensure that the workers involved in our supply chain – the people that make our books – are treated with fairness and respect.

Responsible Forestry
We are committed to ensuring all our papers come from environmentally and socially responsible forest sources.

**For more information, please visit our website at
www.egmont.co.uk/ethical**